OPERATION TEXAS

A NOVEL

ANITA LAMPEL

Hardcover ISBN: 978-1-965253-73-1
Paperback ISBN: 978-1-965253-74-8
Ebook ISBN: 978-1-965253-75-5
Library of Congress Control Number

DartFrog

301 S. McDowell St.
Suite 125-1625
Charlotte, NC 28204
www.DartFrogBooks.com

CHAPTER 1

*S*kills *in German and Slavic languages, some college desirable.*

This job was meant for her, and Rosalind was determined to have it. She shoved the token into the farebox for the streetcar. There went fifteen minutes of pay at her lousy job at Woolworths. She certainly hoped it would be worth it.

She slid onto a seat next to the window. Outside, one boarded-up store followed another—the place she'd bought a pair of cheap shoes, the little used bookstore she'd liked. Nearly half the stores in Austin were out of business.

A tall, middle-aged man in a blue plaid suit too hot for the day and too tight for his thighs sat down next to her despite the open set of seats just opposite.

"Howdy," he said.

"Mmm."

"You off somewhere important?"

"Yes."

He draped his arm over the back of the seat, his fingers dangling down toward her freshly ironed best blouse. His finger tapped her shoulder lightly, as if by accident.

"Sir, I'd appreciate it if you could move your hand away from me." Rosalind kept her voice low and continued to look out the window as if the man and his actions meant little to her.

He snickered, emitting a whiff of mid-day booze, and tapped harder. "I'm trying to have a friendly talk."

"Again, don't touch me."

He moved over so her hip and shoulder were pressed against the side of the bus.

Rosalind slid her hand into her purse and gripped the handle of her Derringer. "Mister, you get away from me now," she said in a low voice. "You don't and this pistol I have will come out."

That seemed to do it. The man got up and moved to the opposite seats.

Rosalind took a breath. Then another one. Her heart quit pounding just as she reached her stop, where the Federal Courthouse rose up in Art Moderne glory of smooth walls, windows in rows like horizontal bands, and three federal eagles looming over the entrance. She'd use the short walk to her interview there to calm down.

***

"I see you speak German and Polish." Mister Wright, the young man conducting the interview, put Rosalind's resume down on the desk and stared at her.

"Yes."

"Any other languages, Miss Fisher?"

"Spanish. I grew up in Galveston and absorbed it more than studied it. I passed out of fourth year Spanish by testing at university." Rosalind kept her hands folded in her lap. She opened her mouth to add more, but he interrupted.

"You never studied it in school and yet you mastered it?"

"Yes." She began to rub her right thumb with her left. The fan above her head made a slight clicking noise and ruffled the resume's two pages with a breeze, which did little to alleviate the heat and humidity in the office.

"How'd you learn German and Polish?"

"From my parents who immigrated here. Then I studied the languages more formally at the university."

"Did you study any other languages besides those?" he asked, then waved his hand to indicate he wanted her to continue speaking, despite the fact that all of this information was in the painstakingly typed papers he had in front of him. The framed certificate over his head read "YALE." Maybe that explained it…or maybe it was just men, she thought.

"Russian, French, two classes in Portuguese. I find it easy to learn languages, Mister Wright." She felt oddly reluctant to confess her skills to this athletic-looking guy who had in all likelihood landed this job in Lyndon Baines Johnson's office because of his family connections.

"You have an ear for them, obviously. How well can you read them?" His wire-rimmed glasses slid down his nose and he shoved them back up and squinted at her.

"At the newspaper and novel level. Probably not anything technical without a dictionary." She tried a slight smile, nothing flirty, and a quick nod to urge the conversation along.

"You are a citizen of the United States, right? So if we offer you this job working for Representative Johnson, you can take it? No problems with background of any sort, no Reds, no Wobblies?"

"Born in Galveston." What else could she say to convince him she was perfect for this job?

"You can provide documentation of your birth." This came out as a statement, not a question.

Rosalind nodded. Her copy of the birth certificate was in a desk drawer in her single room at the boarding house where she lived. Rosalind Fisher, born in Galveston Texas, to Sophia Fisher and Michael Fisher. That her father had legally changed his last name from Fishbein to Fisher and his first name from Moishe to Michael was no one's business.

"And you are not married? If you are married, we won't hire you," Wright said. "Not enough jobs for men these days, let alone women."

"Not married, not engaged. I support myself and have since I graduated high school."

"Why aren't you married?"

Rosalind shrugged and stared at her hands in her lap hoping he would move on to the next question, if there was one.

Wright rustled papers on his desk as if to fill the silence, then said, "Tell me more about yourself."

She looked up and focused on a spot just over his left shoulder. "I got my diploma from Austin High School in 1930 when I was sixteen. I took summer classes to have enough credits. Now I'm taking classes at UT Austin at night and working during the day." She rubbed her thumb harder to quell her impatience. It had been an eight-year slog towards a college diploma, and Rosalind was just two classes away now. The list of what could prevent graduation leapt into her head. She blinked to refocus.

"Ah. Yes, I read all that. Admirable."

Rosalind nodded.

"Just one more thing. You're Jewish, correct? Related to the Fishbein family here, even though the name on your birth certificate is Rosalind Fisher."

"Yes. My cousins." The slight smile remained frozen on Rosalind's face. Why had Wright gone to such lengths to find out that information? She felt the job slipping out of her grasp. But then she remembered that Jim Novy, the most prominent Jew in Texas, was an outspoken supporter of Lyndon Baines Johnson. Maybe Johnson wanted to please his rich supporter by hiring a Jew? Rosalind had never met Novy, but he'd given her a small scholarship to the university and renewed it every year. Perhaps that counted for something.

"The Representative wants to have someone from that part of his constituency for this job assignment," Wright said, confirming Rosalind's hunch. "I'd suggest for now, though, that you keep your religion to yourself. Your qualifications for the position are superb. You're hired, Miss Fisher."

It took her a few seconds to process what the man had said. Rosalind shook her head, then smiled brightly. "Thank you so much, sir."

He leaned across the desk and offered his hand. "Oh, Miss Fisher. Do you speak that Jewish language, too? Sorry, meant to ask it before."

"Hebrew?"

"No, I don't think so. Yidle?"

"Yiddish. I speak it and write it. It's the lingua…" She uncrossed her legs, which were now sticky from the silk stockings combined with humidity, and nerves.

"Lingua franca of European Jews," Wright said, nodding. "It'll come in handy."

Handy for what? Rosalind wondered. Jewish immigration from Europe had dried up like a creek bed in August.

"Well, you've got five hours to pack up and be at the train station. Here's a roundtrip ticket to Washington, DC and directions on where to go when you get there. There's twenty dollars, too, for you out of the representative's special fund. It's for meals and whatever else you might need." He picked up an envelope from the blotter on his desk. "The representative's central office wants to talk to you once you get there—some kind of special assignment that you'll get more information on. You'll check in with Miss Eleanor Lassiter."

Rosalind stared at the envelope in his hand. She didn't want to go anywhere near the Atlantic Ocean, and a train trip was at least two days. "Possibly there's a misunderstanding, Mister Wright? I applied for a position in Representative Johnson's district office here in Austin. I have plans—"

"Miss Fisher," Wright said, dropping the envelope back on the desk with a smack. "What plans would interfere with a job for a great Texas member of the United States House of Representatives?" He shook his head.

Rosalind was in no position to toss this opportunity away, particularly if doing so meant crossing a congressman and Jim Novy. She could kiss her scholarship and maybe her whole future in Texas goodbye if she did that. She took a deep breath and steadied her voice.

"Please let me explain, Mister Wright. I've signed up for a course on education at UT. I need just that and Russian Level Two for my BA. Since it wasn't going to interfere with the hours you wanted me to work, I made the tuition payment two days ago."

"Russian? Be careful with that. Commies are not welcome in this great state."

"I took the loyalty oath, sir. But if we don't understand the Russians, how can we fight them?" Rosalind thought back to the ceremony in which she had held her hand high along with the other UT students and had sworn her allegiance to the United States and denied ever having had any ties to communism. She'd done that twice, once for the general curriculum and once for signing up to learn more Russian. She hadn't thought twice about it, since she had no intention of stepping out of line.

"Yes, well, I doubt teaching Russian in Austin will help anyone understand our biggest enemy."

Rosalind wondered if Wright had ever considered that Germany, a country that had just marched into and over Austria and claimed it as Germany's own, was actually a much bigger threat to world peace than the communists in Russia. The situation for German, Austrian, and Polish Jews was disintegrating by the second. She read the papers and listened to the radio, and the news reports made that very clear.

"I'm sure we can get you your money back," Wright said, "or at least make sure they keep it and let you in next semester if you're somehow delayed getting back from DC. The question right now is whether you are taking this" —he extended the envelope towards her— "and the job?"

"Yes, of course," Rosalind said. "And thank you." She was in no position to turn down the job if she wanted to finally move out of the boarding house and eat decently for a change. A little delay in finishing her classes was worth it. And besides, her life was a slow crawl as it was.

She tucked the envelope with the ticket and the money into her purse and stood. The phone on Wright's desk rang as she turned to leave and she heard the secretary say, "Charles Marsh on the line."

Rosalind recognized the name. Charles Marsh was a newspaper magnate, publisher of the two newspapers in Austin as well as three others in Texas. Johnson sure was well-connected.

Wright snatched up the receiver. "Mister Marsh," he said, "how good of you to call. She meets all of his criteria. No, I didn't tell her…" He dismissed Rosalind with a wave towards the door.

Was Wright talking about her? Why would Marsh want to know if she'd taken the job?

Wright's secretary made a "shut the door" gesture as Rosalind stepped into the small waiting area. Rosalind could hear Wright saying, "Yes, Mister Marsh," as she pulled on the handle and felt the door click into place.

***

On the streetcar back to her boarding house, Rosalind decided to focus on the winning lottery ticket she'd just been handed and not think more about the mystery of the trip to DC and the oddness of Marsh's call. She imagined herself standing in front of a class of high school students, calling on one after another to translate Cervantes' *Don Quixote* into English before returning to her own little one-bedroom apartment, where her closet would hold more than five changes of clothes.

Rosalind began to plan. She got off and walked as fast as she could, trying to decide how best to prepare for the trip ahead. She wouldn't have time to wash her hair, she decided. It would never dry in the humidity and would frizz up, leaving her looking like a red dandelion going to seed. Blue eyes and red hair made her stand out too much, that's what her mother had always said, as if Rosalind could do anything about the traits she'd inherited. She checked her pocket watch. She had enough time for a quick bath and packing.

A guy shouted out of his car window, "Hey, toots. Quite a looker. Need a ride?"

Rosalind ignored him, like she did most men. She'd long ago decided that finding a good guy with a job and a future was—much like looking for an intact seashell after a storm in Galveston, which Rosalind had done one weekend as a child—a totally futile endeavor.

As she walked, Rosalind considered the upcoming train trip. She'd have to change trains in Chicago, which meant it would take almost two days to get to Washington, sitting up in coach, trying to sleep.

She had limited wardrobe options. Two white blouses, two black skirts, two modest day dresses—one pink, one blue—and a daring pair of very modern trousers, a splurge that she thought looked good on her long legs.

She would also need books for the trip. They were her favorite form of entertainment, followed by movies, when she could afford them, and student arts shows. Her sociology professor called such activities "escapism," as if anyone could escape from Austin. The city was isolated, plus it had endured seventy-two dust storms in the past year alone. Thank God

Rosalind loved to read. She enjoyed both real and imagined adventure stories and had closely followed the preparation for Amelia Earhart's flight and been devastated when Earhart's plane dropped out of the sky into nowhere. "Let that be a lesson to you," her cousin, Hannah, said. "Stop dreaming and learn to be content where you are."

Rosalind mentally scanned her bookshelf as she walked. She'd already read all of the best sellers, *Brave New World, Of Mice and Men,* and Eric Ambler's *Epitaph for a Spy,* which was the best of the bunch. Luckily, she'd just checked out *Rebecca* and could take that along.

A frisson of excitement ran up Rosalind's spine as she walked to the boarding house. The neighborhood had once been genteel, a popular area where lawyers, doctors, and successful merchants lived with their wives, children, and pets. Her boarding house had been an elegant family home straight out of a Grimm Brothers' tale, with a steeply pitched roof, intricate carving on the door, and a gnomic knocker. Now every available room bedded a woman or two, except for the small sitting room, dining room and kitchen. The formal garden that had once surrounded the home was now forlorn, full of dandelions and not much else.

Rosalind let herself in and climbed the stairs. In her dormer room, she took off her blouse, skirt, and stockings and hung them on hooks inside her wardrobe to air out. Then she reread the instructions Wright had given her. She was due in Representative Johnson's office in Washington in two days to meet with a Miss Lassiter at 11 a.m.

Rosalind had just paid the rent for the month so the tidy, ten by ten-foot room with its dingy curtained window was hers for now. She'd just need to be back by August 21 when September's rent was due or Marcella Agostini, the widowed owner of the house, would empty out her things and give the room to another single woman.

As if summoned, she heard Marcella's heavy step on the stairs and then three quick taps on her door. "Rosalind, there's that Jewish minister's secretary downstairs to see you."

"Thank you, Mrs. Agostini." It did no good to correct Mrs. Agostini by reminding her that Jewish men of God were rabbis, or even that synagogues were not churches. Mrs. Agostini was content to be willfully ignorant. "Yeah, yeah," she'd say and then go right back to using the wrong word. She knew Rosalind was Jewish yet routinely loaded her plate with bacon at breakfast, which Rosalind would choke down since breakfast was included with her rent and often her only meal until dinner.

The "Jewish minister's secretary" Mrs. Agostini was referring to was Hannah, Rosalind's cousin, who was ten years older and had taken her in when she was orphaned at age twelve. As Rosalind smoothed her hair and pulled on the skirt and blouse she'd just hung up—no pants for conservative Hannah—she wondered what could have brought Hannah to see her? The Jewish High Holy Days were coming soon, at the very beginning of September, so maybe she needed help again in the office. Rosalind sighed as she descended the stairs. She owed Hannah everything for giving her a place to live when Rosalind was orphaned at twelve, but she had begun to resent the weekly requests to put in hours at the synagogue office or watch the two youngest children of Hannah and Harold's seven.

"How nice to see you, Hannah," she said, stepping into the small sitting room.

Hannah rose from the overstuffed burgundy wing chair. "I hope I'm not disturbing you, Rachele," she said, using Rosalind's Yiddish name. Her smile, normally lustrous, was gone.

Rosalind forced a pleasant expression onto her face. "No, of course not," she said, and braced herself for whatever request was coming. The train left in a few hours, so whatever Hannah wanted, it would have to be quick. She took the wing chair opposite her cousin. "How are the children? Harold?"

Hannah flicked her hand in the air to dismiss the question. "All fine. This came in the mail Friday. I'm bringing it to you to see if you can translate it for me." Hannah pursed her lips as if restraining a sigh. "It's from our cousin in Warsaw. He sent a photograph of the family, too."

She pulled a folded sheet of onion-skin paper from her purse. Rosalind took the letter, which was covered front and back in tight, small cursive, the handwriting of the educated. The letter was in Polish and signed by someone named Jakub who she'd never heard of.

"Let me try to read it to myself first." Without looking at Hannah for agreement, Rosalind studied the text. An apology for writing after so many years of silence. A hope that the letter found Hannah and Harold well in the safety of Texas of the United States with their children. A remembrance of the infant Hannah being whisked away by her immigrating parents, and a reminder of how very close Hannah's father and Jakub's father had been. A regret that Jakub had not kept that up, but he had been busy with university and now with his medical practice. His wife had died, and their daughter was now fourteen and their sons were twelve and eight. That was the first side.

Rosalind turned the letter over. The time to leave his beloved Warsaw with his family had come. Jakub needed a visa to the United States, where Hannah was his only family.

Jakub asked Hannah to please do what she could. He was—or had been—a highly regarded pediatrician, but now his practice was restricted to Jews, he wrote, and he'd lost his office in the heart of the city. The children were hounded by the rising tide of anti-Semitism every day. *I am desperate, dear cousin, and our lives are at risk.*

Rosalind looked at the photograph. Jakub was a solid looking, middle-aged man with a trim beard, wearing a tailored herringbone suit. The older of his sons, in long trousers and a cuffed shirt, looked shockingly like a photograph Rosalind had seen of her father around the same age. The younger son held a small dog by a leash, and both boys' expressions suggested they'd rather be anywhere else. The girl, with curly hair like Rosalind's, gripped her father's shoulder. Rosalind could sense her white knuckles, the effort she was making to smile.

Rosalind paused. She was also Jakub's cousin because they were both related to Hannah, and she wondered whether Jakub remembered her father. But perhaps they'd never met, since Jakub was from the educated and assimilated side of the family, not the ultra-Orthodox side her father had fled. Her father had never spoken of his torn family ties and had always put her off when she'd asked questions. Then he died and so did his version of family history. *Sic fugit gloria mundi*—or close enough.

"Jakub wants to come to the United States," Rosalind told her cousin. "He needs a visa for himself and the three children."

"It's not possible," Hannah said, shaking her head. "No one gets family out of Europe now. Only those people, those Einsteins of the world, get out." Hannah began to cry.

Rosalind forced herself to ignore her cousin's tears. She had no time to comfort her or engage in a lengthy conversation; her train was leaving soon, and she still needed to bathe and pack. "I'm afraid you'll need to tell him that," she said, holding the letter out towards Hannah.

She had intended the words to come out soft and soothing, but Hannah reacted with shock. "No! You write him that Harold and I will do whatever we can. Which is nothing, but don't tell him that. Tell him to leave word at the American Embassy there and run." Hannah gripped her purse and stood up. "You're good in Polish, Rachele. Keep the letter in case… I don't know. Give me an English translation."

"Of course. It's just…I'll be leaving Austin for a few days for job training."

"But the Holy Days are coming?"

Rosalind sighed. Hannah had never understood that the Jewish calendar did not control Rosalind's life the way it did hers.

"It's only a few days, Hannahle."

Hannah left without asking any questions about Rosalind's life, well-being, or the job training that was taking her out of town, and Rosalind was grateful for that.

She started up the stairs to her room. She'd have to get an airmail stamp to send a letter back to Jakub in Warsaw, which would cost three times as much as a regular stamp. At least she'd be in Washington, where airmail was probably readily available, and the letter would certainly reach Warsaw in less time.

A little shudder passed through Rosalind as she entered her room. She'd write what Hannah had instructed, but the outlook for her cousins was grim. Almost no Jew left Europe now. There was nowhere to go. The girl in the photo would probably never graduate high school, and what kind of future would there be for the boys?

Rosalind shook away these dark thoughts and turned her attention back to the task at hand. She pulled the shabby, black suitcase her father had bought used almost four decades before from under her bed and began to pack.

When her clothes were neatly folded in the suitcase, she put Jakub's letter in its envelope on top of them. Then she closed the suitcase and sat on the bed to inspect the contents of her purse. She had the twenty dollars Johnson's office had provided, plus six dollars left from her week's wages at Woolworths. She also had the train tickets, a handkerchief, her gun, and the directions she'd been provided. She picked up *Rebecca* and checked the due date. It was due in nine days, more than enough time. She dropped the book in her purse.

***

"I have to go out of town, Mrs. Agostini," she said, poking her head into the kitchen where the landlady was having a cup of tea. "I've locked my door and have the key."

"Now, you know when the rent is due."

"Yes."

"If you're not back timely you'll find your belongings, such as they are, in a box in the cellar. I'll hold 'em for a week." Marcella stared at her. "And no coming back sick." She got up and leaned close to Rosalind to whisper, "If you're delayed in a feminine way, try Molex pills, or Cote. Or see a doctor."

Rosalind felt her cheeks flame, the curse of being a redhead. "No, really, no. That's not the reason. It's a job. I have to go to the capital."

"This here is the capital."

"Of America. Washington DC."

Marcella took a step back and looked Rosalind up and down as if she were on sale. "My, my, my. A job that takes you to Washington DC. Well, good luck."

As Rosalind closed the door behind her and lugged her suitcase down the front steps to the sidewalk, she could hear Marcella's laughter. Good luck indeed.

By the time she'd walked the twelve blocks to the railroad station, she was hot and damp from the top of her head to her toes again, all benefits of the quick bath erased. She'd no sooner sunk onto a bench than the station master announced the departure of the train to Chicago in five minutes.

Luggage safely stowed, Rosalind stared out the train window. She watched the landscape change from buildings to dry pastureland and cattle. Then she picked up *Rebecca* and began to read.

CHAPTER 2

"Miss Lassiter?" Rosalind tapped on the doorpost of Representative Johnson's office suite in the Longworth Building. She'd ridden up in a jeweled box, a polished walnut and gold-trimmed elevator, and then walked down the corridor of lavender and green marble. That the Longworth Building had come in at one million dollars under budget—a fact touted by the Democratic administration and therefore lauded in Marsh's newspaper—was amazing, especially now that she could see its gloriousness.

According to the clock on the wall, Rosalind had managed to arrive two minutes early for her appointment after traveling across half the United States and walking from Union Station. The blonde woman sitting at the receptionist desk raised her head and pointed sternly to the telephone handset she had pressed against her left ear, then pointed to a chair. Both gestures carried the authority of a stern fifth grade teacher. Rosalind sat down, wedging her suitcase next to the chair and wishing she had a sweater she could drape over its worn corners and peeling cover.

"Yes, sir. Yes. I am making a note of that as we speak. Yes, I will be sure Representative Johnson sees this. Yes, I will be sure he gets back to you. Do I have your telephone number correctly?" The woman recited a prefix and numbers from a note pad. "Yes, sir, I will ask the representative to call you from his private office."

From her vantage point, Rosalind had a good view of two of the office's walls, one of which had an ornate mirror and clock, and the other a painting of long-horn cattle kicking up knee-high dust on a trail. Typical boring Texan décor. Rosalind preferred the young, progressive artists of Austin with their wild color palettes and modern themes, but she guessed Johnson either didn't like that kind of art or couldn't afford to have folks think he did. She glanced at the woman at the desk.

Mid-thirties, she thought, with impeccable make-up, a blush-colored blouse in a satiny material, and no sign of wrinkles or sweat stains.

"Thank you, sir. Goodbye to you as well." The woman hung up and looked at Rosalind. "I'm Miss Lassiter. What can I do for you?"

"I'm Rosalind Fisher. Mister Wright of Representative Johnson's Austin office instructed me to come here."

"Hmm."

"I was instructed to be here at eleven."

"And so you are."

Rosalind waited for a first name, a smile, any statement that Miss Lassiter knew why Rosalind was there, but Miss Lassiter continued to look at her as if appraising her value. Rosalind tried counting her breaths to keep from opening her mouth and letting her thoughts roll out.

"Well, Miss Fisher, it appears that you are to stay at my small apartment for" —Miss Lassiter shook her head as if she could not believe what she was about to say— "as long as it takes."

"As long as what takes?"

"How do you think I would know that, Miss Fisher? You may sit there until you and I can go home, which will be around two. You'll sleep on my couch, which is really a day bed. I have no roommate, so I guess that's why you're my honored guest and not someone else's." She rolled a sheet of paper into her typewriter and opened a steno pad. "I have work to finish for the representative. The women's lounge is out the door. Turn right and keep walking. Maybe you want to wash your face." The last sentence was an order.

"Yes, thank you." Rosalind especially wanted to wash her face now that it was flushed from the impact of Miss Lassiter's words.

She spent the next two hours and twenty-nine minutes in a combination of tedium and tension, staring at the pages of her novel, each word like the tick of a clock, nodding to show her alertness whenever Miss Lassiter glanced her way, and wondering what it was that would take as long as it took. She had no idea what she was in for and was grateful that whatever it was, it couldn't take longer than two days, when her return train left.

***

"Here we are. Hold my purse while I get the door unlocked." Miss Lassiter pulled a key ring with seven dangling keys out and handed the purse to Rosalind. The keys looked as if they weighed a pound and the purse pulled on Rosalind's arm. She put down her suitcase.

"I thought Texans were tough, Miss Fisher. You look a bit woebegone, if you don't mind my commenting." Miss Lassiter undid what Rosalind hoped was the last of a series of five locks, each requiring a different key.

"I could use a real washcloth and towel after being in that train for two days. It also does appear that the women who live here in Washington face more threats than rattlesnakes and rifles," she said, trying to lighten the mood. "I only need two keys in Texas."

Rosalind saw the corners of Miss Lassiter's mouth twitch upward.

"And I want to thank—"

"Don't bother. These are the boss's orders. He speaketh and we doeth." She pushed the door open and motioned for Rosalind to enter.

The daybed, with a pink throw and two matched pillows, took up the entire wall on one side of the room. A sink, a counter-high refrigerator that was protesting loudly in the heat, and a four-burner hot plate held one wall opposite a window, under which a gateleg table and two chairs stood. The fourth wall was half-hidden by a screen, but Rosalind could see the end of a twin bed with a yellow cover, corners tucked tightly under the mattress. Tidy. And meant to stay that way.

"You can slide that suitcase under the daybed. The bathroom's a bit austere." Miss Lassiter looked at Rosalind with an eyebrow cocked, as if assessing whether she knew what *austere* meant. Rosalind nodded. "Toilet and sink and a small cast iron tub. Better than sharing like some do at the Y."

"Do you have any clue, Miss Lassiter, as to what my coming to Washington is about?"

"All I have heard is that you are…quite talented in middle-European languages and that is an asset for the specific task at hand. There are many capable people here who also are proficient in those tongues, but it is not my job to wonder why you were chosen."

She certainly wondered why Rosalind from her tone of voice. And what specific task? Rosalind started to ask but Miss Lassiter kept talking.

"After the task is done, it will be office work for you, I suppose. Like any position with a politician, especially one of Mister Johnson's caliber, you will be required to stretch yourself. And I do not need to tell you, I'm sure, that as a woman you will need to stretch further and longer, or you will find yourself in the typing pool or teaching or…"

Or what? Rosalind bristled. She *wanted* to be a teacher. Just let her teach at Austin High School, that would be aces.

"In the meantime, wash up. Possibly even bathe. I'll grab a towel for you. We'll be expecting a guest in about an hour."

The lukewarm water available for the tub was perfect for the warm day. Rosalind sank low, her legs dangling over the end, and then dipped her head backwards into the water and rubbed at her scalp. The sensation was delicious, and she stayed in the bath as long as she dared. As she was climbing out to grab a towel, she heard a loud knock at the apartment's door.

"Just a minute," Miss Lassiter called. Then the bathroom door opened, and she threw a towel on the floor along with Rosalind's pants and underwear from the suitcase she must have opened, and an azure blouse Rosalind didn't recognize. "Make yourself decent and hurry up about it. The blouse should fit. Yours is a bit damp."

As the door closed, Rosalind heard a man's voice say, "We'll talk here," to which Miss Lassiter replied, "You're almost forty-minutes early. Sit down."

After that, no one spoke loud enough for Rosalind to hear.

Fully dressed, with the blouse that was only a little bit too big and bare feet, Rosalind opened the door to see Miss Lassiter sitting on the daybed and a slim, suited man who looked to be in his mid-thirties sitting in a chair opposite her. A leather briefcase sat on the floor next to him. The tailoring of the suit, the briefcase, even the artful haircut all whispered *rich*.

"If you think that's best," Miss Lassiter said.

"I do, Eleanor."

Eleanor Lassiter did not seem pleased by whatever they'd decided, Rosalind thought. "Eleanor, the bath was perfect," she said, awkwardly standing in the middle of the room.

A smile lingered at the corner of Eleanor's mouth. "Good. But let's not be on a first name basis in case something happens."

Rosalind slipped her bare feet into her shoes and felt her cheeks redden. She had the job, didn't she? Was it really necessary that Eleanor keep putting her in her place?

"I'm Frank Baron," the man said. "I've come to speak with you on behalf of Representative Johnson."

Rosalind sat down next to Eleanor on the daybed. "Here?"

"The matter is delicate."

"Oh." Rosalind was baffled. She began to rub her left thumb with her right forefinger and tried to take a deep breath.

"Before we go further," Frank said, "you need to agree to keep our conversation private. Please know—and I don't mean this as a threat in any way—that if you somehow let slip what we are talking about, you'll not be able to find a job here or in Texas."

"Goodness. That certainly does sounds like a threat," Rosalind said, willing herself to stay seated.

Eleanor shook her head and again Rosalind felt like a chastened child.

"The task you're needed for involves accompanying the representative's very good friend, Jim Novy, and Jim's sixteen-year-old son, to Poland," Frank said. "You're to make sure the representative's friend is appropriately taken care of, and that his concerns are addressed. You speak Polish fluently, of course, along with several other languages that may come in handy—including Yiddish, I understand? —and you look like a nice young woman, a representative's clerk. And you are Jewish, so you understand what that situation is for Jews."

Rosalind considered how to respond. She was a Jew, yes, but she was no expert in Jewish issues and kept her distance from the Jewish community as best she could. The news out of Europe was horrifying, but what could one woman who was not even out of college do about it? "I do know the outline of the political situation," she said finally. "But only just what anyone can learn from the papers and the news broadcasts. I'd never assume to understand the fear European Jews are experiencing, much less know how to help them."

"Of course. None of us can, to be honest," Frank said. "But this will be just a couple of weeks out of your life for an important job. Then you can go back to Austin and Representative Johnson's office there, I promise." Frank sat back in his chair.

"I don't think I'm the right person for this job," Rosalind said, wishing very much she had never left Austin. Johnson's office could find someone else, surely, and she'd mail the letter to Jakub and head back to Texas in time for classes to start at the university. She'd chalk the whole thing up to an adventure and be right back where she started, no worse off than any other young single woman.

"I think we need to let Rosalind eat something and get a good night's sleep," Eleanor said, standing up. "I imagine this is an awful lot to take in. There's a decent little place around the corner that serves spaghetti. Let's eat, and then you and I can talk more about this in the morning, Rosalind."

***

The spaghetti dinner was filling and the conversation at the table was light, mostly Frank and Eleanor speaking about local affairs. The daybed was surprisingly comfortable after the train, and Rosalind woke to the smell of coffee and the sound of the percolator.

"I'm frying up eggs for us, Rosalind. I'm due in the office in about an hour. Boss gave me some leeway because I've got you here," Eleanor said.

"I'll go to the station to see if I can get my return ticket changed to today. I'll rinse out the blouse you loaned me and hang it in the bathroom." Rosalind pulled her last fresh set of underwear out of her suitcase.

"Sure." Eleanor took four eggs from a carton. "We can chat a bit more over coffee about how that might work."

Rosalind heard the butter sizzling in the pan. "Is there a post office nearby where I can buy an airmail envelope?"

"We're near DuPont Circle, and the main post office is on Pennsylvania Avenue. Not terribly far. What do you need it for?" Eleanor slid the eggs into the pan. "Over easy is how I make them. There's bread in the refrigerator."

"To send a letter to Poland," Rosalind said, taking Eleanor's cue and retrieving the bread. She put a piece on each plate.

"Then the main post office is what you want. I'll point you in the right direction. Do you have relatives there?"

"A cousin."

"Ahh. Bad time to have a Jewish family member anywhere near Germany. Bad time, really, to be anyone anywhere near Germany. Look at poor Austria and Czechoslovakia…"

Eleanor put two mugs of coffee on the table then plated the eggs as Rosalind pulled up a chair.

They ate in silence for a few minutes, then Eleanor said, "So I understand Jim Novy recommended you for this interview. Why is that?"

"Mister Novy is a kind, generous, and very rich Jew in a state where being generous and rich helps enormously. But I don't know him personally." Rosalind felt a sense of satisfaction that her suspicion Novy had recommended her was confirmed.

"Hmm. Tell me more." Eleanor took a bite of her eggs and wiped up the yolk with a piece of bread.

"He's the most prominent member of the synagogue where my cousin, Hannah, is the secretary. They're acquainted and Mister Novy knows that she took me in after my parents died. He also knows that I finished high school early, at age sixteen. Apparently, he thinks I'm smart, because he's given me a scholarship to help with tuition every year. But I've never met him."

"So, an arms-length relationship to you. He didn't give you a job himself?"

"No." Rosalind considered explaining that she would never publicly ally herself with Jim Novy. All she wanted was to fit in. She was a red-haired, blue-eyed woman who was four years older than her fellow students, unnervingly good at languages, and liked art, all of which made her enough of an oddity among the girls at UT. If she ever wanted to be invited into their circles and continue to share the occasional cigarette, publicly outing herself as a Jew wasn't the way to go about things.

"What brought you to the representative's office then?" Eleanor asked, cleaning her plate.

"I responded to an ad looking for particular language skills. And I'd like to have a steady job with the government, as long as I can finish my bachelor's degree and take the courses I need to teach. If I can't get this job, I'll go back to Woolworth's."

"You should do something that taps into your talents a bit more than filing papers and typing someone else's letters, or, worse, selling at a five-and-dime. Let me explain what Representative Johnson—and Mister Novy and Representative Johnson's good friend, Charles Marsh—have in mind for you."

"Thanks, but I just have a year left and then I can teach."

"Maybe you want to do more than teach. This would be an oppor—"

Rosalind shook her head. "Teaching is what I want to do. And why would Charles Marsh and Representative Johnson even know me, let alone have a job for me? They're famous and powerful. Surely there is someone else who can take Jim Novy and his kid around Poland?"

Eleanor got up and, without replying, cleaned the dishes and mugs in the small sink.

"It's time to get to work," she said, drying the last of the coffee cups. "Here's the deal, Rosalind. I figure I have until a little after lunch to persuade you to take this job. If I can't do that, then I'll put you on that train back to Austin. I will tell you this much, though: You're right that there are other people, but no one has your specific skills. I've read all the resumes, and yours stood out. And you're Jewish." She placed the mug in the cupboard. "All of that could prove very helpful for situations that can't be predicted." She turned to Rosalind and smiled. "So, we'll stop at the post office on the way in. Ready?"

Rosalind grabbed her suitcase and followed Eleanor out the door, her mind spinning over what unpredictable situations Eleanor could possibly be referring to.

***

The post office building took up the entire block.

"I didn't expect it to be this big," Rosalind said, hurrying to keep up with Eleanor. People surged in and out of buildings around them, all of them in a hurry.

"Your tax dollars at work. It just opened about five years ago. The art inside is interesting. Lots of murals, courtesy of the WPA."

"Washington makes Austin look small."

"You have oil and all those resources," Eleanor said with a thin smile, "but we have everyone's resources." She pointed to the crosswalk. "Your relative's in Warsaw?"

"Yes. But I've never met him."

"Why does that matter?"

Rosalind shrugged. "I think it's normal to care more for people you know in person than strangers far away. Anyway, I'll be as quick as possible." She left Eleanor in front of the post office and walked up the steps to the looming main entrance with her suitcase bumping against her thigh.

"How long will it take for a letter to get to Warsaw by air?" Rosalind asked the man at the counter as she set the suitcase between her legs.

"We can get a letter to Warsaw in forty-eight hours or less, but we're not responsible for how fast the postal service in Warsaw gets it to any address." He spoke with a tone of exasperation which, in Rosalind's mind, did not bode well for any post office clients coming after her as the day progressed.

"How much is the stamp?"

"Ten cents. Do you need an envelope and paper, Miss? You've got people waiting in back of you."

"Yes, all of that." Rosalind reached into her purse and pulled out a dollar bill from her wallet. As she handed it to the clerk, she felt a light tap on her ankle and whirled around. A thin figure was crouched with its hands around her suitcase. Rosalind grabbed the back of the figure's collar and dragged it upwards. It was a young girl with short-cropped hair and a grimy face. "Oh no, you don't," Rosalind said.

"Security, over here," the clerk called out.

The two people standing in line behind Rosalind shook their heads. She moved her grip to the shoulder of the girl, who now had tears running down her cheeks.

"My ma got no money." The girl couldn't have been more than ten or eleven and spoke with a deep Southern accent.

Rosalind let go of the girl's shirt. "Go on, then. Security is on the way." She grabbed a quarter from her change. "Take this."

The girl ran out the main door. The clerk shook his head. "Okay, then. Just stand aside, Miss, so the folks in back of you can take care of their business."

Rosalind moved over to an unoccupied counter, keeping her suitcase in her grip. "No need," she told the security guard when he came over. "Just a kid scrounging for change."

***

"Good reflexes and an interesting choice to give her some change and let her go. Especially as you have so little money yourself," Eleanor said when Rosalind rejoined her. "I was watching from over there." She pointed to just inside the post office's main entrance.

"Can I trust you to mail this letter for me tomorrow?" Rosalind asked. "I'll write it before I leave and put the stamp on it."

"Still going back to Texas?"

"Yes. I'll just walk to the train station and get the ticket changed for today this afternoon, if possible."

"If that's really what you want, Rosalind, I'll have one of the clerks do it if you give me the ticket. It'll save you the to-ing and fro-ing."

Rosalind scanned Eleanor's face for signs of deception, but her expression was the bland mask she'd first seen in Johnson's office.

"I think I'd rather do it myself. But thanks."

Eleanor smiled half-way. "You don't trust me."

Trust? Rosalind wanted to laugh. Trust had gotten her a boyfriend who'd tried to skip town with five of her dollars, a professor who'd tried to fondle her during office hours, and a so-called friend who'd tried to spread nasty rumors about her because she was Jewish.

"Don't take it personally," Rosalind said. "I don't trust most people."

"Another asset for the work we have in mind. You're so raw though," Eleanor said as if she were thinking aloud. "Makes it hard to see if you have the right mettle for this."

Rosalind bit her tongue and walked alongside Eleanor back to Representative Lyndon Baines Johnson's office.

***

Dear Jakub,

I am Rosalind Fisher, also your first cousin on your mother's side. My father was Moishe Fishbein of blessed memory. I am replying on behalf of myself and Hannah Fishbein, to whom you wrote. Hannah does not read or write Polish. I do, which is why you are hearing from me. We are following the terrible news from Europe. Hannah wants to assure you that she will do everything she can to bring you and the children over to the United States. She and her husband will submit the paperwork to act as your sponsor and hope they are accepted. It is helpful that you are a pediatrician, because that shows you are able to earn a living here once you pass the required tests.

Rosalind studied the English text that she had written as a draft for the letter. Once she started to write it on the air mail letter in Polish, she was committed. And she'd told Hannah she would provide a copy, so the message needed to be gentle and hopeful, but promise nothing.

Have you made an application for immigration to the US Embassy in Warsaw? We know that the number of people allowed into the United States is very limited. If you have not, do that as soon as you receive this.

She could have written "Your chances are slim to nil, as almost no one from Poland, much less a Jew, is allowed to immigrate." The Evian Conference of thirty-two countries and twenty-four voluntary organizations had met in July to discuss the Jewish immigration problem—the "problem" being that Jews were desperate to go anywhere, as long as it was away from Germany. The countries refused to do anything more than offer sympathy, except for, oddly enough, the Dominican Republic.

Other countries, especially the Dominican Republic, are open to immigration, Rosalind wrote. *We are pleased you sent the picture of the family. The children look delightful, smart, pretty and handsome. How sad they have lost their mother. We send belated condolences.*

Rosalind tried not to think about her own mother as she wrote. It was important to keep those floodgates closed lest the memory of her mother's smell, coupled with the aroma of fresh baked bread and the feeling of her mother's touch—the calloused fingers making a delightful scratch as she rubbed Rosalind's back—came pouring in.

Eleanor's shadow fell on the page and Rosalind looked up from where she sat at the edge of Eleanor's desk, trying to take up as little space as possible. Eleanor had allowed her to use the desk as she stepped into the inner sanctum of Johnson's private space ten minutes before. When she'd opened that door, Rosalind had glimpsed a blue leather couch and an enormous desk, suitable for a man over six feet tall representing the great state of Texas. Eleanor had quickly shut the door behind her, restoring the cushion of velvet silence.

"Good thing Mister Johnson is out for August recess so you can violate protocol and be so close to my work," Eleanor said, leaning over to look at what Rosalind had written. "We've put you on the payroll. Temporarily. Count that twenty you got in Austin as an advance."

Rosalind took a deep breath. Eleanor wasn't going to give up on trying to persuade her to take the job.

"So, you'll continue to bunk with me for the next few days until we get it sorted out," Eleanor continued, returning to her chair. "Again, this is America and so, of course, you are free to refuse this decently paying job. You are not my prisoner. But you might want to consider the larger picture. The representative wants you, and even I think you are beginning to show a hint of promise." Eleanor smiled and began to type notes from her steno pad.

The weight of the letter Rosalind was drafting to her cousin dragged at her thoughts. If she went with Jim Novy to Poland and helped a bit with the paperwork and translating for him, could she at least see Jakub and his family? And maybe a few weeks of traveling safely under the umbrella of the United States of America with a very important man and his son at the request of another very important man would help her build some connections, which she currently did not have. Maybe it would lead to financial aid for graduate school, and possibly even a UT professorship. She wouldn't be a Margaret Meade, but she'd be somebody.

"I'll think about it more," Rosalind said. "But I can't lose my room at the boarding house."

Eleanor looked up. "Really? That's what's worrying you?"

Rosalind tried to hide her anger. "I have very few things that are mine, and they are all in that boarding house. My photographs, my books, my texts from my classes at UT, my high school annual. If the rent isn't paid on that room by August twenty-first, I'll lose everything I own." She took a deep breath. "My world is precarious, Eleanor, and not just because I'm a woman and a Jew."

Eleanor pointed to herself. "Black Irish, potato famine, 'no dogs, no Irish, no Jews.' I don't talk about it much, but it scarred my gran, and my ma after her. I'll make sure your room's taken care of."

Rosalind managed a thin smile. "Thank you. Just… Could you do it discretely, so my landlady doesn't think I'm… Well, whatever she'd think I was? That would make it very hard when I go back."

"Understood."

"And if I do this, I want permission to find my cousin and his children and help them with paperwork at the embassy."

"That can be arranged. Just don't promise them anything."

"I wouldn't."

So it was settled, Rosalind thought. She would do this special assignment for Johnson, translating for Jim Novy and his son. She would definitely be helpful to Mister Novy, who might think he remembered Polish well and was fluent in Yiddish, but likely didn't realize that when you're in your fifties and haven't spoken or read either language in thirty years with any regularity, the fine points slide away. And the fine points counted. So yes, she'd definitely be useful.

As for her cousin and his children, she'd do her best to be sympathetic, but what could she promise them except a bleak future? Some in the Jewish community in Europe and America were likening what was happening to pogroms, the tornadoes of hate that ripped through the Jewish sections of eastern Europe and Russia for centuries, leaving those who survived to rebuild and renew. Others thought Jews who remained in Germany's path were simply all doomed, and would have no chance to rebuild their lives. That certainly seemed likely to Rosalind.

She returned to drafting the letter to the cousins whose photograph sat before her. *It is possible I will travel to Poland in the next few weeks.* Should she mention that she worked for Representative Johnson? She decided not to. She didn't know who would read the letter before it got to Jakub, if it ever did, and besides, it might give her cousin the wrong idea about what she could do for him. *If I do, I will try to come and see you and do what I can to help with the paperwork.*

"Eleanor, when I send the copy of this letter to my cousin Hannah in Austin, may I put your address as somewhere to reach me if she needs me?"

"God, no. I'll add getting you a post office box to the list."

"What list is that?"

Eleanor tapped her head. "In here. Your boarding house landlady, new clothes and more of them, post office box, passport. Get a refund on the return ticket to Austin. You best get used to keeping lists only in your head for the work you're going to do. And now that I think of it, get used to running your own errands in DC."

She pulled open the top drawer of her desk and pulled out a trifold map with a US government logo. "Take this. Go to the train station first, which is here, and get the refund. You can use that cash to go back to the post office, there, and get a box. Call me from a payphone when you're done. Here's the number." She grabbed a sharpened pencil from the drawer's tray and wrote it down. "I'll meet you and we'll go clothes shopping."

Rosalind stood up, took the map and the draft of her letter, the air mail stamp and stationer, and put them all in her purse. Then she reached down for her suitcase.

"For heaven's sake, leave that thing here. And one last warning. We don't discuss this job anymore here in the office. Or with anyone besides you and me unless I'm there to clear it."

"What about…" Rosalind began to say Frank's name.

"Absolutely not him. He sees himself as State Department material, so who knows who he'd tell about this to move over there. What he thinks he knows now is too much."

"But this is just escorting Jim Novy to Poland, right?" Rosalind said.

"It's about that, sure. Hurry up and get to the post office, then remember to call me," Eleanor said. "Leave the suitcase in the corner."

Rosalind pocketed the paper as Eleanor went back to typing and walked out. She felt more weighted down by her sudden decision than she ever had by the suitcase she'd just left behind. Why would Frank want to tell people about her? Did Eleanor just suggest that Jim Novy's trip to Poland and Representative Johnson's involvement was salable knowledge that could move Frank up the government chain? What did Eleanor not want Frank to know more about?

Too late now. She'd agreed to take the job. Rosalind sighed and consulted the map. The first thing was to get her ticket refunded and then send the letter on its way to Warsaw.

***

Back at the post office, Rosalind wrote her letter to Jakub on the extra-thin paper and slid it into the envelope to which she'd affixed the air mail stamp. After delivering it to the counter, she walked over to the row of mailboxes and tried her key in the box that had just been allotted to her. The door to the box opened and she peered in. Of course, there was nothing but the interior of the post office itself. She locked the door and walked to the bank of payphones and sat in one of the booths.

"I'm done," she said to Eleanor when she picked up the phone.

"Wait for me. I'll be there soon. An important friend of the representative's called with an unexpected invitation that requires explanation."

Before Rosalind could say anything, the phone clicked to silence. She shrugged and went to sit on a bench at the entrance. How unexpected could anything else be today?

CHAPTER 3

"We're more slow-paced than New Yorkers, but twice as fast as folks in Texas from what I remember," Eleanor said as Rosalind raced to keep up with her as they walked on 11th towards F Street.

"That's because we ride our horses everywhere. Kind of bow-legged when we actually walk, so we try to avoid it."

Eleanor smiled. At the corner, a building that looked eight stories tall took up half a city block in each direction. "Welcome to Woodward and Lothrop, affectionately known as Woodies," Eleanor said as she pushed a revolving door to enter. "We've got higher-end shops, but this is the place for girls like us."

"We've got Nieman Marcus in Texas, but I've never ever shopped there," Rosalind said, looking at the floor devoted almost entirely to cosmetics and shoes. She'd been in Scarbrough's in Austin, in the basement where the bargains were, but they were never discounted enough for her. Woodies looked similar to Scarbrough's—open, high ceilings, glass display cases for jewelry, escalators, unaffordable goods. "Do I really need to spend money on clothes for this trip?"

"Well, you could wear your schoolmarm drab and fit right in with the office typists. Or you can have clothes that let you travel with Mister Novy and fit in with that group."

Rosalind considered replying but decided to practice the skill of keeping her mouth shut.

They rode the escalator up to the third floor where Rosalind was confronted with four mannequins wearing midi and knee length dresses in soft floral prints and solids. She fingered the fabric on a dotted Swiss dress. The cut was good enough, although it wouldn't have passed her father's judgement, and it would fit her small waist and long legs just fine. She looked up and saw that Eleanor was eyeing her. "My father was a tailor."

"Grab the one you think's the nicest in your size and go try it on. We need it for today."

"Where am I going?"

"Tell you once we have you in a dress and shoes and a new purse and hat. Meantime I'll find travel clothes to supplement your—"

"Wait a minute. Who is paying for all of this? Is it coming out of my paycheck?" Rosalind gripped her purse against her chest.

"Hey, calm down and relax." Eleanor motioned Rosalind away from the mannequin and the three women who'd just stepped off the escalator and were staring at them. "Sorry to bother you ladies," she added and smiled. The trio walked off towards the lingerie section.

"Learn to not blurt out the first thing that comes to your mind. Can you do that?"

Rosalind nodded, cheeks flushed. She had been trying to do exactly that since the minute she walked into Johnson's Austin office. "Sorry."

"Good thing you can say that word in seven languages, sweetie, or I'd probably be done with you. Stop carrying your purse like a shield and come on." Eleanor walked deep into the women's clothing section and held open the door to the Ladies Lounge. "Time for a very quiet chat," she said, pointing to a red chaise sofa. "Sit."

Instead, Rosalind walked over to the closest sink faucet, turned the water on, and used her hand as a cup to drink. When she'd had enough, she splashed cold water on her face and stared at the white-faced person in the mirror. "I really need something to eat. Soon." She walked over to the couch and sank down next to Eleanor. The only conspiratorial whispers she'd ever heard were at the movies, so she tried to mimic Greta Garbo. "What do I need to know?"

Eleanor laughed. "First, that is a horrible accent. Just talk in a quiet voice. Or can't you Texans do that?"

Rosalind remembered the first day of first grade, when she'd entered the classroom in the dress her father had hand-tailored for her in the exact style of a proper European school uniform. Except no child in her class wore anything like it or spoke like her or had long red hair woven into two braids and piled on top of her head.

She'd overcome it all, not easily, not quickly, but quite thoroughly by the end.

"I can do exactly that," she said in a soft voice from which she stripped any Texas accent. "Now you tell me why I need an afternoon dress."

"Alice Glass."

"That's a name, not a reason."

A woman pushed the lounge door open and walked towards the toilet stalls. Eleanor stood and turned towards the full-length mirror, adjusting her hair, with her back to Rosalind. When the woman exited the stall, she stared at Eleanor as she washed her hands, then finally left. Eleanor sat back down.

"We need to be careful of what we say and where we say it. The woman who just walked out, I recognize her from Secretary of State Hull's office. Seems like she might have recognized me too. Maybe I should have said 'hi'. Hard to know." She sighed.

That was the second time Hull's name had come up. "Hull?" Rosalind asked, leaning towards Eleanor.

"Among other areas of exceptional importance, the State Department handles all embassy business. Poland, for example. Hull is, to say the least, not sympathetic to the plight of Jews. Not an admirer of Hitler—I wouldn't say that—but absolutely not inclined to let Jews into the United States, even if they are exceptional, like Einstein. We don't want to bring ourselves to Hull's attention." As the door to the ladies' room opened again, Eleanor stopped talking.

Rosalind had the same sense she'd had several times since arriving in DC: of walking down a dark hallway toward an unknown danger. In a whisper, she said, "I have the distinct impression that this job is what we call 'a wolf in sheep's clothing.' Unless you tell me what exactly is going on, and what I'm supposed to do, I'm returning to Texas." Maybe she would be blacklisted from getting a job there, as Frank had threated, but she had nothing much keeping her in Texas and she could go any-where. North Dakota or Nebraska, anywhere a high school wanted a foreign language teacher, even without a degree. She wanted nothing to do with sneaking and secrets and high-level government officials.

"Listen, I'd hoped a department store full of women who were shopping on a workday would be a safe place to talk, but I was wrong. Let's get you a dress and go back to my place."

"Not the office?"

"We can't talk there. Have you not been listening to me?" Eleanor grabbed Rosalind's hand and squeezed tight. "Pay attention here. Too many government people with agendas of their own pass in and out of House and Senate offices, eager to know what anyone in power has on his agenda. There are enormous conflicts between folks who want to confront Hitler and folks who believe communism is the worser of the two threats. Plus rabbits who want to hide in holes and pretend there are no wolves out there at all."

Rosalind considered what Eleanor had said. Clashes at high levels over what to do about Hitler didn't surprise her. Isolationists, folks beaten down by the Great War, people who saw Europe as 'the great other' that had slaughtered decent American boys—they all wanted nothing to do with Europe, and they elected politicians who felt the same. There was also the pro-Nazi American Bund, anger over efforts to boycott German products, and a rampant fear of communism. The country was so divided and on edge that you almost had to swear an oath of loyalty to America to get a job pumping gas.

"We still need to get you a passport." Eleanor's voice intruded into Rosalind's thoughts. "Did you happen to bring your birth certificate with you, by any chance?"

"In here." Rosalind patted her purse. "Too important to risk my landlady tossing it if I didn't return on time to pay my rent. Not that she'd mean any harm, but she is thorough when she cleans."

"Good for her," Eleanor said. "Now let's finish shopping."

✳✳✳

Rosalind carried two bags—one with a mid-calf baby-blue day dress, new pumps and a small clutch, the other with two dresses and a new blouse Eleanor pronounced suitable for travel—into Eleanor's apartment and put them on the daybed. Her suitcase was on the floor. Had Eleanor had it delivered from the office or dropped it off while Rosalind was at the post office? She glanced at Eleanor's face, now with a sheen of perspiration that made her look like a dewy rose, and decided not to ask.

"Food in the 'fridge," Eleanor said. "Help yourself. But we have to be at Charles Marsh's by 4:30. And there'll be food there, I promise."

"I'm starving," Rosalind said, and went over and took out two pieces of Wonder bread. The bread tore as she tried to spread cold butter on it. "So, I'm listening."

"We're meeting with Alice Glass at the DC home of Charles Marsh. I don't know if Representative Johnson will also be there, but Marsh is a close friend of his. So maybe you'll meet everyone. Be prepared and look your best. Take the dotted Swiss out before it wrinkles." Eleanor pointed to the bags of clothes.

"Is Alice Glass really Marsh's mistress? It's what I hear. Folks read about her in the paper—at this gala, attending that thing—and they talk." Rosalind put the sandwich on the table and grabbed the baby-blue dress from its bag, shook it out, and laid it on the daybed. Eleanor handed her scissors and she clipped off the tags.

"You hear correctly…sort of. Mistress implies someone hidden away and whispered about in polite circles. Alice Glass is none of that. She's… unique. You'll see."

"And why do I need to meet them?" Rosalind asked, picking up her sandwich and biting off another chunk of it.

"Mister Marsh and Miss Glass went to Germany and heard Hitler speak. It turned them vehemently anti-Nazi. They are convinced that our State Department is not doing enough. No surprise to me."

"All of Roosevelt's Jewish friends can't move him, so isolationists like Lindbergh are winning."

"If you'll pardon me for saying, the entire continent of Europe and England are at risk from Hitler. We won't move on this to help anyone, not just the Jews," Eleanor said.

Rosalind didn't respond.

"Getting back to Alice Glass. She wants to meet you," Eleanor said.

"Why?"

Eleanor shrugged. "She didn't tell me. I just get the command, and I obey. When you're ready we'll take a cab. After Miss Glass, we'll see what's next to do."

With that, Eleanor ended the conversation. Rosalind felt that her agreement to accompany Mister Novy made her into a game piece being pushed along the board with no control over when she was picked up or put down, or by whom.

***

The cabbie drove about a mile before stopping on a side street in front of a four-story, gray stone townhouse with darkly varnished double doors. The townhouses on either side and across the street also had the hard shine of wealth.

"We're just off Embassy Row," Eleanor said as she opened up the taxi door and motioned for Rosalind to follow her.

Laughter rolled out of the open window of the townhouse in front of Rosalind and a man's deep voice caught her attention. "And then I told him a Texas rattler would've been twice as big." His laughter mixed in with other, softer tones. There was no mistaking Johnson's voice, which she'd heard on radio broadcasts.

"You're getting quite a reception, it appears. I thought maybe he and Missus Johnson were out of town." Eleanor knocked on the door. A uniformed maid opened it wide.

"Miss Glass is expecting us," Eleanor said as she stepped inside. Rosalind, feeling like Dorothy finding herself in the Land of Oz, followed.

The foyer was the size of Rosalind's room at the boarding house, with a gleaming marble floor, an oil painting on the wall bearing the signature of Renoir, and a carved drop leaf table with a bouquet of roses in the same tones as the painting underneath. That scene, combined with the air-conditioned coolness, made Rosalind dizzy. She wondered what it would be like to be so wealthy that you could have the air conditioner on and the windows open at the same time.

"I think I need to use a bathroom," she said, whispering the words as if she were at the theater.

In silence, the maid opened a paneled door with a small brass inlaid knob. Rosalind had never before been intimidated by a bathroom, but this one was incredible. The flush was soundless. The hand towel felt like cashmere and the oval mirror was spotless. When she exited, Eleanor was alone in the entrance, waiting for her.

"Miss Glass is the taste behind the décor. If Charles Marsh is here, call him Mister. Never call her Missus, always *Miss* Glass. If Mister Johnson is here, Lady Bird may also be. You call her Missus Johnson."

"How will I know the difference between the two women?"

"Trust me, it'll be obvious."

***

When Rosalind entered the room at the top of the stairs, it glowed with sunlight from the French windows. Over the fireplace hung a large painting of a soft blue pond with floating white waterlilies. Two large sofas and four armchairs, all covered in a cream-colored fabric, were placed around the fireplace, with large decorative pillows in hues of blue that matched the painting beckoning you to sink into them. Each of the tall narrow tables and small end tables held a vase of mixed flowers. Rosalind recognized peonies and snapdragons in surging reds and violets.

Lyndon Baines Johnson—tall, lanky, with dark hair and a piercing, brown-eyed stare— was leaning against the fireplace mantle. The newspaper photos Rosalind had seen failed to convey how magnetic he was in person. "Well, I do believe our guests are here," he said.

An older man, wrinkles settling into permanency around his mouth and hair graying at the temples, rose from the couch and turned around. At the same time, a figure stepped in front of the

French windows, indistinct against the sun until she stepped into the shade. Alice Glass was almost six feet tall, with reddish-gold hair that flowed onto her shoulders and large blue eyes. Other than movie stars on the screen, Rosalind had never seen a woman as breathtaking—or as well-dressed. No wonder Eleanor had fussed over her clothes at the store.

"How nice of you to join us," Alice said in a soft Texas drawl. "I so look forward to discussing our concerns. I'm Alice. Charles, darling, introduce yourself."

Charles Marsh held out his hand for Rosalind to shake. "Happy to meet you, Miss Fisher. Eleanor, good to see you again. Lady Bird, you know Eleanor Lassiter, of course."

At those words, Rosalind saw a slim, dark-haired woman about her age stand up and smile, which lit up her face. She was lovely, but despite this, Lady Bird was newspaper next to an illuminated manuscript when compared to Alice Glass.

"Good to see you out of Lyndon's office, Eleanor. And you are Miss Rosalind Fisher, our impressive linguist. Lyndon says you will be so helpful to our good friend Jim."

At that Lyndon Baines Johnson nodded, leaving Rosalind with the impression that he was completely prepared to take all the credit for her appearance. "Indeed."

"Please sit." Alice waved Rosalind and Eleanor towards a sofa. She picked up a silver bell from an end table and rang it twice. "We'll have some iced tea and light refreshments."

Charles Marsh said, "Lyndon is fully up to date on the concerns Alice and I share about Hitler. He—and his charming wife, Lady Bird—have read *Mein Kampf,* that egregious piece of horse shit, excuse my Texas."

"And Lyndon rescued the conductor, Eric Leinsdorf. Have you heard of him?" Alice asked Rosalind.

Rosalind shook her head.

"One of the best young classical music conductors in the world, my dear. Jewish. Our government almost sent him back to that Nazi hellhole, but clever Lyndon got him into Cuba, got a new entrance visa for him there, and now Eric is safe in the United States. I'll have to take you to one of his concerts." Alice offered a warm smile, a queen bestowing a favor.

Rosalind was not going to slip and use anyone's first name. "Miss Glass, Mister Marsh, Representative Johnson and Missus Johnson, thank you so much for asking me here. Yes, I am keenly aware of Hitler's evil…" She paused, then decided *evil* was sufficient. Adding more would be like painting a pig.

"Roosevelt is not of a mind to push intervention as a US policy," Lady Bird offered in a soft drawl.

"Speak up, darlin'. We're among friends." Lyndon laughed. Lady Bird blushed and, watching the reactions of the others, Rosalind guessed this was not the first time Lyndon had pointed out what he thought were his wife's deficits in public. In front of someone as gorgeous and poised as Alice Glass, such a comment would smart even more.

"We know," Lady Bird said in a firmer voice, "our citizenry wants nothing to do with Europe and its woes. This is a mistake."

"Hear, hear." Charles Marsh nodded. "Even if that son of a bitch bombs every capital on the European continent and throws in London for good measure, Lindbergh and his cronies will make sure we never enter a war."

The door to the living room opened and the maid entered the room with a tray of fresh cut fruit and pastries, which she put down on the coffee table next to a short stack of plates and cutlery that were already there. Everyone remained silent until she had returned with a pitcher of iced tea and then left again.

Alice shut the living room door behind the maid. "Words carry," she said. "Please, let's eat."

The peach quarters tasted as if they'd been just plucked off the tree and the iced tea refreshed Rosalind, but she still had no idea why she was included in the conversation. The occasional question bounced her way, directed at understanding her employment from age sixteen on and whether there were issues of dialect and accent in Polish or Yiddish. Alice asked most of those questions, leaning toward Rosalind as if Rosalind had been whispering her responses. Rosalind stiffened and sat up straight, forcing herself to meet the woman's intense gaze and maintain a normal speaking voice. Marsh sat next to Alice, his eyes fixed on Rosalind when she spoke.

"As you travel to Warsaw, Rosalind, I'd be interested in your observations of people, the feeling of places. Details my reporters could use for what we call 'color.' If you're in the middle of a breaking story, lots of detail. In fact, you could call or telegram someone on my staff. Eleanor will give you the number. Could you do that?" Marsh asked.

Johnson nodded at her.

"Of course I can, sir." 'In the middle of a breaking story' sounded nightmarish, a situation she and Novy and his sixteen-year-old son should avoid at all costs.

Johnson smiled. Small favors for big friends, Rosalind guessed.

Forty minutes later, Eleanor indicated it was time to go. Rosalind stood up, smoothing her skirt, and she and Eleanor said their goodbyes. As they passed the Renoir, Rosalind still had no idea why she'd been invited except to be given yet another task—providing color for Marsh's reporters.

A cab waited, door open, by the curb. Before she slid inside, Eleanor looked around and then nodded to Rosalind. "Do the same."

Remembering Eleanor's caution at Woodies, Rosalind made a slow, careful sweep of what she could see. Expensive houses, well-maintained tiny front yards with miniscule flower beds. One car parked across the street three doors down. The sun was in Rosalind's eyes blurring the details and making it hard to see. The driver of the other car reached out and adjusted the mirror, then retracted his arm. Rosalind waited, counted to fifteen. Then she slid in next to Eleanor.

"Here's the address of where we are going. When you start, take the route that way." Eleanor pointed up the street past the occupied auto.

The taxi driver nodded. As the taxi passed the other car, the person in the driver's seat leaned over towards the passenger side as if fumbling for a package on the floor.

"Go around the corner and stop," Rosalind said. Eleanor's concern about the car and driver oozed intrigue that was too tempting to ignore and Rosalind wondered whether the whole thing was a set-up, a challenge organized by Eleanor to test Rosalind's mettle.

"Ma'am?" The driver looked at Eleanor in the rearview mirror.

"Yes, fine. Follow her direction."

As soon as he'd brought the cab to a halt, Rosalind opened her door, got out, and walked towards the other auto. She could see now that it was a dark blue Ford sedan, not black. It had Washington DC plates, but she could only see an M and 23 before the driver pulled out and drove in the opposite direction.

Rosalind returned to the cab, dreading Eleanor's reaction.

"What possessed you to do that?" Eleanor asked.

"You told me to pay attention, so I did. Whoever was in that car was waiting for us to exit. License plate was DC, M and a 2 and a 3. I couldn't see it quick enough." Rosalind shrugged. "I read detective novels, like Dashiell Hammett. Eric Ambler for spies. It's what those guys do in the books. But here's my question for you, Eleanor: What the hell is going on and what do you really want me to do?"

Eleanor laughed. "My dear girl, you are surprising. It's true there are more reasons to go with Mister Novy to Poland. But don't make the serious mistake of confusing fiction for real life. That can be very, very dangerous."

"I understand, but again, what the hell is going on?"

"I'll explain more when we're back at my apartment."

Lurking men who sped away. Reasons to stick with Novy beyond just translation. Gathering 'color'—whatever that was—for the powerful Charles Marsh. For the first time, Rosalind felt lifted above her life's horizon to see a complex future not smothered by chalk dust and the sound of restless students.

***

Eleanor shook Rosalind's new midi length dress on the hanger.

"It needs ironing," Rosalind said.

"Iron is under the sink. Ironing board pulls down from that fake cupboard. You've got a dinner with the congressman, Lady Bird and Jim Novy tonight at the Johnson's apartment. Your job right now is to persuade Novy that he needs you to go with him. Why he's taking his sixteen- year-old son too is beyond me, but that's not your concern. Once he's convinced, I'll give you the most complete rundown I can of the darker side of DC. And a few other things we'd like you to do while traveling and once you're in our Polish Embassy. You've already gotten Mister Marsh's agenda—give him stuff his reporters can make into stories. But Novy is the important matter."

"Novy hasn't agreed to take me along?"

Eleanor shook her head. "Johnson insists. Novy…"

"I don't believe it." All this and the main character hadn't agreed to the other characters or plot line.

Eleanor shook her head. "If Novy doesn't agree… Well, I've never seen anyone resist the congressman when he leans in. He'll agree. But you'll go to our embassy in Poland for the main job regardless of whether Novy takes you along to wherever else he goes. Or whether he even wants to have you there. That's not up for debate. We want you to stick by Novy as much as he'll let you for several reasons. Especially on the ship. I'll explain later."

After getting the creases out of the dress, Rosalind retreated to the bathroom to splash cool water on herself before changing to go out. She opened her purse and checked that the twenty dollars Johnson's office had given her was still there. That was her security. She could use it to get back to Texas, or somewhere else entirely.

As Rosalind checked one final time to make sure she was present-able, she thought about what leaving Texas would mean. She'd have to abandon Hannah and her family, plus her plans to finish college. Both of those things seemed doable. At the moment, however, she would just have to go along with whatever came up. She was too far in to turn back, and too far from the end to know what lay ahead.

CHAPTER 4

Rosalind had never met Novy in person. Yet here they all were in the small living room of LBJ and Lady Bird's one-bedroom apartment, drapes closed against the day's lingering heat. Novy sat on a red upholstered sofa, LBJ in a leather armchair, and Rosalind in a high-backed wing chair dragged over from the dining room table, which was set for dinner for four with fine china and silver.

The room was not big enough to contain the men's personalities. Lady Bird had retreated to the kitchen after she greeted Novy with a kiss on his cheek and Rosalind wished she, too, could have followed the inviting dinner odors.

LBJ was taller than Novy by six inches at least, even sitting, so he leaned towards Novy so that their heights were almost equal. Novy was balding, muscled under the shirt like she'd expect of someone who'd made his money in the iron and steel business. He had blue eyes, and what was left of his hair was cut short and fading from brown to gray, and his skin had the colorlessness she associated with almost every immigrant she'd known who came from the area known as the Pale of Settlement in Europe. Novy's English was a mix of Texas and Yiddish accents, with Yiddish vying for first place. Each man was wearing a tie and jacket, as if journalists were waiting to photograph them—which they might have been, as far as Rosalind knew.

"I tell you, Lyndon, I will go myself with my son to Poland. I do not need a babysitter."

"Jim, David is sixteen. He can't be of much help if there's a real problem. You can use someone who is fluent in all those languages. And I still think you shouldn't take him. Or even go yourself, for that matter."

"I snuck across the border between bloody Russia and Germany. I found my way with immigrants to Bremen. I took a ship to the United States, may it be blessed for a million years. I came to Texas to be with my brother who was already here—on my own. I was sixteen! The same age as my dear David." Jim Novy snorted. "Only the presence of this lovely young woman keeps me from saying to you everything I suffered. Let me remind you, my good friend."

Novy's story was the same one that came out of thousands of mouths over decades of flight from Europe's bleeding, starving, oppressive forms. He'd left his parents behind at their insistence, only to never see them again—the baby bird thrust out of the nest to safety as the hawks swept in to eat. Of his four brothers, the two eldest had been almost fatally injured in the pogrom that compelled his escape, and they remained in Poland, supported by Jim, and he was desperate to see them before... Well, before it was too late. And he did not want to have Rosalind with him.

"Mister Novy, if I may speak." Both men turned to look at Rosalind as if they'd forgotten she'd been placed in a chair just twenty-five minutes before.

She began in Yiddish. "Times are difficult in Europe. The place you came from has changed hands from..." She switched to Russian, "Russians who went through their own revolution." She switched to Polish. "And as for Poland, what do we know about what may happen? We do not know when or if the Germans, may they rot in hell, will have a hand in the future of all those countries," she finished in German. "You will need to communicate, possibly at a high government level, if you wish to help your kinsfolk," she added in English. "And I can do that in most European languages, even Portuguese. And I can write in those languages, as well as read them."

"I see you've put my scholarship money to good use, Miss Fisher." Novy nodded.

"Thank you again for believing in my future. That you have had such exceptional success in the years you have been in Texas is a testament to you..." Rosalind began.

"And to this great country of ours," Novy added.

"Hear, hear," Johnson said. "So, it's done, Jim. Miss Fisher will accompany you as a member of my staff."

Novy looked as if he was swallowing cod liver oil, but he said, "Sure, okay, Lyndon. But what'll I tell my missus? Suddenly I'm taking a young, unmarried woman to Europe with me?"

Then he turned to Rosalind and said, "*Aoyb epes geyt falsh, ir vet zeyn nebekhdik.*"

"Yes, sir." Rosalind didn't need Novy telling her, in Yiddish or any other language, that she'd have hell to pay if anything went wrong.

"What did he just tell you, Rosalind?" LBJ asked.

"He wished us all luck."

Novy smiled. "Excellent translation."

"Let's get back to the issue of Missus Novy. Lady Bird, darlin', come here a bit. We need your help," Johnson said.

Lady Bird walked out of the kitchen, smoothing her apron. She and Lyndon were known for their hospitality, but she still struggled to cook, according to Eleanor. "Yes?"

"I need for you to call Missus Novy and assure her that Miss Fisher here is going on my behalf to handle some issues for me as part of my staff. There's no hanky-panky going on. And there won't be. You tell her that. She'll hear it better from you. Miss Fisher can get on the line with you and do some smoothin' over. Part of her job training."

Rosalind considered that, tilting her head. She probably would have to talk to people and explain what she didn't really understand. Might as well start now.

"Happy to help after dinner is done. What is Miss Fisher going to do there? Have you told Jim about what you have planned?" Lady Bird's Texas accent softened the sharpness of the question like a knife sleeve over a blade.

"Just getting to that. Have a seat beside me." LBJ patted the couch and Lady Bird sat. He addressed Jim Novy. "Lady Bird, Alice Glass, Charles Marsh and I want you to get your family and friends out of there. We're in the process of finalizing the details. It'll involve our embassy in Warsaw. Forty-four visas to the United States."

Rosalind's breath caught. Visas were like alchemist's gold.

Novy shook his head like a stunned animal. Then a tear trickled down his cheek. "You are an incredible friend, Lyndon."

"Just one thing about any publicity," LBJ said.

Ah, here it came, Rosalind thought. The reckoning, the positive publicity for being a savior, a beacon of light.

"Absolutely none of that, Jim. Keep your mouth shut. No one is to ever know that I am arranging this. It could mean my political career. My sources tell me that we could give Poland ten times as many visas as they have now, which is under two thousand, and still not fill the demand. And we know some State Department people are slow-walking the few applications we've allowed to delay filling as many as they can. They're anti-Eastern European, anti-Jewish, just like we are completely against Chinese immigrants and hated the Irish. What can I say except—for God's sake—no publicity."

Rosalind sat back with force, her surprise almost tipping her backwards. Lady Bird looked at her and smiled.

"And I'm to do what, sir?" Rosalind asked.

"Help get these visas through the embassy. With as few people knowing as possible," LBJ said. His lips smiled, but his voice was firm and his eyes were fixed on her.

Rosalind suppressed a shudder. "How?"

LBJ shook his head. "You're smart. Like my missus here, who's way smarter than me. We're relying on you to figure that out."

"As I go along?" Surely he couldn't mean that. Throw her into an embassy and send her scrounging for help for something not-quite-legal at best?

"No. We don't expect the impossible. Eleanor will give you names of contacts at the embassy —Poles and American. People who understand the scope of the problem and want to help, if they can. You'll talk to them and assess how suitable they are. When you find the right person, he'll help. Also, if interesting information comes your way—without you looking for it, mind—let me know. If we have potential traitors among the Americans or Poles who are in favor of that Hitler fellow at the embassy, I want to know that, too. And Mister Marsh would be pleased, as you know, to have eyewitness accounts of what is really going on in Poland's capital to print in his newspapers."

Johnson was speaking in mysteries, a knot of "ifs." True Texas bull-shit if she'd ever heard it, Rosalind thought.

"If you want me to be a spy, sir, just say it."

"Do I want you to be a spy?" Johnson chuckled. "No. Absolutely not. I want you to do what I said—find a suitable person or two at the embassy to help with the visas, keep your ears open. Look around. Just like you'd do if you were here in my office in DC. The word 'spy' was never spoken. Jim, did I ever say 'spy?'"

Jim Novy shook his head. "No, my friend. But if she doesn't want to go, Lyndon, we should leave her be."

Rosalind detected a note of hope in Novy's voice, a route to disentangle himself from her. But her future rested now on taking this job. And besides, Rosalind thought, how could what she had been through—being orphaned and sent to live with her older cousin in the safety of Austin—compare with the horrors her parents and kin had lived through? They were the survivors of pogroms, starvation, ships' bellies, and more. They were from the generation of despair. And here was the chance to help other Jews—a chance she'd neither sought nor wanted, and given to her by what God, she did not know.

"I could do this on my own at the embassy," Jim Novy said.

"We've settled this. You'll have enough to do, Jim, to find who you want to get out. You'll need to select who gets the visas. It'll be on you." LBJ let out a sigh and shook his head. "Just let the lil' lady here handle what she needs to. *If* she agrees here and now, that is. Which I note she has not done yet." He nodded towards Rosalind. "Maybe Eleanor was right. Let her find the right person to send who knows his way around. I just thought for you, my good friend, you'd like a fellow Texas Jew to help."

Rosalind could see that Jim Novy would be too visible wherever he was, whether in an embassy or small town—a tough guy, like LBJ, muscling his way through the clerks, not speaking the language fluently, demanding, a millionaire. A grab-your-arm sort of fellow, leaning over you to be sure he got his way, with a Texas attitude when he got mad. Rosalind had heard rumors. He wasn't as fluent in Polish as she was, and certainly not in German. Mister Novy would need her.

"Like I told Miss Lassiter earlier today, sir, I will go," she said.

"It's settled then." LBJ leaned back in his chair and crossed one leg over the other. Novy shrugged. The smell of scorching potatoes hit the air.

Lady Bird jumped up. "Not again!" she said as she ran into the kitchen.

Rosalind followed her. She needed a break from the men. Plus, it was the right thing to do, a young woman helping her hostess, who was the same age as her. Lady Bird had the handle of the pot in her toweled grip and was setting it in the sink, where the bottom steamed. "I think it's just burned on the bottom," she said.

"I'm sure," Rosalind said. "Point me to a bowl and a spoon so we can scoop out the good stuff."

"Thanks. Grab a towel, too," Lady Bird said, as if directing the cook at her father's house. "Please," she added and smiled.

Rosalind smiled back. "Nice kitchen." Large black and white linoleum tiles, counters on each side, a full-size refrigerator, a four-burner gas stove, and storage cabinets—one with a glass front displaying a large, green, geometrically-patterned Art Moderne vase.

"True but small as an outhouse, my Daddy would say. You're an Austin girl, I hear. What were you doing before you got hired by Lyndon's folk to do this excitin' job?"

"I was working as a clerk at Woolworth's and trying to finish up my bachelor's at UT at night."

"UT Austin? I got my bachelor's there in history and then did a year of journalism. Great time." Rosalind detected a forlorn note in Lady Bird's tone.

Lady Bird finished scooping potatoes out, leaving a thin layer of char in the pot. "I'll throw butter in. Maybe that'll hide the overdone bits. Would you mind checking on the chicken? It'd be just my luck that would burn too."

Rosalind used a second towel to open the oven door, releasing the aroma of chicken perfumed with apricot and prune. Her mouth watered. "Yum. Smells perfect, Missus Johnson."

"Oh, please call me Lady Bird. Do you know how hard it is to get a kosher chicken in this city? I didn't want Jim to be offended if I served the wrong thing."

Lady Bird wouldn't know that mixing meat—like chicken—and something with milk products—like the butter she proposed for the mashed potatoes—was not done. Best to stop her before the dinner was ruined.

Rosalind sensed that Lady Bird was treading carefully in the thicket of Jewish feelings and behaviors. Coming from wealth, she wouldn't have met many Jews socially. Maybe, before LBJ, Lady Bird would have heard of Nieman Marcus, or even shopped there, or had a few Jewish students in her classes…but maybe not. She'd more likely have thought Jews had horns growing out of their heads, a hand-me-down from the historical—and possibly deliberate—mistranslation of "radiance" to "horns" that Michaelangelo sculpted for eternity on Moses' head.

"Best not putting butter or milk in the potatoes then," Rosalind said gently. "Jews don't mix milk products and meat, including chicken. Maybe some of the chicken gravy?" If she didn't find them so boring, Rosalind could have gone on and on and on about the intricacies of kosher cooking.

"Thanks for the tip." Lady Bird spooned gravy into the rescued potatoes and mashed with surprising vigor. "I never knew many Jews growing up, Rosalind, but the ones I know now are all fine folks. We're bound for a war with Hitler. No one wants another one but there you go. Lots of things in life no one wants but must suffer through for the sake of a greater good we hope will come."

Lady Bird lifted the chicken out of the roasting pan and placed it on a platter with the apricots and prunes. "I think we're ready to eat. But I'd better make that call first."

She cleaned her hands on a dish towel and consulted a small address book on the counter. Then she lifted the black handset for the rotary phone and dialed. "Missus Novy? Edna, Lady Bird Johnson here. How are you?"

Rosalind couldn't hear any reply.

"Yes, Jim's here for dinner. When he's gone back to the hotel, I'm sure he'll call you. He's fine, really, Edna."

There was a pause while Lady Bird nodded to whatever Edna Novy was saying on her end. "Yes, a long-distance call is alarming. Now, Lyndon wants you to talk to a member of his staff, a very trusted member, Edna. Lyndon's given her an important assignment. Rosalind Fisher is her name." With that she handed Rosalind the handset.

"Hello, Missus Novy. I'm Rosalind Fisher, one of your family's scholarship recipients. I am very grateful to you both for that. I am a fluent linguist in all the languages that belong to the countries Mister Novy and David will visit. Because of the…well…the situation…"

Rosalind heard Edna Novy sigh all the way from Texas. "Ma'am, Representative Johnson wants me to go with your husband and David to help."

"Miss Fisher, my husband will do what he wants," Edna Novy replied. "I have expressed my regrets to him over this planned trip, but he will do what he wants. So if he wants to take you, he will. Good luck." With that, Edna put down the handset on her end.

Rosalind stared at the receiver in her hand and then gave it to Lady Bird.

"Not what you expected?" Lady Bird asked.

Rosalind shook her head.

"When you marry, Rosalind, you'll see what the world looks like from there," Lady Bird said, smiling with everything but her eyes.

***

As Rosalind stepped outside LBJ and Lady Bird's apartment building to wait for a cab after dinner, a man, his face obscured by his hat's brim, walked towards her at a brisk pace. He brushed by her and muttered, "I'd be careful if I were you."

"Who…" As she turned towards him, the man pulled the brim of his hat tighter around his head and tilted his face away from her. All she could see was a clean-shaven jaw line. She began to walk after him, trying to be as quiet as possible. A car horn tooted next to her in the street.

"Are you the gal who called for a taxi?" she heard the driver say.

The man stopped and turned. Middle-aged, glasses. He watched her as she got into the back seat. Then he turned and began walking away.

"I'd like you to drive slowly down the street. Don't pass that fellow, if you can do that," Rosalind said to the driver.

He nodded. "I could make a U-turn if it's about that guy botherin' you." His accent was deeply Southern.

"Thank you. I want to see where he goes before you take me where I need to be."

Rosalind waited to see if the mystery man would turn around to see where the cab had gone. He just strode on, turning right at the next corner.

"What's there?" she asked the driver.

"Two blocks down is a bus stop."

"Is there another route to that bus stop?"

In response, the cab driver made a U-turn and headed towards the previous intersection, where he turned right. A minute more and they were at the bus stop where her mystery man sat.

"I want you to drive slowly past and get a good look at him, if you can. I'll tip well for this."

"Yes, ma'am."

Rosalind lay down on the back seat.

***

At Eleanor's apartment, Rosalind, now upright, held out fifty cents more than the taxi meter called for. She'd be reimbursed. "What did you see?" she asked the driver.

"Maybe dark brown hair. Dressed like an office guy, you know. Hard to see his face with the hat. And the lighting. Ordinary except…" The driver paused and looked at the coins in Rosalind's hand. She reached into her purse and got out a quarter to add. "Looked like his nose had been broken. A bumpy bridge." He pointed at his own nose. "But I really couldn't be sure what with driving and trying not to be noticed."

Whether he was making all this up or not, Rosalind couldn't tell. It was her first foray into paying for information. She didn't have a truth-o-meter or anything other than her wariness built up, like a callus on her feelings, over years of being on her own, plus the information she'd gleaned from spy novels. Was that enough to keep her alive in her new career?

CHAPTER 5

"**L**ady Bird likes you, Mister Novy agrees to take you. Now we have to shape you up." Eleanor sat back on her kitchen chair, drinking her morning coffee, early sun sliding under the window shade.

Eleanor seemed content, but Rosalind felt like she was going to jump out of her skin. She took a bite of toast, melted butter sliding onto her tongue and soothing her momentarily.

"I was followed and warned. By whom? And who is the 'we' you keep talking about?" she asked.

Eleanor sighed. "Yes, I'll get to that. We need just a small addition to what the boss wants you to do. Now, let's look at the possibilities." She held up her left hand, fingers up. "One…"

"Should I take notes?" Rosalind chewed off half the remaining bread, stuffing her mouth with it as if the food would keep her from wanting to shake the implacability out of Eleanor. It didn't.

"Mental notes. Learn not to put much in writing."

"Really, Eleanor, what am I supposed to do for the mysterious 'we'?" Rosalind asked. Knowledge and remembering facts had gotten her As in school and a leg up on anything she'd wanted to do so far, and she wasn't about to just let this go.

"You'll find out about that later. A small thing, really. Now, please pay attention." Eleanor sounded like an exasperated professor explaining calculus.

Later did not sit well with Rosalind, but what choice did she have? She nodded, keeping her eyes on the table.

"Who is following us? One, it is possible that somebody from our homegrown American Bund is spying on the representative. Possibly a Bund member from Austin told to follow LBJ around since he's known to have a good relationship with Novy and other Jews. Sees you and decides you are new fodder."

"Directed by Kuhn?" Rosalind asked. Kuhn was the guy who called himself Bunds Führer, dressed like a Nazi, and wanted the United States to stay neutral in any European issue involving Germany. It was even said that Kuhn was building a headquarters for Hitler's use on the coast of California after his inevitable triumph over the world.

"Yeah. He has lots of followers and is not to be dismissed. Two, it could be someone from the State Department."

"Spying on me? Spying on Representative Johnson?"

"Well, Secretary of State Hull wouldn't say spying. Certainly not on US soil! That would be completely illegal. He'd say his guy was 'just in the area.' Most probably not him, honestly. And three, it could be someone from the FBI."

Rosalind rose out of her chair feeling as if her hair was standing on end. "Hoover spying on me? Oh, no." The FBI was for gangsters, mobsters, traitors, and communists!

Eleanor made a sitting motion with her hand. "Down girl. The FBI watches lots of people. Guys running around like Dick Tracy. It's a paperwork generating mill, out of which nothing much to help America comes. So, my money is on the Bund." She went to the sink and poured water into a glass which she handed to Rosalind.

Rosalind sipped the water and tried to slow her racing heart.

"There's another possibility," Rosalind said, setting the glass on the table. "Someone from a Jewish organization. Maybe the Hebrew Immigrant Aid Society or the Anti-Defamation League knows Mister Novy is going to Poland. He hasn't made a secret of it. So they are being watchful over *him*, not me."

"They don't want a kidnapping or a different problem for the State Department that features a Jew, that's what you mean?" Eleanor asked.

"Yes, a high-profile problem." A low profile did not even begin to describe what Rosalind, and most other Jews, sought.

"Possible. Overall, what we have to prevent—that is, what *you* have to prevent—is an episode with Novy in Europe. No matter who wants to cause it. Let him go, smile, pass out money. And you help get a few Jews out of Poland without notice." Eleanor's lips smiled but her eyes narrowed as if a threat were just inside her apartment.

"I want to know who's following me, though. Not speculation. Maybe we can find out." An enemy needed a face and a name. And an address, if possible. "And I want bullets for my derringer and another, more serious gun."

"Gun!" Eleanor laughed, spitting out her just sipped coffee.

It was not the reaction Rosalind expected, but she wasn't surprised, either. Her parents never even owned a rifle. But Rosalind had seen what bullies would do, what men would try to do to women, unless the less powerful found power—and a gun was just that. She knew how to use rifles and pistols, knew how to slide a small derringer into her purse when she had to go out alone or work late. Life was a narrow bridge, and someone always wanted to push you off to get the right-of-way.

"I didn't bring more bullets with me," Rosalind said. "They're still in my room in Austin."

"Adding bullets and a gun. Preference?"

"Something more serious than a derringer. What do you suggest?"

"Me? I don't suggest anything. But I'll ask around. Anyhow, all easy to come by. There are lots of gun stores in Virginia. But I do want to know how you came to be so tough, Rosalind! It's not what I expected."

"Tough? Because I know how to use a gun?"

Eleanor said, "I've been around folks from the western states. The good representative and his wife are not the first. Guns are like clothes to them. You, though, seem ready to slide into this assignment now without a backward glance. And with armament, no less! Decide to do it and move on. My kind of gal."

That was almost true, Rosalind thought. "I'm not tough," she said. "If I were a man, no one would bat an eyelash at what I'm doing…or the fact that I carry a gun when I do it."

Eleanor stood up. "Then let's be on our way."

"Where to?"

"We need to get you the passport. You need a bit more training in preparation for the trip, to help you spot potential problems. After all, you're just a few days out now."

"We'll get the bullets and the gun, right?"

Eleanor nodded. She went to her phone and dialed a number. "Bullets for a derringer and another gun." She laughed and listened before adding, "Surprised me, too. See you soon."

"Who was that?"

"You'll find out when we get there."

***

Rosalind stood on the lowest step of the Lincoln Memorial. Eleanor had told her to act like a tourist, which wasn't difficult. Lincoln loomed above her, a giant of stone, his deeply etched face and large hands conveying a compassionate power that the words of his speeches, engraved in the walls, only emphasized. Rosalind thought of Jewish folklore's *golems*, non-human creatures brought alive to protect the community, and wished Lincoln were alive right now, in 1938.

"Miss Fisher?"

Rosalind started at the light tap on her shoulder. If she was going to do the job right, she'd need to rein in her reveries. She turned to the man standing just in back of her. "Yes. And you are?"

"John Smith." John was a few inches taller than Rosalind, with brown eyes and brown hair and nondescript clothing. "I'll tell Eleanor you need to do something about your hair. It makes you way too noticeable, Miss Fisher. Walk with me."

He started up the stairs. "A tourist would move up these stairs quickly to see the great man close up. And, equally as quickly, would head back down to see the next sight on the agenda. Learn to act like everyone around you does."

Taking the steps at a quick march, Rosalind assessed Smith from the side. He wasn't bad looking, with an athletic build under the drab clothing, and a slight and almost bemused smile on his lips. Even in the mid-morning heat, his cheeks were pale, as if the exercise he got was not in the daylight.

Smith turned towards her. "I was able to get you a small box of bullets for the derringer. But I don't think we can get you a second gun quick enough. The store had hunting rifles and two Colts, all too big for you."

She followed Smith towards the corner furthest from the entrance to the statue's left. "The next person who approaches you and casually asks your name may not be a friend. You must learn to be guarded and far more alert about everything you say and do. Is that clear?"

"Yes." Rosalind positioned herself away from Smith and closer to the stairs, in view of a family of five who'd moved into the shade and were encouraging their oldest child to read Lincoln's words. As the boy began, "Four score…" Rosalind took another step backwards, putting herself in sight of the father of the crew.

"Now, John," she said in a loud voice. The father gave her an annoyed look as the boy stuttered to a stop.

"Go on, Mikey," the mother urged.

"Please do. So sorry," Rosalind said, raising her voice to just below a yell. "John, dear, I really must be getting back to the office. Where is the package for me? In your pocket you said? Let's not bother these lovely folk anymore."

Smith walked up to her, reached into his suit pocket, and brought out a small box. "Here you go," he said. "Let's meet again, my darling, at the usual place around six." He turned and trotted down the stairs.

"A little birthday present. Isn't that sweet?" Rosalind waved at the family and walked down the stairs.

By the reflecting pool, Rosalind sank onto a bench and took a deep breath. Smith was right. She was too naïve and too memorable with her red hair. Weren't most Polish women blonde?

A hand came down on her shoulder from behind. "Never let your guard down," a man's harsh voice whispered in her ear. "Now I'm coming around to sit next to you."

The gun was buried in its packaging and sat at the bottom of her purse, useless. There were tourists around—lots of them—including a few children, which gave her some relief.

Smith slid onto the bench. "Me again. Learn to be aware of your surroundings. If you tell someone to leave, that's often not the end of the story."

"Mmm. So, John Smith, am I going to be a spy or what?" Rosalind said, burying her feeling of relief that it was him under a terse response.

"An influencer, a greaser-of-palms, a seeker for someone who would do the right thing, even if for a price. We have a list of potential people. We don't want state secrets…probably. We want someone who will put those visa stamps on the right passports and not say a thing to anyone. You need to find our little ace in the hole in our embassy. And, if you're up to it, more information gathering. More about that, not here."

"I don't get to be Mata Hari?" Inside she felt a combination of relief and odd disappointment. Then she felt a twinge of shame that saving Jews wasn't at the top of her list.

"No, you get to be Rachele, now Rosalind. You see, we've done a bit of homework on you."

Rosalind controlled a wince when she heard that old name, dropped by second grade, at her insistence. Now that she was older, she could imagine how hurt her mother must have been to give up a cherished Yiddish name in the face of a hostile child determined to be an uninflected American.

If someone had dug that far back into her past, who and what was she dealing with? She remained silent, staring out at the reflecting pool, breathing the moist DC air. After a minute had passed, she said, "I need to be able to trust you and whoever has sent you, Mister Smith. The lives of innocent people are at stake, along with mine and Jim Novy's and his son's. Just because you brought me that present doesn't mean you have those interests at heart."

Smith sat, hands folded in his lap.

"I'm not a twit or a patsy, Smith. You know a lot about me, it seems, but I know nothing about you or the group you are with. Until that changes, I'm not talking to you. Or dealing with any of this." She reached into her purse and put her gun and bullets on the bench between them. Then she stood up and walked away.

On her left, just barely in her peripheral vision, a woman began to keep pace with her. She peeled away as Rosalind got to the sidewalk, heading off in the opposite direction. Still, Rosalind wasn't calm as she stood at the bus stop between two families, one with a child wailing for an ice cream, the other with two scowling boys.

She saw the bus coming their way and integrated herself into the families as she got on. Whoever Smith was and whoever he worked for, he was unlikely to grab her in front of innocent Americans.

***

Rosalind arrived at Eleanor's apartment and used the keys she'd been given. As she opened the door, she felt something hard poke into her back.

"Move in quietly," Smith said.

"I wonder, Rosalind, if you are going to be more trouble than you are worth," Eleanor said from her seat at the kitchen table. "You had a simple assignment. Stay with Smith and learn from him. But you didn't. You flounced away, as if you didn't need the help. Dragged me out of the office, too."

Rosalind gripped the back of a kitchen chair and said nothing.

"For heaven's sake, sit down—all of you. And put that gun away, Smith."

"Or give it back to me," Rosalind said, holding out her hand.

Smith gave the derringer to her. "I'm going to brief you on our little group and what we want, in addition to what the good Texas representative wants. That is, if you'll take a little instruction and not get huffy and suspicious."

"And you didn't even get your passport. Now we have to go downtown again," Eleanor said, then sighed.

Rosalind sat on one of the kitchen chairs.

John turned one of the kitchen chairs around and sat down on it backwards. "I'm going to finish my briefing on Bixel, the embassy and the visas. Then, we'll talk about other matters," he said. "Ambassador Bixel surprises people. You may meet him because Mister Novy is not just a wealthy Texan with deep ties to Poland, but also a good friend of Representative Johnson, who is a friend and protégé of Charles Marsh."

Rosalind nodded at Smith's explanation.

"Bixel is a patrician East Coast millionaire, known for being one of the best-dressed men in the world. First class tennis player, served in the Great War. He has shown a surprising aptitude for being a diplomat, maybe because those types know how to hide feelings well under a smooth smile. Probably does not do much direct supervising of staff. And that's your best bet, Rosalind, for getting your tasks accomplished. To approach someone a few rungs down on Bixel's team."

"What can we offer someone who helps?" Rosalind asked.

"If you persuade a US citizen who's staff there to help, you can promise you'll never tell," Eleanor said.

Rosalind waited for a smile, a sign she was kidding, but it never came. Of course, anyone who violated State Department policies on visas would be fired, if not also charged with a crime.

"Embassies are interesting places," Smith said. "A mix of our folk and trustworthy citizens of the country we're in. I think—and Eleanor tell me if I'm wrong—you'll need to meet the two or three people doing the initial interviews and document checks. They are the funnel to the final arbiter. That last person, at the bottom of the funnel, he's likely to just want to push the visas out the door—too much work to send the applications back and much easier to trust your staff. So, it's the interviewing clerks and their secretaries who are critical."

"Those clerks are drowning in applications for visas already," Eleanor said. "Poland received even fewer US visas for each year than Austria or Germany, and they only got about twenty-seven thousand each. The waiting list to get out is seven years."

"So the Polish Embassy clears about a hundred-and-twenty visas a day?" Rosalind asked, feeling the need to wrap herself around a pillar of facts.

"Sounds about right." Eleanor got herself a glass of water and sipped it slowly.

"I have forty-four visas to get processed in how long?"

"Novy plans to be in Warsaw for four days after he visits a few smaller towns. He'll be seeing the sights. He and you and his son will have been in the countryside in a town called Knishin, where his relatives are. I assume that's where most of the names for the visa applications will come from."

"And he knows who all his relatives are, and that forty-four is the final number?" Rosalind said, hoping he didn't know the actual number and that there were four visas she could pilfer for Jakub and his family.

"Good question. You'll have to ask him since I have no idea how Mister Johnson came up with that number," Smith said. "I'm going to get you the best list I can of our staff and the Polish staff at the embassy, plus whatever limited information we have on them. I'll try to organize the names with most likely leads on top. I'll have it for you before you get on the ship." He looked at his watch. "I have to go soon."

"Tell her what else we want her to do now," Eleanor said, "so we have time to put someone else in if she backs out. We still have to get her passport."

Smith sighed. "Rosalind, Eleanor and I are part of a loosely organized group of committed anti-Nazis in and close to our government. We try to cooperate when we can with the Brits who feel the same and who still— God love 'em—have an active spy network. All we want is for you to keep your eyes and ears open on the Queen Mary. Lots of Germans traveling from here to there with secrets to share with Herr Hitler, especially in first-class, where Mister Novy and his son will be. He'll ask you to join them at dinner and you'll have the whole ship to wander around in. We'll have a fellow as contact on board. Just listen and let him know if you hear anything interesting. No cloak-and-dagger, no going out of your way. It's just a matter of being in the right place at the right time."

"How will I know this person to give the information to, if there is anything to give?"

"Better if we tell you closer to departure. Are we good on this?"

"Just keep my eyes and ears open and give a little report before I get off the ship? I can do that." Rosalind felt as if she were sliding into a seat in the movies, into an unreal reality.

Eleanor nodded. "That's it. Are you still in?"

"I'm in."

Smith walked to the door. "Good. Bye for now," he said as he closed the door.

Eleanor had just reset the locks when the door clattered against the frame in a sudden, fierce fashion. Rosalind grabbed the gun, slid two bullets into the chamber, and pointed it dead center on the door. Eleanor grabbed a kitchen knife.

"Unlock the door, dammit." Rosalind recognized Smith's voice.

Eleanor nodded to her. "Do it. I've got you covered."

Rosalind handed her the gun and pointed to the wall next to the door. "Over there, where you get a shot at whoever comes in the door first."

Eleanor moved to the wall.

"Coming," Rosalind said.

She opened the door with precision, bracing herself for getting slammed by it. Smith stepped in and pointed down. "Let's drag him in."

The women stared at the limp body on the doorstep.

The man was clean-shaven, with an average build, wearing summer pants and a jacket—a standard issue kind of guy, Rosalind thought, as she tied his hands behind his back with Eleanor's bathrobe belt. No wedding ring. Smith was going through the man's wallet. Eleanor retrieved the man's hat from the hall floor and brought it inside, then shut the door and locked it.

"Anything?" Eleanor asked.

"Sucker punched me as I started down the stairs," Smith said. "Never seen him before in my life. No identification."

"So, the attack was planned. Good news is that if he's dead we can just dump him in the Potomac because the police won't know who he is either without his wallet." Eleanor was looking for something sturdier than a cloth belt in her wardrobe. "Aha. Leather is the thing."

Rosalind took the new belt, tightened it around the stranger's wrists, and loosened the other one.

The man began to lift his head and open his eyes. Rosalind grabbed the skillet. "One hard whack and you'll be out again. So no yelling. Just a nice conversation among friends. Understand?"

The man nodded.

"Who are you working for?" Eleanor demanded. "Anti-Defamation League?"

As the man shook his head, Rosalind wondered why Eleanor started with the least likely group, the Jewish group. Was it to act as if she didn't really have an idea? Soften the guy up somehow?

"FBI?"

The man shook his head again. Rosalind lifted the skillet, and the man began to speak.

"Name's Jeff Fitzroy. The Bund hired me as a private detective," he said, with an accent Rosalind couldn't place.

"What does the American Bund want? Do you understand how dangerous it is for you to be following decent citizens around, attacking them, especially ones employed by the federal government of the United States?" Eleanor's tone had the smooth, flat hardness of polished granite.

Rosalind knew Eleanor was digging for information now, playing as if she didn't know much, but of course she'd already identified the Bund as a likely group to follow them; a group wanting its own information on American anti-Nazi groups that it could send to the Reich for points with Hitler.

"You'd have to prove I knew you were all government people. The Bund hired me to follow the moneybags, Novy. It's not about government secrets. Just that Jew and that big newspaper person, Marsh, and any stuff they're up to together. And who did I see coming out of Marsh's door? You two broads."

"Watch your language, bud," Smith said.

"So, I see where you go." He nodded at Eleanor. "It's a curve—this guy coming out of your apartment. Look, it's just a job for me. And it sure doesn't pay well enough for me to get damaged. The boss's a cheapskate."

"Who is?" Rosalind asked.

"Kuhn. The head guy."

"Hmm. You don't like Kuhn. So what do you think of Father Coughlin?" Rosalind asked. The priest's anti-Semitic, pro-Fascist radio broadcasts made her blood boil. She squatted down to look Fitzroy in the eyes. Fitzroy stared back.

"Not crazy about him neither. Stirring up all the Cath-O-Lacs. As I said, I'm just a private dick anyone can hire—even you. So untie me, right?"

"Nope. Who do you check in with here?" Smith slapped his hand on Fitzroy's shoulder as if to remind him there was a guy there.

"I'll give you the telephone number which is all I've got. You gotta untie me though because the number is in my pants pocket."

"What are you going to tell the Bund?" Rosalind asked.

"Screw 'em. I'll just say you two had tea with that Alice Glass woman. And I followed you here, where you had a male friend visiting."

"The phone number." Smith untied Fitzroy and held out his hand.

"Here." Fitzroy reached into his trouser front pocket and pulled out a crumpled white note that Smith grabbed. Then the man struggled to his feet and quickly walked out the door, closing it behind him.

"We should let Rollins know," Eleanor said to Smith. "At least give him the phone number to follow up on. Could be a lead."

"Who is he?" Rosalind asked.

"Rich Rollins. Our New York off-the-books American Nazi hunter. He's trying everything he can to take Führer Fritz Kuhn down. But that is not our focus here. Smith, time for you to go. I will take it from here. We've used up a lot of time on the Bund and Fitzroy that I could've used getting Rosalind up to speed."

Smith shrugged. "I'll take care of Rich getting the number. You'll go over the list with her?"

Eleanor pursed her lips. "Of course."

"What list?" Rosalind asked as Eleanor watched as Smith walked down the stairs and then peered out the window to check on his departing torso.

"The possible embassy contacts," Eleanor said. "We have a lot to do."

CHAPTER 6

A short list of four embassy employees, with their addresses, sexes, ages, marital status, and nationality lay on the kitchen table. The names had been carved out from a list of fifteen by Eleanor and Smith as the ones most likely to help, based on reports from a vaguely labeled "set of interested parties" who'd visited the embassy in the last several months. The "parties" had noted the listees' courtesy to applicants, slight shudder when Hitler was mentioned, and warm mention of a Jewish friend. Ephemeral information from casual contacts, and now they were the most promising candidates for facilitating Novy's forty-four visa applicants and blending them into the general pool.

Rosalind committed their vitals to memory, then asked, "Again, is there a tit-for-tat here?"

"No." Eleanor looked up from a comfortable spot on the daybed. She'd been reading *The Atlantic* while Rosalind memorized the list and closed it now.

"Fine. So I say to Andrzej in my best Polish, 'Save a life, maybe lose your job.'"

"I'd stick to 'save a life' and not mention the job."

"How am I supposed to do this?"

"Rosalind, I do not have the answer to that, as I tried to make clear. Your job is not espionage, which I honestly know even less about. No one wants information from Andrzej. Jim Novy and Lydon Baines Johnson want to rescue a paltry forty-four Jews. Andrzej does not need to shelter, feed, and clothe a Jew. He only needs to approve the application for the person jumping the line and send it up the chain immediately."

"And he gets what in return?"

Eleanor pointed a finger at Rosalind. "You'll make him feel like doing this little, tiny favor for an unnamed member of the House of Representatives is heroic. That upping the visas for the week by a measly forty-four is nothing because of how many go unclaimed by the end of the year. Think of something. For crying out loud, you're supposed to be smart."

"I'll ask Mister Novy if he can spare three or four-thousand *zloty*."

"That's your idea of smart? Bribes? You don't think you can appeal to the milk of human kindness?" Eleanor shrugged. "Suit yourself. It's your operation."

Rosalind couldn't tell if Eleanor was being sarcastic or honest, but either way, it was clear Eleanor didn't worry about job security.

"I think that people need to put food on the table. I think that if someone will risk their job to do this, I need to have the ability to offer something in return."

"It would be a better world, by far, if that wasn't the case."

"Maybe." But money made the world go round. How did Eleanor not see that? Rosalind took a deep breath and asked, "Eleanor, what is your position with Representative Johnson, exactly? I don't think I ever asked."

"I have flexible assignments. And extended interests somewhat beyond the confines of that particular office space. When I'm not doing those, I am doing the normal senior staff stuff."

Rosalind pushed her chair away from the table. Eleanor's vagueness drove her crazy. She bit the inside of her cheek and took a deep breath. "What do you mean by extended interests? And who works with you on those?"

"Smith told you about one interest —getting more on what the Nazis and Nazi sympathizers are up to here in our country and in our embassies. Verifiable information we can discretely send up the chain."

Rosalind refocused on memorizing the list of names before turning her attention to the rest of the staff, noting who reported to whom, who translated Polish to American English, and what their citizenship was.

"Relax, Rosalind. You find us a good contact in the embassy and get those visas handled. That's the primary assignment. By the way, your cousin has nice looking kids—I took a look at the photograph. You can't afford to be less than all-in on this, and following our directions to a tee."

Rosalind nodded. "I'm in. Definitely in." She ignored the fact that the photograph had been tucked in her suitcase to send back to Hannah, which meant Eleanor had snooped—and wanted Rosalind to know that she had.

"Good." Eleanor stood up. "Time for a walk. Let's enjoy this peaceful DC scene while we can."

***

Eleanor walked with the long steps of someone late for a train. Rosalind matched her, looking up at black rainclouds.

"Here." Eleanor turned. "Department of State building."

They ran up the steps just as sheets of water began to fall from the sky.

"Where are we supposed to be going?" Rosalind asked.

"Second floor," Eleanor said, striding up the stairs. "He's waiting."

Smith smiled as he stepped out of an office and shut the door behind him. "Here it is." He reached into his beige linen jacket's breast pocket and pulled out what looked like a small, thin book. "My present to you and now I have to run."

Eleanor took it. "Thanks."

"Hope it's the magic amulet you seek." He strode off down the hall.

"Let's sit there on the bench. The second floor is quieter than the first." Eleanor walked down the hall and sank onto the empty seat. When Rosalind joined her, she said, "Here—it's your passport."

Rosalind took the little booklet from her hand. Inside, in elaborate cursive, she read: *I, the undersigned, Secretary of State of the United States of America, hereby request all whom it may concern to permit safely and freely to pass, and in case of need to give all lawful aid and protection to...* On the blank line, someone had written *Rosalind Fisher.* That was followed by *a citizen of the United States.* It was signed "Cordell Hull." The opposing page gave Rosalind's vital statistics under the "Description of Bearer."

"The signature is blank."

"You will need to sign it. Also, we'll need a suitable photograph. Why didn't I think of that yesterday? Add that to the list. I know just where we need to go. And we'll do it after the rain lets up. Smith will bring the photo to us tonight."

Eleanor smoothed her skirt and looked around. "Not everyone has a passport to travel, but we thought you needed this extra layer of safety. Jim Novy and his kid will have them, too, plus visas to get them into Palestine when they are done in Poland." She sighed. "Poland and Palestine in one trip as Europe descends into chaos. Does the man have a death wish?"

"It's Novy's problem if he does," Rosalind said.

"Until it's your problem," Eleanor replied. "You have a ticket on the Queen Mary for tomorrow's departure. Second class, which is how the government travels. We'll make sure you have what you need for when Novy invites you up to the first-class dining room."

"I've only got what I brought with me and the few outfits we bought here."

Eleanor nodded. "Back to the salt mines as soon as the rain let's up a bit."

A loud thunderclap sounded overhead.

"My dad was in the Great War," Eleanor said. "Artillery. Big booming noises like that made him shake all over."

"Does he still do that?"

"He killed himself when I was fourteen."

They sat in silence, until Eleanor said, "Enough sharing. We have dead dads. Smith has one too." She got to her feet. "Let's get to the passport photographer right now. He'll rush the job."

***

"That's a sad suitcase, Rosalind." Eleanor shook her head as she nudged it with her toe. "But it is perfect for who you are going to be, our nondescript agent. I just wish your hair was a different color."

"Blonde, anyone?" Smith waved a bottle of peroxide as he came out of Eleanor's bathroom. He'd arrived with Rosalind's passport photo just after eight p.m.

"No." Rosalind capped her hands around her head as if protecting every strand.

Smith stepped closer. "It won't hurt a bit."

"Rosalind's right. Peroxide is awful." Eleanor wrinkled her nose. "I've got this new stuff, just out on the shelves—"

"No. I'll wear a hat or cover my head with a scarf if I have to. Anyhow, women can tell if you've dyed your hair. I don't think I'll be trusted as much as if I'm just natural."

"And men may be so enchanted by those springy little red curls that they'll help you." Eleanor walked back into the bathroom with the bottle of peroxide.

"I just wish there were more women on the list. Women understand families. Men want something in return and it's usually not just money," Rosalind said.

"You'll have money, though. It'll arrive in your cabin on the Queen Mary, the equivalent of one hundred American dollars, compliments of Jim Novy," Smith said. "What I'm going to say next is very important, Rosalind. When the porter brings your bags, he's our guy. Well, he's the Brit's guy. He'll give you the money. For heaven's sake, hide it in the cabin, and figure out how to get it into Warsaw without it being found."

"I know how to hide money."

"If foreign agents decide to watch you, you need to be clever. Especially going through Germany on that train." Eleanor returned from the bathroom and resumed folding Rosalind's clothes and putting them in the suitcase.

"Yes." Rosalind reviewed the itinerary to calm herself. They would sail the Queen Mary from New York, then they would go from England, where the Queen Mary docked, to the port of Ostend, Belgium by boat. The three of them would then travel by train through Nazi Germany to Warsaw. Days of travel, the exact time hard to estimate.

Rosalind was to stay away from Novy unless he asked her to join him for dinner or otherwise needed her. If asked, she was to identify herself as vaguely as possible as an employee of the United States government on her way to check on some issues at the embassy in Warsaw. Once they got to Europe, she was to step in more, as needed. She would travel in first class with the Novys on the train.

"By the way, the Queen Mary has a Jewish chapel. The Brits, who are really not known for being philosemites, just wanted to stick it to Hitler. Anything else to pack?" Smith said.

***

The crowd seemed glued together by the heat and the sheer numbers on the wharf. Rosalind was overwhelmed by the salt smell, the enormous ships all around, the cacophony of the crowd punctuated by a tugboat hooting, and porters with luggage carts weaving between lines of passengers.

The Queen Mary accepted a river of people walking on the gangway. Rosalind, freed of her suitcase by a porter who confirmed her cabin number, joined the onboarding passengers.

When she arrived on the main deck and waited to check in, people began to differentiate into solitary units and small groups. Ahead of her, she saw Jim Novy and his son, David, who was about her height, slim, clean-shaven, and leaning attentively towards his father. Novy put a hand on his son's right shoulder and patted, then turned and spotted Rosalind. He waved her over.

"Hold my place, please," Rosalind said to the man in back of her. He nodded half-heartedly and she walked over to Jim Novy. "Mister Novy, how good to see you here."

"Where else would I be?" he replied.

When Rosalind started to say, "Oh, of course…", he smiled and said, "Miss Fisher, never mind my little teasing, please. Please meet my son, David Howard Novy. My scholar, who insisted on coming to Europe with me to see the sights."

David held out his hand and Rosalind shook it. "You're the translator who works for Representative Johnson. Pleased to meet you. My father said how multi-lingual you are, but he didn't say you were also young."

Rosalind felt herself blushing. Was this child flirting with her or just being politely observant?

"I'm twenty-four. Mister Novy, David, I will see you soon."

"I've arranged for you to sit at our table tonight," Novy said.

Rosalind nodded and gave what she hoped was a grateful smile, then returned to her place in line with a whispered "Thanks" to her reluctant place holder. Soon, she was processed onboard.

"Welcome on board, Miss Fisher. Here's your key. Third floor down. You may take the stairs or use the elevator." Then the key was in her hand, and she was walking on the deck of the Queen Mary, the smell of ocean air mixed with women's perfume and diesel oil around her.

***

Rosalind found her cabin on the first deck of the second-class cabins, after she walked by the pool dedicated to tourist class, the shuffle-board court, and a hair salon. Her room had a single bed with a mahogany headboard, and a Pullman-style bed above it, a desk and two chairs, a wardrobe, a washroom with a built-in shower, and two portholes for a view. At that moment, all she could see was the side of a building on the wharf. A steady throbbing sound came from the ship's engines, a few decks below.

A knock at the door was followed by "Your bag, Miss." Rosalind opened the door to the porter, whose nametag read *Sidney*, holding her father's ancient suitcase.

"May I?" he said.

Rosalind stepped back into the cabin.

Sidney waved her away from the bed. "This portmanteau slides under the bed like so."

Now that he'd said more than two words together, Rosalind detected a thread of a German accent twisting around his gutturals. Leftover from childhood, possibly.

"I was told you have something else for me." She held out her hand.

With a slight smile, Sidney reached into his uniform jacket and pulled out an envelope.

Unsmiling, she took the envelope and opened it. Counting the currency and hiding it would have to wait until Sidney left the room.

"We need to have a brief talk," Sidney said.

"You can begin with your real name," Rosalind said.

"It's Sidney, really. Hill is my last name, courtesy of my British dad. Mum is—or was, depending on how you look at colonial issues—Boer. She raised me in South Africa after they lost the war, of course."

"So I'm hearing Afrikaans in your voice?"

"Is it still there? I spoke nothing but King's English from the time I entered boarding school on. Thought it was thoroughly driven out." He smiled broadly. "You're very attentive. It's a good thing for a spy."

"I'm no spy."

Sidney shrugged slightly. "Here is the situation, Rosalind. As you ply your zlotys among the Polish and American clerks at the US embassy, we would like information on who seems loyal to the West and who can be swayed towards Nazi Germany. But only if the information comes your way easily, by observation, for example, and not questioning anyone. Those rats need to be flushed out of the system before they can do damage."

"Who is 'we?'"

"Ah, well… We are a group of cooperating concerned Brits and Americans who engage in discreet information gathering to aid our mutual governments."

He'd told her just what Eleanor and John had—an unofficial group, nothing else. But the Brits had spies, real spies.

"But you're a steward," Rosalind said. "You're hardly highly placed."

Sidney shook his head. "I'm not offended, but a person in your situation must separate what you think from what you say even to someone you believe is your ally. And for your information, the best information is collected by the invisible class. People in service. Stewards, for example."

"Right." Rosalind folded her hands together and sighed. A steward would not be noticed in the stateroom doing a task, like turning down the bed. Plus, he had the keys to everything in his pocket.

"If it helps you understand even better, we found guns in a case of hollowed-out German Bibles being shipped on a vessel like this one to the American Bund. Not that Herr Hitler wants to drag the United States into European issues. Quite the contrary. He wants you neutral," Sidney said. "Hitler was not pleased and demoted the spymaster responsible. And we got notes identifying highly placed Nazi sympathizers in New York in the suitcase of a prominent socialite traveling to Berlin." He chuckled. "Now that was helpful to a certain person sympathetic to us in DC."

The ship's engines roared up and Rosalind felt a slow forward movement.

"I have to get back to my steward duties." Sidney stood up. "Be sure you join Mister Novy tonight at dinner. The cuisine is grand and there are people you can listen to in a way that I can't. Especially the German duo, but be careful of them, the woman in particular. I'll need a report tomorrow. Don't let anyone know your secret talents, Rosalind. Novy's been told to go along with whatever you say and do, and he will."

***

The two evening dresses in her suitcase were borrowed from one of Eleanor's friends, who seemed to have spent a month's wages on each of them. "For business purposes," Eleanor had said. "Lightly worn, appropriately used, fitting for the occasions. She'd like them back when you're done. Dry-cleaned, please."

Each dress had the natural waistline, slightly exaggerated shoulders, and hip-hugging silhouette Rosalind had seen in the women's magazines and the department store. One pair of evening shoes, one small clutch, and one fascinator for her hair completed her wardrobe.

From the limited view of herself Rosalind could see in the mirror, she looked suitable in the green dress. She smoothed the skirt and headed toward the second-class deck hall, where six or seven couples, all dressed in their finest, were heading towards the stairs up to the first-class deck and dining room.

***

"Miss Fisher, you look lovely. Everyone, this is Rosalind Fisher." Jim Novy stood up and pulled out a chair for her. David Novy and two other men stood when Jim Novy did, and two women remained seated, each giving her a quick up and down. One pursed her lips and twiddled her oyster fork and the other made eye contact with Rosalind.

As she took her seat, Rosalind smiled at the women in turn, giving her particular attention to the one who'd pursed her lips. That was a woman who did not care much for social graces, which made her noticeable.

The table held a bottle of champagne, which David picked up and poured into his glass. Novy put a hand on his son's forearm but removed it when David shifted away in his seat.

"Lest we forget our manners," one of the men said with a slight New York accent, "I'm Art Wallace and this is my wife, Bernice." Bernice smiled in the quick manner of women accustomed to being introduced by their husbands and then ignored for the night.

The other woman put her fork down. "I'm Hedda Becker," she said. Her English was weighted with German. "Heinrich is my husband. His English is not as good as mine."

"Your English is excellent, ma'am. I wish I understood German." Rosalind picked up her napkin and put it on her lap. She waved off a waiter bearing a freshly opened bottle of champagne and caught Jim Novy's glance. "Isn't it just like our government to send someone like me over to Poland and here I don't know anything except good ol' American."

Hedda turned to her husband and whispered in German, "First this horrid Polish Jew who is at least rich. Now this girl. Who is she to sit at this table?"

Heinrich Becker shrugged and poured himself a glass of champagne. "Maybe Novy's mistress? Maybe just a secretary for her government? Or both?"

The next set of waiters brought oysters on the half-shell and shrimp cocktails. Novy and David waved them off. "I ordered the fresh herring for an appetizer," Novy said in a firm voice. "I am Jewish. No pork. No shellfish. We'll eat fish and vegetables every night."

"And drink the champagne," David said.

Rosalind could almost hear the German couple's teeth grinding behind their set lips.

Then the waiter was next to Rosalind. She'd never eaten shellfish in her life. "Thank you. I'll have four oysters."

She picked up the little three-pronged fork sitting at the furthest end of the array of five forks next to her plate, just as Bernice had done. Smiling at Bernice across the table, she said, "Isn't this lovely?" Dipping her head down towards the plate, she stabbed at the rounded mound of grey-white flesh in the first shell and plucked it up. She lifted her head and smiled at Bernice again. "Bon appetite." When Bernice swabbed the oyster into a red sauce, Rosalind did the same after counting to five. Then she popped the cold spicy mass into her mouth and chewed. Her eyes watered from the sauce.

"I don't believe these are as tasty as the ones we can get in Boston," Art Wallace said to Bernice.

"Well, beggars can't be choosers," she replied.

Rosalind ate the oysters remaining on her plate with less of the sauce and hoped the next course wasn't pork.

"Did you enjoy your trip to the United States?" Rosalind asked Hedda.

"No."

"What a shame." Rosalind had turned towards Hedda, the pose of someone expecting continued exchange.

"Why not?" Bernice had a now half-full glass of red wine in her hand. Art patted her shoulder, but Bernice shrugged him off.

"New York is disorganized and full of…"

"Oh, I do understand what you mean," Rosalind said. "Yes."

The ship gave a distracting lurch. Bernice downed the last of the wine in her glass and waved at the waiter. Rosalind leaned in towards Hedda. "I am so looking forward to seeing Berlin."

"You are not traveling with that Herr Novy?"

"No. Well, not really. I have a job with the…ummm…the House. Representative…ummm…Johnson." Rosalind let her voice trail off.

"A young woman like yourself working in your country's government. You must know how the wheels are oiled, as they say." With that, Hedda turned her attention to the next course.

With relief, Rosalind looked over at Bernice. "Sauteed filet of sea bass in a reduction of white wine and mushrooms," Bernice said, poking at her fish. "Hope it's better than the oysters."

"Oh, yes." Rosalind picked up the next fork in line and cut herself a small slice. The fish was delicious.

***

The two American men adjourned to drink whiskey and smoke cigars with David doing his wobbly best to follow. Careful to modulate their tone, Heinrich and Hedda quarreled in German about whether he would go as well. Hedda said to her husband, *"Stellen Sie sicher, dass Sie fur die morgige Lieferung gerustet sind."* He rose, gave Rosalind and Bernice a small bow, and left.

Rosalind noted Hedda's admonition to her husband to be ready for "tomorrow's delivery," whatever that was, and she also noted that Hedda used the formal version of "you." Rosalind took a small spoonful of her silken chocolate mousse, suppressed a small sigh of delight, and considered what delivery Heinrich might be getting on the Queen Mary, now chugging her way through the Atlantic.

Rosalind excused herself from the table pleading a slight stomach problem. "Too much heavy food the first day out," Bernice announced with the conviction of someone who'd traveled many times.

As a steward walked towards her, Rosalind said, "I need to find the man who brought my bags to my room today."

"Is everything all right, Ma'am?" She assured him it was and wrote down her cabin number on the pad he provided.

***

"You got me in trouble with the chief steward." The mass of Sidney's body took up most of the cabin's small floor space.

"I hope that's not true. I just said what I needed to get you here. We should figure out a way for me to contact you."

"Fine, Miss Fisher. Why don't we pretend I've taken a shine to you and vice versa? Happens between crew and tourist-class passengers all the time. Then I can seek you outside and even slip in here. I also need to emphasize that you are just to observe carefully and report to me. Same at the embassy—observe, report. You're not—under any circumstances—to play Nancy Drew, girl detective, sneaking around everywhere and following your own hunches."

Rosalind's cheeks pinked. It wasn't up to this man to tell her what to do. "Look, Sidney, so far as I'm concerned, I'm here to observe and share with you what I see and hear, just as you said. That's it. Let's fake a romance, but let's make it a sedate flirtation. Novy's a very traditional man, so nothing to distress him. It'll be bad enough because he'll know you aren't Jewish and I am."

"Sure thing. I wasn't thinking torrid."

"Good. Here's information for you. Heinrich and Hedda Becker are expecting a delivery of some kind tomorrow morning, early enough that she was upset he planned to go have a scotch with the other men at the table. That also suggests that he understands more English than they'd like anyone to know or he wouldn't have wanted to plant himself with all English-speaking men. Also, they are flat-out Nazi supporters. It was all they could do not to leave the table when Mister Novy made his Jewish identity known."

"Good. May I sit? This is awkward—you and me standing in this small space and staring at each other."

Rosalind waved at the bed and Sidney sat. "The most likely delivery would be from an American wanting to get something into Germany without sending it by mail or going himself," she said. "Or herself."

"Agreed. A Nazi-sympathizer. I haven't seen any likely suspects in first-class. Any ideas on your end?"

"Not yet, but I've only met the people at Novy's table. I'll keep my eyes open. By the way, is there any man traveling alone, probably second-class?" Rosalind wondered if Jeff Fitzroy was still following her, if perhaps he had a bigger role in the Bund, and described him to Sidney.

"No. Can I ask why?"

"He followed me in DC and works for the Bund. I just have a feeling about him."

"I'll keep a lookout." Sidney then pulled a penciled list out of his jacket pocket. "Besides the two charmers at your table, there are three German citizens on their way back from business in New York. But they'd have no need to give something to our pair since they're going to Berlin."

"How do you know that?"

"I look at luggage tags. My job. There's a New York socialite who was seen by a colleague exiting the Bund headquarters there, too. Blonde hair, wears it in a bob, and sunglasses even inside most of the time. She's around your age, I'd guess. About four inches shorter than you. Her family makes money supplying the Navy with office supplies."

Rosalind hadn't seen the woman in the dining room, but she'd been focused on her table. "I'll look more on my end, but I can't promise much."

"Just hang around the German speakers as much as you can without looking too obvious. Especially the couple at your table. That's the best job for you."

She smiled and in her best Texas belle drawl said, "I learned a long time ago how not to stand out."

"Well, there is your curly red hair." Sidney put out a hand as if to pat her head then withdrew it.

"That is one of many reasons my talents for unnoticeability have been honed to perfection, Sidney."

CHAPTER 7

Rosalind tried to stroll, but even in August, the piercing Atlantic wind on the open deck drove her back inside to retrieve her jacket. Day three of the journey and nothing to report to Sidney except banal exchanges between Hedda and Heinrich at dinner about news in Berlin that anyone could read in the paper. No further mention of the mysterious delivery, and Sidney hadn't been able to get into their cabin to look, either.

Rosalind was bored. Enforced inactivity, sitting and pretending to read, pretending to drink beer, listening to nothing. She'd had a brief sighting of the blonde New York socialite Sidney had described getting her nails done in the first-class deck salon, but all the other chairs were filled, so there was no way for Rosalind to get close enough to eavesdrop. She'd hovered like a seagull around the salon until the manager came out and asked her if she wanted to book an appointment, then she left. The next sighting was the socialite playing gin rummy for money after dinner at a table stocked with men of varying ages and eligibility. Then swimming in the pool, but Rosalind had no bathing suit and simply sat near the pool's edge, pretending to enjoy the sea air.

"Do I know you?" the socialite had asked, swimming up to Rosalind and propping her arms on the deck. "You were staring."

Smiling, Rosalind shook her head. "You look like a sorority sister of mine. Sorry."

The woman had nodded and returned to doing laps. Wondering how better to approach her next time, Rosalind headed towards her cabin to get a wrap for the breezy air.

***

As Rosalind headed towards her cabin to retrieve her jacket, she noticed a man ahead of her. He was walking down the stairs, away from her. Because her eyes hadn't quite adjusted to being inside, his silhouette was all she could make out. She slowed her pace, then stopped altogether as his face became clearer to her. Despite the fact that his body seemed to be padded under his clothes and his hair looked gray, it was clearly Jeff Fitzroy.

When he reached the landing of her second-class deck, Fitzroy turned left. Rosalind walked down the steps and waited for the count of five before peering around the corner. He'd disappeared.

As she turned and started to walk to her cabin, a hand clapped onto her shoulder. "Just keep walking, Miss Fisher."

"Mister Fitzroy, what a surprise to find you here." Rosalind stepped down, planting one foot sideways and bracing herself as best she could against the wall with her shoulder.

"Here I thought my disguise was better than that. Keep moving."

Rosalind felt something poke into her waist–the muzzle of a gun or perhaps just his rigid fingers. Nodding her agreement, she walked down the hall.

"Your cabin." Fitzroy jabbed her again. "We'll talk nice and private in there."

As Rosalind unlocked the door to her cabin, she thought of the two bullets in her derringer, which she'd slid into the magazine before tucking the gun into a newly constructed compartment in her ancient suitcase.

Fitzroy shoved her in almost hard enough to make her fall. Rosalind fell dramatically onto the floor, her arms outstretched. "Is this payback for my friends knocking you around a little?" she asked, reaching back towards her leg with her left hand. "Ouch. My knee." With her right hand she found and then fiddled with her suitcase lock.

"Just get up already."

"Yeah." She rolled over and covered her left knee with her hand. "My knee's bleeding, Fitzroy. Can I clean it up in the washroom? Happy to leave the door open."

He grunted.

Rosalind made a show of cleaning off her knee, wincing as she tapped a wet washcloth on it. "Still bleeding. And my pant leg has blood on it. I have to rinse it out and hang the pants up."

"Fine."

"And I don't want to sit here with you in my pantie briefs so I'm going to get a new pair of pants out of my suitcase."

"Just hurry the fuck up." He waved the hand he'd kept hidden in his pocket. No gun. "I don't care if you sit here naked. You got until I count to ten."

In her pantie briefs and the top, Rosalind turned so Fitzroy had a full view of her long legs, her left knee wrapped with a knotted washcloth, and her small waist. "Just let me get into my suitcase," she said. "Would you move?"

He stepped aside. She put the suitcase on the bed, raised the lid and pulled her gun out of the loosely basted lining.

Pointing it at the now-paling man, she said, "Sit down, Fitzroy." He perched on the bed.

"Back against the wall."

He scooted until his back was against the wall.

"You're following me again. All the way to Europe this time. Why?"

"You have a link to Charles Marsh and that Johnson guy. And the Jew, Novy. That's all."

"Nope. Not all by a mile. Who's interested?"

"You're not going to hurt me, sister."

She tilted the muzzle towards his left knee. "I wouldn't try me, if I was you."

He continued moving, pulling the bed covers with him. As his body turned towards her and he began to stand up, she pulled the trigger.

The small bullet tore into Fitzroy's thigh. Blood spurted out as he wrapped both hands around the wound.

"You fuckin' bitch." He stumbled back and sank onto the bed.

Rosalind pointed the gun towards his groin and hoped Fitzroy wouldn't play a game of chicken. Her heart had left her body, and nausea had taken its place. She'd shot one bullet in a gun that only held two, which he certainly knew. The rest of her bullets were in the suitcase's compartment, and she'd need two hands to put a third and fourth one in the gun. What was she going to do with this wounded man who would report her the moment he could?

She swallowed hard. "You want to answer my questions and I'll get help, or keep bleeding on my bed? Your choice."

His hands were slimy and crimson with a surprising amount of blood and his face was ashy. Rosalind tried again. "Talk and I'll get you some help."

"Know your enemy."

"What?" Was the man dense or had he just lost too much blood to think?

"The Bund, you fool. Who plans to turn America against us? Who are the other Jew lovers? Help me. I'm…" The words came out whispered just above the engine throb. Fitzroy's head lolled against his chest, eyes closed.

Rosalind tapped Fitzroy's wound with her gun but he didn't react. The pool that had formed on her bed kept filling. She went into the bathroom and vomited into the toilet. Then she rinsed out her mouth, washed her hands, and put her trousers back on so she could find Sidney.

✳✳✳

Sidney stared at the corpse lolling on Rosalind's bed. "Any ideas?" he asked.

"I was hoping you had some. I pretty much exhausted myself shooting him, putting on clean clothes, and finding you. And I didn't mean to kill him, if that means anything."

"You hit the femoral artery. Bleeds out in six minutes or less. Do you know how to apply a tourniquet?"

"I'm not planning to have this happen again."

"Successful espionage—getting the secrets and not getting caught—is about anticipating what you don't think will happen. Of course, you're not a spy. Not even close." Sidney was patting down Fitzroy's jacket. "Just a packet of Camels and his cabin key." He handed the cigarettes to her. "Go through that carefully."

"Why?"

"No matches. And his cabin didn't smell of smoke."

She went back to the tiny bathroom, sat on the toilet, and emptied the cigarettes onto the last dry towel. Each white cylinder, tightly packed with tobacco, seemed just as she'd expect it to seem until the last one—the one that had been tucked into the rear corner, hardest to get out intact without tearing the packet. She'd seen enough men hand-rolling their own cigarettes to know this one wasn't factory issue.

"I have something."

Sidney nodded. He was stripping the corpse. "Leave it for now. We have to come up with a plan for the dead guy. And I have to report this to ship's security before he starts to go cold."

"He saw me in the hall and then snuck up behind me as I opened my door."

"Keep going."

"I recognized him from… No, that won't work. I didn't know him at all. He planned to force himself on me. Why did I have a gun?"

"Who said this is your gun, Rosalind? It's his gun. You struggled with him and he shot himself in the leg. After all, he's dead on your bed."

Sidney took the gun and slid it into Fitzroy's hand, posed the trigger finger, and stepped back. "I need to put his pants back on his ankles. It has to look like he was just about to…you know. Help me."

She grabbed the blood-sodden trousers and began to work at her task. The heavy weight of the fabric, the drag as it went over Fitzroy's shoes, how the red stained her hands—details her mind grabbed onto.

***

The Queen Mary's Director of Security sat across from Rosalind in his office. "You work in the Office of Representative Lyndon Baines

Johnson of Texas. Don't bother to respond; our wireless communication is superb. The senior secretary there was alarmed, of course, but we assured her you were relatively unharmed."

Rosalind nodded.

"And your sworn statement, which you will sign, is that this man, who we identify as Jeffrey Regal Fitzroy of Baltimore, Maryland, propelled you into your cabin at gunpoint with the intent to force himself upon you." He paused to look at her.

Rosalind nodded again.

"You struggled with him and he discharged the gun, fatally wounding himself in the left leg. After vain attempts to staunch the bleeding on your own, you then contacted the steward, Sidney Hill. Why again did you contact him and not a higher level of crew?"

"I'd only seen him and waiters. I've never been on a ship before and I don't know the hierarchy." Her voice was as steady as she could balance on edgy nerves.

The man leaned back in his chair. "A young woman, distressed and all, I can see that. And Mister Hill confirms what you've said. I'm closing this matter, Miss Fisher. We do not want an incident even indirectly impacting a member of your government. We…just don't. Do you require any assistance from our medical doctor or his team?"

"Oh, thank you. Possibly they could look at some bruising I have. Do you need to know where?"

"No, not at all. On behalf of our crew, we are of course very sorry you had to go through all of this. How can we know who our passengers are, really?"

Rosalind nodded. "Thank you again. May I go?"

Rosalind returned to her cabin. The small paper cylinder was in her cosmetic case where she'd put it before Sidney replaced the pack in Fitzroy's pocket. She took it out and sniffed. Pungent. Not gunpowder. Slowly she untwisted one end and then the other. Just leaves, no writing on the paper.

"Mary Jane, how do you do," she murmured. Then she rerolled it, just as she'd seen guys do with their cigarettes. She'd give it to Sidney the next chance she had. He could look at the paper again, toss it in the ocean, or smoke it, his choice.

***

Less than a day remained until they docked. For twenty-six hours, Jim Novy had kept his distance as the investigation into Fitzroy's death occurred, sending a brief handwritten note of support, but not inviting Rosalind back to the first-class table. Even though he'd resumed contact with her, mostly at lunch when the seating was looser, he remained distant.

As a result, Rosalind had nothing to report about the German couple, whether they'd had a reaction beyond the typical to Fitzroy's death, and what they might have received in the mysterious package. She also no longer had her gun, and she missed it. Sidney had vanished from her life and despite herself, she missed him, too. But she understood. If she were in charge of the crew, she'd assign him somewhere else, too.

Rosalind rested on a chaise lounge, gazing at the green-gray ocean and taking careful glances down the deck to where Heinrich and Hedda Becker sat, nursing mid-morning drinks.

The non-communicative blonde, wearing the fifth bathing suit Rosalind had seen her in, walked by, then she stopped where the Beckers were and sat down. Rosalind stood up and strolled in their direction, the soft swaying of the ship no longer noticeable to her.

"…useful to you, my father…" The blonde, leaning in towards Hedda Becker, stopped speaking and sat up as Rosalind passed. Hedda stared at Rosalind.

"Oh, how nice to see you again." Rosalind smiled at them all and walked over to the bar. Just as she sat down, a steward came over and said, "Mister Novy would like to meet

with you in the ship's library."

"Of course. When?"

"I believe, Ma'am, the matter is important, and he is waiting for you."

When she entered the library, Jim Novy rose from a deep leather chair and waved her into the chair across from his. The room—with its built-in, book-lined mahogany shelves, a round table with a gleaming green and turquoise world globe, and the Art Deco sconces in the wall—was otherwise empty of passengers. At another time, Rosalind would have been delighted to sink into the chair, book in hand, and read.

"I hope you have recovered fully from the episode, Miss Fisher." His voice was neutral and the word 'episode' conveyed almost nothing about his thoughts, except for the merest pause, as if he'd shifted through word choices before landing on that one.

"Yes, I have." Rosalind matched her tone to his. The truth was, even with a complete change of mattress and bed linens, she'd been unable to sleep without nightmares since she'd killed Fitzroy. But there was no reason to share that with this man.

"That's what comes out of strong immigrant stock. Resilience. To the point, then. I've been warned to turn around and go back. I intend to go on, nonetheless. I'll make arrangements to send you back to New York the minute we dock in England, if that is what you want."

"No, thank you. My job is to assist you and that's what I'll do. Who's warned you, Mister Novy?"

"I received this note. See, it's on ship's stationery. Unsigned of course." He pulled a piece of paper from his jacket pocket and handed it to her.

You are a rich Jew. Do not create problems. You are better to not proceed.

She stared at the penmanship, done in an elegant and well-trained hand. It reminded her of the letter sent by her cousin. "German or Polish, probably," she said. "The English is, of course, correct. However, the person who wrote this was educated in one of those countries. No one in America has handwriting like this or uses such formal grammar. It's hard to tell from how it's worded if this is from a friend or a foe." She looked at the note again. "But I do think from the boldness of the script that it was written by a man." She'd seen the difference in how men and women wrote when she'd helped her professor of Germanic languages grading freshmen papers. No matter how many mistakes the men made, they made them in black, forceful lettering.

She handed it back and Novy refolded it and tucked it back into his pocket as if it was a linen handkerchief needing careful attention.

"There are a handful of men on the ship who I'd suspect of this. I'd consider the passengers first, although there might be a few crew-members who'd qualify. Is it important who sent it, sir? And, if there is a clear and specific threat to you, not Jews in general, would you consider returning David to the United States instead of me? He's only sixteen."

"Miss Fisher, my son is my concern, not yours. Of course, your recent experience and then this note have heightened your—"

Rosalind stood up. "Yes, sir. I apologize. It's not my business. But I have no intention of returning to the United States, thank you. I will finish my assignment with you. Now, if you don't mind, I'll excuse myself and see you when we disembark."

"Since you are insistent on continuing, Miss Fisher, will you look into this? Someone should, after all."

She'd been going to stomp off, but it was Jim Novy who'd gotten the warning from someone and Novy and David were her responsibility.

"I apologize, Mister Novy. Of course I will."

She had to have a gun for protection. That meant locating Sidney. And she needed to consider who would have sent such a note.

***

"I hear that your interview with our head of security went well."

Between the wind and the noise of the engine room below them, Rosalind could just make out what Sidney was saying as they stood on the outside deck. "Yes." She nodded for emphasis.

"Bad reputation for a ship to have women attacked."

"I want my gun." She cupped her mouth with her hands and shouted right at him.

"The Captain's got it locked up because you said it was Fitzroy's and he turned it on you. I want Fitzroy's phony cigarette that you still have." He smiled at her. Under other circumstances she might have appreciated the dimple, the white teeth, even the warmth. Now it just conveyed a sad ending oozing with sympathy for what a boob she'd been.

She wrapped her arms around herself as the wind kicked up. The ship seemed to shift and buck in the water like a bull in a rodeo. One dead man, no gun, nothing to show for it except a reefer.

"The cigarette is just marijuana. I recognize the smell. There's nothing on the paper."

"Toss that stuff overboard first chance you get. Keep the paper for me just in case there's a code or something on it."

"Fine. But Sidney, that blonde gave Hedda and Heinrich something she thinks is important. I don't know what."

Sidney stopped smiling. "Anything else?"

"Right now it's vague. Novy got a threatening note from someone. Please, get me a gun or tell me how to find one when we disembark."

"Don't do anything on your own, Rosalind. And I don't have a gun for you here. When I get off the ship…"

Always have something to offer that is less valuable than what you want. Never let the other guy know that. Rosalind knew how that worked from the torrid summer she'd spent behind the counter of her cousin Hannah's husband's pawn shop, watching him deal with the luckless. Fair, above board, profitable, and ruthless. She had the reefer paper, though she was pretty sure it was just that and had no code hidden on it, and she had the vague information about the blonde American, and she had the threatening note to Novy. Sidney might have a gun for her. Right now, Sidney might have the better end of the bargain, but who could say.

"Let me consider these possibilities," Sidney said. "Just don't act on your own."

"So, the deal is a gun when we disembark. I'll give you the reefer now and when I have information about the threat to Novy, I'll give you that, too." She reached into her pocket and held the joint out.

Sidney shrugged, took the small white cylinder, opened it and let the wind take the dry leaves. Then he turned and walked away. As he yanked open the door to reenter the ship, Rosalind saw the edge of a cadet blue coat whipped into view and pulled back by an unseen hand. Then the door closed. She stayed, holding onto the rail, looking towards England, and thinking about her next steps. She knew who her prime candidate for author of the note was and she had very little time to prove it. If not telling Sidney who she thought it was constituted yet another mistake, she'd find out soon enough.

***

Two hours later, when the sun was at its warmest, she promenaded around the first-class deck and cursed the fashion arbiter who held that mid-heel pumps were anything close to safe on a rolling ship with her mother's favorite oath: *May he grow like a potato with his head under the ground.* Halfway around the deck, she spied the Beckers, now in swim clothes and with Heinrich carrying a blanket under his arm, headed for the sun-drenched chaise lounges.

Rosalind watched them settle in. Then she walked to the deck's bar and said, "We'd like to send Heinrich and Hedda, over there, a lovely bottle of champagne. Please just tell them it's compliments of the Captain. We want to surprise them, so no telling them it's us, please." She smiled as if she sent innocent yet expensive gifts routinely. The bartender nodded. Rosalind wrote down Mister Novy's cabin number and added a hefty tip.

The champagne cork made a barely audible pop. Heinrich and Hedda held up their flutes for the pour as Rosalind slipped away, changed her clothes in her cabin to office drab, and proceeded to the first-class deck.

She found a steward for the first-class cabins and said, in English as heavily accented by German as she could choke out, "My employers, Herr and Frau Becker, require an item from their stateroom. I must get it for them."

The steward, who looked to be in his early thirties, pursed his lips and shook his head in the age-old posture of "close, but no cigar." She put her hands up to her eyes in the classic posture of a woman in distress and fell back against the wall. "I will lose my job. Do you know what it is like?" She began to keen.

"Go get the key from them, Miss."

"Ahh. That is the problem. They are on deck in bathing attire and have no key upon themselves. That is what I must obtain."

"For cryin' out loud. Ya should'a said that at the beginning." The words came out in a Bronx accent as thick as mustard.

"Yes, yes. I am but the fool."

"Hurry up. Just close the door behind ya and it'll lock up tight."

"You will not embarrass my employers over this?"

"Lady, we never embarrass the first-class passengers."

***

The suite was four times the size of Rosalind's, maybe five. Bigger than the house she'd had as a child, anyway. The sitting area had Art Deco-style furniture she'd only seen in movies, made from burnished wood and upholstered in yellow and gold material that felt like cream.

She searched the desk but found only paper and a pen. Making a small mark on a paper, Rosalind looked at the ink. It could have been the ink on the note to Jim Novy, but it could just be the standard ink in all these first-class rooms. She sighed, folded up the paper she'd marked, and stuck it in her pocket. The coffee table was bare and the wastepaper basket, empty. Very efficient crew.

In the bedroom, Rosalind wanted to lie down in the white-satin-covered twin beds and sleep. Instead, she searched the nightstand drawers with no luck. Then she returned to the sitting room, which had two more doors to explore. She opened the first to see a fully outfitted bathroom, rifled through the medicine cabinet and, for good measure, checked behind the bidet and inside the toilet tank.

The second door opened to a luggage room with four steamer trunks, one open, and a set of poles where over a dozen dresses and an equal amount of men's clothes were hung. Based on the amount of clothing, Herr and Frau Becker had been in the States for a long time, much longer than their casual comments at the dinner table suggested. Hanging to the far left, in Herr Becker's section, was a cadet blue coat. The pockets were empty.

Rosalind heard the door to the cabin open and Heinrich's voice saying, "Yes, I know where I left it" in German. She slid into the hanging clothes, hoping Helga's long sable coat at the end of the rack was not what he wanted as she stood behind it. The door to the luggage room swung open and banged against the wall as the ship hit a turbulent patch of water. One of the Beckers walked over and slammed it shut. Rosalind stepped out of her hiding spot and took a post by the door to hear what they were saying.

"Why did that steward say he was pleased we now had our key?" Helga's irritation was obvious. "We should have asked him."

"And we would have sounded suspicious. Just like we sounded when we asked why we received that bottle of champagne. The Captain sent it? I don't think so. As for our steward, there are already spies on this ship for England and maybe he is one, like that steward, Sidney Hill. The less we say, the better."

"Yes, the more suspicious we act, the more suspicion we draw in, like dark clouds gathering together. Still, you keep an eye on this steward." Helga was in charge of whatever they were doing, Rosalind thought. No *please*, and again, use of the formal "you."

"What about that Rosalind Fisher girl Sidney met with on the deck?"

"I think she's a twit. Hired for her looks." The *twit* was in English. Rosalind hadn't heard it before but in Helga's mouth the word was dismissive. That was good—she was not a threat, as far as Helga was concerned.

"Wrong. She's involved in Fitzroy's death. That man the Bund hired. Whatever she told the Chief Security Officer was certainly a lie," Heinrich argued.

"You may be right. Maybe the officer didn't believe her, but he didn't want to arrest a member of the US government, even a lowly person. We'll watch her for now." With that, Helga seemed to pull rank and shut down the discussion.

Rosalind bit the inside of her cheek and refocused on the conversation.

"Now let's get the list. I need to make additions from our last two days in New York and the couple here. I need to know for sure it's up to date in case someone else dies." After she said this, Helga began to laugh in a low rumbling way that made Rosalind's mouth go dry.

Rosalind saw the handle to the luggage room door begin to turn. She took four giant steps backwards towards the fur coat, ducking behind it just as Heinrich said, "It is too dark in here to see," and turned on the light.

Rosalind stood as far back in the corner as she could, holding her breath. She heard the soft, creaky sound of the trunk lid rising, and then rattling as Heinrich lifted the tray out of its place.

"Yes, here. The first trunk towards the door and just under the tray. Exactly where I said it was." He walked out, leaving the door open and the light on. Minutes passed, then he returned, replaced the tray in the trunk, and left, turning out the light.

Rosalind felt her lungs screaming for a deep breath.

"I'm lying down now. Then I will bathe and dress for dinner. You will find out more about Fitzgerald's death and more about our red-haired *mädchen*." That seemed to be Helga's parting shot at her partner.

"Yes. Fine." There was the sound of the main cabin door opening and closing.

Rosalind waited for what seemed like enough time for the ship to have reached England and returned to New York. Then she peered out and saw the bedroom door was now shut. As quickly as she could, she opened the trunk and found a tightly folded paper under the tray. In the dim light coming in under the door, she could see that it had over a dozen names and addresses, all written in the fine European script she had seen on the note given to Jim Novy. Beneath the paper was another object, which felt like a metal cylinder. She slipped the paper and the cylinder into her pocket, refolded the paper she had taken from the desk to match, and put that in its place. As long as neither Heinrich nor Helga took the paper out, the decoy would work and hopefully camouflage both missing objects.

***

Rosalind took her dinner in her room. "Just leave the tray outside the door," she'd called to the person who dropped it off. She planned to stay in her room for the few hours remaining in the trip, pleading neuralgic symptoms from Fitzgerald's assault and his death.

She studied the list of names and addresses and recognized no one. They were people in New York City, Chicago, and Detroit—no recognizable names, no Father Coughlin, no Henry Ford. But someone would track them down and figure out why they were important to Helga and her masters.

After Rosalind copied the list, she refolded the original paper. She tried to think of how to get the original back into the trunk. With Helga and Heinrich suspicious of Sidney and watching both of them, he'd have no direct access to the trunk on the ship. And by early afternoon tomorrow, they'd be docked and preparing for their trip across the English Channel and to the train station for the overland section through Germany to Warsaw. When and how could she talk to Sidney about this?

She tried to pry open the metal cylinder, but the top was too tight. Was this the package the Beckers had talked about, the "something" from the blonde?

The cylinder would remain with her until its secrets were unlocked. She tucked it into the side of her suitcase where her gun had once been and added plyers to her mental list of things she needed for Warsaw.

***

At seven-twenty the next morning, Rosalind startled awake to a loud banging on the door and the voice of David Novy calling, "Are you alright, Miss Fisher? We're worried about you."

"I'm fine. Just resting."

"My father thinks he should send you back to the States immediately when we dock. He worries that you're ill."

"Stop shouting, David," Rosalind said, unable to hide the annoyance in her voice. Had she not settled this very issue with Novy just yesterday? "If he is so concerned, why did he send you?"

"It would not be correct for my father to come to your cabin, Miss Fisher. But as a young man who is curious about this fine ship and on his first trip to Europe, well…"

Of course. Smart thinking. "I'm not letting you in here."

"Appearances."

"Exactly. Let us talk through the door in the quietest way possible while you keep a look out for anyone suspicious."

"Suspicious how?" His voice was lowered, as she had asked.

"A person as out of place as you are. Someone who doesn't belong on this deck. Someone who isn't busy doing ship stuff. Who is hanging around while we talk. Who—"

"I understand," David cut her off.

"Have you seen the steward, Sidney Hill, around?"

"Not since the unfortunate episode."

"Please ask the steward assigned to your suite where Sidney is."

"Just ask him?" The tone, even through the door, was disappointed.

Just asking would bring attention to David. He needed a cover story that would not make him a target. She wanted to give him one but was coming up blank.

"No. That won't work. What's your suggestion?"

"My father sees himself as your protector, Miss Fisher. He requires a review of the episode in which an innocent young woman was…let's say attacked…and had to defend herself on this ship. I'll suggest he demand an interview with the steward. He'll get it."

"I need Sidney to find a way to put a small piece of paper back in a trunk exactly to my specifications."

"Miss Fisher, let me in so we can work this out, please. I feel like a dip whispering into your door."

With that, she unlocked the door and let him in.

David brushed the hair back from his forehead with his hand as he sat down as far away from Rosalind as he could and not fall off the bed.

Rosalind made sure the cabin door was locked from the inside, then she pulled the curtain across the porthole even though she knew no one could crawl down the side of the ship to look in.

"My father was my age when he left Poland on his own, came to the United States and made his way to Texas. I love him. But he seems to think I can't get out of bed in the morning without his guidance."

Rosalind felt the story in her marrow—immigrants not even eighteen-years-old who made their own way and then forever tried to protect their young from similar hardships. Her parents had tried to protect her. Rosalind knew she had the same grit as her parents and knew that David wanted to prove he did, too.

"I said you could help, David. I meant it. Please tell your father that Heinrich and Hedda Becker are spies. And they aren't married, so those aren't real names. One of them, probably Heinrich, is responsible for the note your father got. That means that Nazi sympathizers will be watching us in Poland. More urgently, your father needs to get Sidney to put this piece of paper back in their trunk." She took the original paper with names off the small bureau top.

David started to put it in his pants pocket.

"No. It has to look exactly the way it looked when I took it out. They aren't fools."

"Of course." David held it between his thumb and pincher finger. "What else does Sidney need to know?"

She stopped, feeling her hands grow cold. Which trunk? She knew it was closest to the door, but that wouldn't help if the trunks were being moved before everyone disembarked. Still, that would be Sidney's best chance, finding the trunk after it was out of the suite. But the trunk looked like the other two trunks, and it would be locked again.

"Miss Fisher?"

She shook her head. "He'll have a problem with which trunk. I'm sure he can handle the locks. He needs to find the one that has a tray on the top which, when lifted up, has a small compartment underneath. Maybe they all have that tray. But…but there will be a slip of folded paper in there like this one but without any writing. Just a line of blue ink. So that's the one he wants."

Rosalind sighed and rubbed her eyes before continuing. "David, I also want you to let Sidney know I have another item that can't be replaced yet. I'll get it to him somehow. Do that out of your father's watchful eye and be careful. This is not a *Hardy Boys* mystery." The little metal cylinder felt like her prize to hold onto as the reward for her first successful venture at spying. She'd get it open.

"Why not just give it to me and I'll get it to him?"

"I have my reasons."

"I'll do what you've asked," David said. "Look, I read the papers, Miss Fisher. I overhear my father's calls to our fellow Jews with family in Europe. I know the difference between real life and a story, even if my father doesn't think I do."

With that, David got up and left the cabin.

CHAPTER 8

David found Rosalind minutes before disembarkation began and muttered in a low voice, "Done." But she decided to check herself as best she could.

She sighted Sidney moving around the stacked first-class luggage like a cougar moving around boulders towards its prey. Then she retreated up the steps to the passenger area to wait for the second-class passengers' turn to leave.

Once down the gangway, Rosalind staggered slightly to keep her balance on the solid ground beneath her.

"Over here, Miss Fisher." A porter held her suitcase by the handle and waved. Behind him, Jim and David Novy stood next to a cart that held their six pieces of matching leather luggage. She walked over.

"Now our real journey begins, Miss Fisher. David and I will be in one first class compartment on the train and you will be in another compartment in the same car. That way, should any of us…"—Jim Novy paused as if shifting through a card catalog of possible sentence endings— "should any of us be in need of assistance, we are together. And we will know quickly if one of us is somehow separated."

Rosalind nodded. With that, Novy had revealed his personal Grand Canyon of worries about traversing Nazi Germany. The three of them followed the porter in silence.

***

Rosalind had the first-class compartment all to herself, with a plush purple sofa that converted to a bed, windows draped with white lacey fabric and a room darkening shade, a table that slid out of the way, and a small commode so she didn't have to suffer the indignity of exiting at midnight for a shared toilet.

For over an hour, Rosalind looked out the train window at the landscape of green passing by, so verdant and multi-hued that she had no names for the colors. Her eyes felt stunned. The scenery slightly eased her disappointment over Sidney, who had failed her spectacularly, with not even a word about the gun, let alone a farewell. That thought eased her feeling of deception at keeping the cylinder.

Fork tines had proved useless in prying off the top of the metal cylinder. Maybe she could find snips in Warsaw, with those sharp, sturdy scissor blades designed to cut through metal.

A sharp rapping on her door startled her. "Yes," she called out.

"Your ticket, Madame. And a word of advice." The voice was male, firm, accustomed to giving orders in English as well as another language whose accent she couldn't quite identify. "Please open the door."

"Of course." She fumbled with the lock, failing her intention to act with the calm directness she thought a woman working for a member of the United States Congress should have.

"Turn it the other way."

With a click, the handle loosened and, red-cheeked, Rosalind pulled the door towards her. A tall, blonde man in a train uniform stood in the corridor, holding a ticket punch. His nametag said Luc.

"The ticket?"

Rosalind dug into her purse to locate her ticket, which she handed over. He punched it and handed it back.

"What language do you usually speak, Luc?" she asked.

"We Belgians have three national languages, Madame. We speak Flemish, the sister of Dutch but with a strong French influence. We also speak German, and some, Luxembourgish. I was raised in the Luxembourgish language until I began school. Now I speak all the Belgian languages, of course. And English, French, and a little Russian."

"Thank you." She paused to consider how many other languages in the world she could have spoken had she not been born in Texas. "Is there a newspaper on the train in Dutch or Flemish or Luxembourgish?"

New languages to learn. That would possibly take her mind off Germany in a way that the small twist-resistant cylinder had not.

"I'm afraid not. Would you like a copy of the *International Herald-Tribune?* I will bring it after we come to an agreement about your passage through Germany." He stared down at her.

"You require my agreement?"

"It would be preferable."

Rosalind detected a hint of a sigh. Best not to push a ticket collector only doing his job. What choices did he have, after all?

"Please tell me what you came to share," she said.

"It is best that Mister James Novy, Master David Novy, and you, Miss Fisher, all remain in your compartments, doors locked from the inside, throughout the time the train traverses German soil. Do not open your door to any person who knocks. I will bring food to you and announce myself. You now recognize my voice. Please use the private commode. Keep your window shades down."

"Has Mister Novy agreed?"

"I have not yet spoken to him. You, as staff of your government, may need to insist. It is…" He lowered his voice to a whisper. "He is a Jew. That is not, of course, on his United States passport, but it is known. We do not believe the German government would do something to him of a direct nature, unless they have an excuse to search luggage and find something they label contraband. We do not know about the thugs with their armbands. They have been known to be on platforms, sometimes to enter the train itself, and…what is the word…"

"Harass."

"Thank you. Yes. Harass. My company does not want that. Nor do we want you, a woman and a representative of the government of the United States, compromised in any way if there is an action within Germany against Mister Novy or Master Novy."

"I see." Rosalind had studied the train schedule. From where they were now, she calculated it was another five hours to Berlin. There was an hour stop there. Then another four-and-a-half hours to Warsaw. All of it inside a small compartment with the shades drawn, quiet and hiding. Would she be a caged animal to be tormented, batons rattling against the side of the car, whispered threats through her keyhole?

We know you are a Jew and vulnerable and we can get you even if you are an American. So be afraid every moment you are here. That was the subtext of the note to Novy, the fear Helga and Heinrich wanted him to feel every moment he was on the continent.

"Yes, I think I should talk to them and explain," Rosalind said, feeling her stomach cramp in an unpleasant knot. "This is a big request you make. Even if it is for our well-being." In her head, Rosalind was hearing her mother scream, as she had anytime Rosalind mentioned wanting to travel to Europe. *Never! Never go there!* She placed her hand against her forehead to make her stop.

Luc nodded.

***

With Luc standing beside her, Rosalind explained what needed to be done. Jim Novy listened, grim-faced, but when David began to protest, he placed his hand on David's knee with decisiveness that offered no room for disagreement. From David's slumped shoulders, Rosalind could tell he was no stranger to his father's force of will. She felt a whiff of longing for the security David had with his father and mother.

"Yes, of course. Whatever is necessary," he said.

"Thank you, Mister Novy and Master Novy," Luc said. "I'll bring food for you now. Then in an hour, we will lock the car at both ends. Miss Fisher will see that this has been done, as a member of your government. Then, you will lock yourself in."

"I will need a key to unlock the car, then," Rosalind said. "For safety, in case of an emergency."

"Yes. I will get that."

***

Two trays of food balanced on the small table in her compartment, along with the current and day-old copies of the *International Herald Tribune*. Rosalind sat looking out the window. Four black and white spotted cows munched on the fresh grass near the tracks while two calves nursed, and as she watched, a swoop of swallows took flight towards a row of trees in the distance, where she could just see the red roof of a barn.

"It is time, Madam," Luc said, stepping into her cabin. He handed her a key.

Rosalind nodded and pulled down the window shade. A thin stream of sunshine snuck out of the edges on both sides. Luc flipped the electric light on, then stepped outside the cabin and closed the door. Less than three minutes later, she heard Jim Novy's door shut, followed by the thud of the door closing at one end of the train car, then the other. She opened her door and moved to the front of the car and locked it from the inside. She then checked that the door to Jim's compartment was locked before moving to the door at the rear of the car. After that, she returned, and with a mounting sense of dread, locked herself in her compartment.

***

The train slowed to a gentle halt. Rosalind peered through the sliver of space between the shade and the window. Passengers were disembarking onto a swept and painted platform. Posters of Adolf Hitler's face and the swastika loomed over each ticket window and the arches that led into the Berlin *Bahnhof*. Three Nazi soldiers in full regalia stood with rifles, watching the passengers.

Rosalind could hear the murmurs of "*Heil Hitler*" used as greetings among the passengers. She sat back against her seat, hoping to remain invisible behind the drawn window shade.

There was a sharp tap at her window, followed by another.

"*Bitte, nein. Amerikaner.*" She recognized Luc, the ticket taker's, voice. "*Reisepass.*"

"*Sie fahren nach Polen,*" Luc said, insisting that the passengers in their compartment were simply transiting through to Poland.

"*Reisepass,*" the German voice responded, demanding their passports again.

"*Ja. Ich verde sie bekommen.*" There was only so much Luc was willing to do, and now he would request their passports. Rosalind's mind spun. She would have to comply, but she also did not want to let their passports leave her sight. Who knew if they'd be returned—or if she and the Novys would be allowed to stay on the train?

She opened her door and banged on the Novy's.

"What?" Jim Novy called out.

"Do not come out. Do not hand over your passports unless I am there and I say it is alright." Rosalind's voice sounded firmer than she felt inside. She swallowed hard and took a deep breath.

"Poppa?" That was David, his voice quivering, once again a child.

"Davidle, it will be alright."

Rosalind walked down the corridor and stood on the lowest step of the train car, gripping the rail with her left hand, knuckles whitening with the effort. The Nazis would have to drag her off the Belgian-owned train if they wanted her badly enough. She only hoped they wouldn't.

In flawless High German, the accent of her once-posh, Berlin-raised mother, she said, "Officer, I am traveling through Germany, with no plan to stop except for this brief interlude. I am a member of the staff of the United States Congress on official business with the United States Embassy in Poland. What is this commotion about?"

The ticket taker, Luc, and the Nazi officer stared at her. She returned the stare, impassive as she imagined a person in authority would be, despite the blood pounding in her ears.

"A moment, Madame," the Nazi said. "I must check your travel documents and those of anyone traveling with you."

"The documents will not leave my possession. I am not on German property. The documents will not leave the possession of those I am accompanying for the same reason. We are traveling through, not stopping in Germany."

"Madame, you are stopped in Germany." The Nazi officer had a slight smirk on his face.

She smiled back, teeth bared.

"You may inspect the passports while I hold them. If this is not acceptable, you will get your commander here, as well as the United States Ambassador's representative. 'Staff member to United States Congressman and American citizens dragged off train in Berlin' may not be the headline the Führer wants."

"We will delay the train, Madame, while I discuss this with my commander." With that, the Nazi turned and marched away.

Rosalind turned and walked back to her compartment. She opened her unlocked door and almost bumped into David, who was peeking out the side of her window curtain onto the platform. As he turned towards her, Rosalind saw his eyes were red.

"My father now wishes he hadn't brought me. Our lives are in danger."

"I wish he hadn't brought you, too." As soon as the words came out, Rosalind saw David wince and wished she could take them back.

"David, I'm sorry. This situation is, I think, a piece of theater designed to frighten us all. The Nazis don't want an incident with our government over us. We are not in a state of war with Germany and we have passports that require our safe passage." She paused. "What I am trying to avoid is the Nazis somehow using your Jewishness and not your American citizenship as some kind of…"

"Pretext," David said, nodding. "To set us up in a scene that makes us look bad or hold us for ransom, right?"

"Exactly."

David nodded, but his expression quickly turned to fear when there was a rap on the door.

"Please, Miss Fisher, you'll need to bring the passports for all three of you to the steps." The accent was New York and the voice was male.

Rosalind opened her door to Luc and a white-haired man in a suit.

"Who are you?" she asked.

"Here." The stranger reached into his suit jacket and pulled out documents which he handed her. "I'm an attaché in the United States Embassy, Miss Fisher. Name is Robert Miller. We'll just flap these at the fellow outside and you'll be on your way. After…"

"After what?"

"They have exerted their right to inspect the luggage. It's now out on the platform. Mister Novy will have to hand over the keys for his. And you'll need to give me your small bag there, and your purse and your coat."

"Sure. What are they looking for?"

"I couldn't say. Some high-placed German woman on the train raised a fuss over something disappearing. Although she didn't specify where or when the item went missing, she seems convinced the thieves were American."

Rosalind pasted a smile on her face. "Of course. I just…" She looked down and sighed.

"Miss Fisher?"

"I have my monthly. May I please just get a change of sanitary…"

Miller could not get the words, "Of course" out fast enough. He stepped into the aisle and shut the door. Nothing like women's blood to scare men away.

She plucked the strange, impenetrable cylinder from its nest in her purse and slid it into a small slit she made with her nails in the side of a Kotex pad, then put the pad into her panties.

"I'm ready," she said, opening the door and handing her suitcase, purse and coat over.

CHAPTER 9

At the *Warszawa Glowna,* the train rolled to a gentle stop. David stepped off first and offered his hand to Rosalind and then to his father. A Polish-speaking deputy from the United States Embassy led them into a section of the new train station in the heart of Warsaw, with the ubiquitous Art Deco ambiance that now signaled modern life. Rosalind looked around and saw construction scaffolding and several hallways blocked off.

"It's not finished. But when it is, it will be the envy of Europe for its design," the deputy said. "I've arranged for a taxi to your hotel. Your bags are just there." He pointed to a luggage cart. "The three of you and two other people were the only ones to get off here. Sad."

"When will I be able to begin my review at the embassy?" Rosalind asked.

"We're expecting you in a few days, after Mister Novy completes his tour with you. I must say it's unusual for a congressman to require that a member of his staff visit and observe operations at an embassy."

"These are unusual times," Rosalind said. The sanitary pad, which she'd dabbed with blood from a paper-cut finger, chaffed her upper thigh. She was short on sleep and so on edge that even David coughing made her jump.

The man nodded. "Let's get you to your hotel rooms for a decent night's sleep. All the Americans stay there. Safe and comfortable."

***

The woman at the hotel desk handed Jim Novy a key. Rosalind watched the bellman whisk their luggage away on a cart while they walked towards the imposing elevators.

"My key?"

The woman busied herself with sorting papers.

"Is there a problem, Miss?"

The woman shook her head. "Madam will please wait. Someone will come."

"Who—" Rosalind felt the weight of a hand on her shoulder.

"Thank you, Matilde." Something about the woman's voice sounded familiar but the Polish the woman was speaking threw her off. "Miss Fisher, I do believe you have something of interest to me. And I have something you want in return. We'll just go up to your room now. Matilde, the key."

Matilde handed it over with a weak smile.

"*Heil Hitler*, Matilde. Come, Rosalind. This will be entirely painless. A reasonable transaction. I know you understand me quite well."

"Missus Becker?" Rosalind thickened her Texas accent. "Ma'am, I don't understand what you are saying in that German of yours."

"It is Polish." Hedda switched to German.

"I'm still not understanding you. And here I am just off the train and dyin' to go to bed—or at least get out of these clothes," Rosalind said in a Texas drawl. "I'd like my key to my room. And I'm certain sure that this young woman does not want to be embarrassed with her boss about this. Do you, Matilde?"

Matilde paled behind the counter. She shook her head.

"I can complain pretty loud when I have the need. And Mister Novy, well…he knows people for sure. Matilde, my key."

Now Matilde was staring out into the lobby, lips pursed, calculating the risk to her job. Hedda nodded and returned the room key to the counter.

"Is there a bar in this here hotel?" Rosalind asked.

Matilde nodded and pointed to a room off the lobby where Rosalind could see shadowed torsos of men and women sitting at a counter.

"Then I suggest we go there. Is your night manager around, Matilde, in case this woman begins to accost an employee of the United States government? A government that recommends this hotel to its citizens, I might add." Rosalind kept her eyes on the vulnerable night clerk.

"Yes, Madame."

"Excellent." Rosalind turned and Hedda followed.

***

"Explain yourself," Rosalind said as soon as they were seated in the bar. "I'm planning to file a complaint with my embassy tomorrow. Against this hotel, that clerk, and you." Rosalind moved the glass of an aperitif she had ordered closer to her mouth and mimicked a sip. The strong licorice aroma reminded her of medicine.

"You entered our suite on the Queen Mary and took papers from us." Hedda took a swallow of lager.

Rosalind smiled. "Ridiculous."

"A woman matching your description tricked the steward into letting her in."

Rosalind shook her head. "A made-up tale."

"She had curly red hair."

"The steward in trouble seeks to blame another person and picks on someone he believes has no supporters and no alibi. Who better than a woman traveling alone and in second-class? Someone easily identifiable. Already known because of her actions defending herself."

Hedda shook her head slowly with a smile. "Clever."

"Hedda—I assume I can call you that, Missus Becker, since you pressed yourself on me in such an intimate fashion at the desk—you might know what that's about. It's rather like what's going on in Germany with certain groups, isn't it? But as I said, I don't know about anything missing from your cabin. The steward has the extra key and he unlocks the door. He still has the key, no? And yet he has put the blame on an employee of the United States government." Rosalind paused and stared at Hedda. "May I remind you my bags were thoroughly searched in Berlin? I suspect you know that already."

"You were not searched."

"Where on my person could I hide... I don't even know what it is you claim to be missing? Papers?" She shook her head, hoping Hedda hadn't noticed the slight pause while she thought of something other than *cylinder* to say.

Hedda drained her beer and set the stein on the table with an audible thump.

"If you don't comply with a body search, I will file a complaint with the United States Embassy and demand they return you to America. A dead body, a witness that you have entered a stateroom not your own from which items of importance disappeared. You won't be untouched and you know it."

"You'll do that, Hedda? Here in Poland? Really? Darlin', what is all this fuss about?" Rosalind took a sip of the absinthe and found it lacking the liquid courage she sought. She sighed. "You can search my bags yourself. Just come to my room now. I am dearly tired."

***

Hedda examined Rosalind's clothes and the interior and exterior of her suitcase, then she held out her hand for Rosalind's purse. She removed each object from it, turned the purse inside out, made a slit in the lining with a small penknife, and shook the purse upside down. Four of the eight US twenty-dollar bills Rosalind had slipped in between the lining and the outer shell floated down.

"You have American dollars and zlotys, my American friend. What is the use?"

"Dinner, a movie, taxi fare, money when I get back to the states. What does it matter to you?"

"Are you planning to stay a long time in Poland? This is a month's pay here just in Polish money. Or are you planning to bribe someone?"

"If the zlotys or the twenties are what you are looking for, Hedda, take them."

"Americans." Shaking her head, Hedda returned the bills to the purse as if dropping a dead rat outside her door.

Rosalind sat on the bed, yearning to lie back on its downy quilt, put her head on the clean, white pillow, and sleep. She felt low cramps and a twisty ache in her stomach.

"You need to take all your clothes off now." Hedda stared at her.

"Now Hedda, I must object. I'll report you to my embassy and to yours. This has gone on too—"

"Get up." Hedda held the penknife, blade out. "I'm not afraid to cut you badly. I'm not afraid to claim you made a forbidden advance to me when I was just being a friend."

So far, Hedda kept talking in English, so she believed Rosalind enough to think she didn't speak or understand German or Polish. But Rosalind had run out of delaying tactics. Hedda would know the difference, maybe, between cut-finger-blood and the menstrual kind. She'd look hard at the Kotex pad.

"Nothin' to see that you don't see in your own mirror, Hedda." Rosalind had lots of practice being naked in front of women—one cast iron claw-footed bathtub and one flush toilet for eight women in a boarding house didn't permit any modesty.

Rosalind stood up and began to strip. She dropped her blouse on the bed, then her brassiere. She undid the waist band of her skirt and slid out of it.

"Your panties." Hedda waved the knife.

"Sure thing." Rosalind stopped and slid them to her knees. There was the Kotex pad, now dotted with clots of menstrual blood. Rosalind hadn't been that happy to see her cycle start since her last, unfortunate, boyfriend walked out. "Want me to hand these over? Want to check my insides too?"

Hedda's nose wrinkled. "Fine. I am satisfied that you do not now have what we seek. I will consider what you may have done with it."

"May I get dressed?" Rosalind knew frustrated determination when she heard it. Hedda wasn't done, just not certain what to do next.

Hedda nodded.

Rosalind pulled up her panties and reached into her suitcase for her nightgown.

"Anything else, Hedda, or are we good?"

"For now, my little *mädchen.*" Hedda walked out slamming the door behind her.

***

Rosalind pried the tube out of the Kotex pad, wiped it dry, and set it back in her purse while she put on a new pad and her work clothes. Sleep was not on the menu. No way to get snips to open the cylinder at almost midnight in Warsaw, but maybe there was another way.

She picked up the heavy receiver on the phone and dialed the front desk. "Matilde, the lining of my purse has been torn. I require a needle, thread, and scissors. A small scissors, please, for the threads. Where could I find that tomorrow before I leave?"

"I will have housekeeping bring up a sewing kit, Madame. It is too late to call a seamstress here. Would Madame like a member of housekeeping to repair it?"

"No, I am able to do this." Rosalind would have to remember for the future that a hotel dealing with wealthy foreign travelers and ocean liners had much in common—well equipped to meet every reasonable need.

***

When the kit arrived, arranged artfully in a basket as if for Easter, Rosalind spied two scissors– one a pair of shears, the other the size of embroidery scissors, with thin, tough blades. A memory of her father hunched over a woman's dress, snipping away threads from the emerald-green and blue embroidery her mother had contributed, rose in her mind. Rosalind took the embroidery scissors and began to force the blade precisely, firmly, and gently between the cap and the body of the capsule. When the cap yielded its grip and popped off, she sighed and shook the cramp out of her hand.

Cursing LBJ, Eleanor, and everyone else she could think of for sending her into this mess, she tapped the capsule onto the table to loosen the paper she saw inside. With her pinkie, she pulled upwards. The paper unwound into the air like the Chinese finger puzzle she'd once seen in Austin's miniscule Chinatown.

Fifteen tedious, breath-holding minutes later, the narrow strip of paper, which was almost a yard long, lay open to the world on the bed. Rosalind placed pillows at each end to hold it down. She'd been unable to keep the paper from staining a light pink in five different places but the letters and symbols on it remained readable, thankfully. Except that she had no idea what they meant.

It was long past midnight, and she and Jim and David Novy were scheduled to leave early the next morning by private car to Knyszyn, where most of Jim Novy's cousins—the lucky recipients of the visas— lived. Mister Novy's uncle, Rabbi Shmuel, had written to him in Yiddish that a great celebration would be held in honor of this visit.

Rosalind began to reroll the paper as slowly and gently as she could. She put it into the topless capsule and forced that between the lining of her purse and its exterior. Then she sewed the lining with stitches that were a distant cousin of her father's elegant handwork. Tomorrow she would think about this cryptic hieroglyphic that she had no idea what to do with…and that Hedda wanted so badly.

CHAPTER 10

Rosalind placed a bright smile on her face and hoped Mister Novy wouldn't comment on her reddened eyes as she stood in the lobby with her suitcase and her purse.

The hotel clerk behind the front desk nodded to her. He was a boy, really, with downy cheeks, probably not older than David. She walked over.

"Do you understand English?"

The clerk nodded. "Yes, of course. May I help you?"

"While I'm waiting, can you tell me where this address is located in Warsaw?" Rosalind wrote her cousin's address on the pad of paper on the counter.

"That is the largest Jewish section in the city. Four tram stops north, then ask for directions. I think it should be near their big synagogue. Is there an interest by your government in this one person, Ma'am?"

Rosalind could sense the cold drift in his voice. She refolded the sheet and stuck it in her pocket. "No. Not at all. He is a doctor, a friend of a friend."

"I hear many Jewish citizens are leaving. If this person is one, I know a man who is buying apartments and other non-portable items in that area for cash."

Thirty percent of Warsaw's population—more than thirty percent of their doctors, musicians, authors, lawyers, professors, librarians, businesspeople, teachers—all selling their homes, breakfronts, and pianos. That's what the *Tribune* on the train had said.

"This has nothing to do with leaving. I've only been asked to say hello. Thank you for the information. Your English is excellent."

"Ma'am, you do have a message in your box. A cable from the Queen Mary. Also a packet of papers from the United States Embassy." He turned and plucked a cellophane envelope from a mailbox cubby and handed it to her.

"Thank you." Turning so he could not see what the message said—unless he'd already opened and resealed the envelope—she read, "*Will be coming to Warsaw quickest. Sid.*"

She turned to the clerk. "My boyfriend. Should he arrive before I am back from…" —she hesitated as if she could not pronounce the word— "well, whatever this town is that I'm going to, please tell him to let me know where he is."

"Of course, Ma'am."

"And the packet of papers, please." She tapped on the counter, trying to temper her concern over what might be in the packet and who might have sent it.

He put a large, sealed envelope with the logo of the embassy on the counter.

"How did this get here?" Rosalind asked with all the authority she could muster while she stared at it.

"Delivered this morning around 7:30 by a courier from your embassy."

"Male, female, young, old?"

"A woman, madame, middle aged, but she left no name." The clerk's voice began to sound tense. The buzzer at the desk sounded and he picked up the phone. In Polish he said, "Yes, Manager. I have the woman here now. She has vacated the room and has her baggage with her. I had no time without being noticed." He stopped and replaced the receiver.

Rosalind did not react. "I do wish I understood this language. It's going to be hard for me at the embassy without it," she said. "Oh, and what's this new greeting that people are using sometimes. *Heil?*"

"*Heil Hitler*, Ma'am," the young man said, straightening his back and throwing his shoulders back.

"*Heil Hitler.*" She made certain her face reflected only a serious consideration of the statement. "So powerful."

"Your driver is waiting outside, Madam."

"Thank you." Rosalind took the package, nodded at the bellman to bring her luggage, and stepped out into the warming Warsaw day.

A Renault Primaquatre, a saddle-brown, four-door family touring sedan, sat at the curb outside the hotel. The driver introduced himself in heavily accented English as Michal Maltin. The exchange was too brief for Rosalind to judge how well he understood English or any other language she might care to use.

He opened the car's back door and waved her in.

"Wait, let me check something," she said in English and held up her hand if he didn't understand her. He nodded. She slid her hand around the interior border of her purse until she found her little secret, still where she'd tucked it into the lining. "I thought I'd forgotten my lipstick, but it's fine."

"Yes, good."

When the Novys came out, David claimed the seat next to Michal, so Rosalind sat next to Jim Novy.

"How do you know your driver, Mister Novy?" She could speak above a whisper thanks to the street noise and the car's vibrations.

"He's the eldest son of a friend of mine, now dead, may he rest in peace. Michal was a concert pianist until these troubles began. You should ask him about his career."

"Is this his automobile?"

"It's been borrowed for a small price." Novy looked out the side window, his tone signaling the end of the conversation.

Rosalind sat back. A career as a pianist told her nothing about Michal's trustworthiness.

***

Once outside of Warsaw, the road narrowed and the pavement gave way to rutted gravel more suitable for farm carts than automobiles. A bus lumbered by as Michal steered the car to one side as far as he could.

"What is that?" David asked.

"An Ursus bus. Very…" Michal paused. "Built for our tough Polish roads."

David and Michal continued a halting conversation in the front. Mister Novy stared out the window on his side.

Rosalind took advantage of the time to unseal the envelope from the embassy. She counted forty-four applications for visas to the United States, with directions in English and Polish. The applications required proof of Polish citizenship, birth certificate, medical clearance, tax documents, police certificate guaranteeing no criminal record, military discharge records, and an inventory of goods and wealth.

Each person had to have one sponsor in the United States who would guarantee that the person and their family would not become a burden on the government. The sponsor had to provide a recommendation letter for the immigrant, a bank letter certifying funds in an account, a tax return, and a signed and notarized affidavit of identity and worth.

Exhaustion seeped into her bones as she considered the paperwork—ephemera, documents hidden or lost in a house, or waiting to be dragged out of drawers or begged from reluctant bureaucrats—that was required.

She pointed out the list of what Jim Novy had to provide. "We won't talk of this now. Later in private," Jim Novy said quietly. "Excellent driving, Michal," he said loudly and in Polish.

"*Dziekuje,*" Michal replied.

"What did he say?" Rosalind asked.

***

"We are arriving," Michal said. The car slowed and a few houses appeared on either side, sitting back from a cobblestone sidewalk. A small truck pulled out of a driveway and headed past them. The driver waved. At the head of the driveway, a three-story brick building bore the name *D. Spiwak and Sons Textiles.*

"Dovid Spiwak. He was, when I left here, a proud father of two young boys and just starting out in his father's business," Jim Novy said.

Rosalind looked out across a hay field towards another factory belching smoke. "There's industry here?"

"Twenty-three textile factories," Michal said in English. "When the Poles kicked us out a hundred years ago, they quickly called us back.

Without us, the factories went into decline and with us, well, they flourished until the Great War ended. The question now is are we Jewish Poles, Polish Jews, or Jews living in Poland waiting for the next exile?"

"What do you think, Poppa?" David turned around to ask his father.

"Our Jewish brethren must leave as soon as they can. Like the song at Pesach says, 'The cat eats the goat, and the dog bites the cat, and so it goes until the Butcher comes.'"

***

The car inched its way behind a horse-pulled cart into the town square, which consisted of five buildings on each side. At a distance, the buildings seemed fresh and open in the August sun, but as they came closer, they were rubbed, worn and closed, except for the Catholic church, where the door was wide open.

"Most of these buildings in the square belong to members of the Jewish community. The two synagogues are up that street. So is my uncle's house," Jim Novy said, pointing to the lane opposite.

Michal drove towards where Novy had pointed, the car moving no faster than a stroll. With the window down, Rosalind heard a child announce their arrival. "*Di Amerikaner zennen do!*"

The street was full of small houses with high-pitched thatched roofs. Jim Novy tapped Michal on the shoulder and pointed to one of the largest homes. "There is my uncle's house. I did not expect such poverty. When I left this was a prosperous community. Still, I am prepared." He patted his jacket.

"Sir?" Rosalind was not sure what he meant.

"Oh, very open and above board, I assure you, my dear Miss Fisher. I brought United States money here and exchanged it this morning at the bank for zlotys."

"Before nine?"

"For a price, almost anything can be done." He patted David's arm. "*Nu*, Davidle, what do you think?"

"Let's meet your family, Poppa. It's what you came for."

Rosalind caught the edge of disappointment in David's voice as he looked at the home in front of them in this almost forgotten town.

A slim figure stepped out of the house. In Yiddish, the man called, "My dear nephew, to see you at last! I am happy."

Jim Novy responded in Yiddish. "My dear uncle. My esteemed Reb Shmuel Shnigewitz! You look the same. I would know you anywhere."

Rosalind saw the creases around the rabbi's eyes and felt sure his slimness was from a lack of food rather than choice.

"You are a flatterer, my boy. And who is this striking young man? Is this your David? He looks like you did at that age."

"*Rebbe*, I am honored." David, speaking halting Yiddish, reached out his hand to shake Reb Shmuel's and was pulled into a tight embrace.

"The generations continue, thanks to America and to God." Jim Novy stepped closer to the rabbi and spoke in a lowered voice. "This woman, Rosalind Fisher, has been assigned by the United States government, no less, to accompany me and make a report. She will be with me at all times."

The rabbi nodded. "Hello, Miss Fisher. Do you understand what I am saying in Yiddish?"

She shook her head.

"Possibly Polish?"

She shook her head again.

"Well, my boy, you will translate for us if Miss Fisher and I need to speak. Not much of a help, is she? Let us first relax and enjoy this moment. We have planned for this day ever since I got your letter. Come in, say hello to your aunt."

Michal slid out of the driver's seat and stood by the car's open door. "Hello, Rabbi. Do you remember me? Michal Maltin?"

"Of course! I did your bar mitzvah. I have your records. When is your next concert?"

"No next concert."

"New records coming out?"

Michal shook his head. "Now I am Mister Novy's chauffeur."

"Ah, yes. I see. Go inside, my boy, and see the *Rebbetzin*."

"My job is to guard this car, which is borrowed, and the luggage and personal items."

"I'll ask her to bring you lunch, then, when we are ready." Reb Shmuel smiled as if Michal was still a traveling concert pianist about to perform. "And we will listen to your records later."

"Good." Michal leaned back against the car.

"Can we first walk by to see my family house, Uncle? I'd like to stretch my legs after the ride here."

Reb Shmuel nodded. "The house is still there. And the stroll in the warm summer air will be welcome."

Rosalind felt more than heard a hesitancy, but Jim Novy smiled. "Great," he said. "I have told David so much about my life here, how I would see you and all my family. How every day of my childhood you would ask me how I did in *cheder*. Always you would give me a little treat."

The sides of Reb Shmuel's mouth tweaked up as if to smile and failed. "Happy memories of the past. Let us walk, then."

The four of them walked up a side lane from the square. Half the houses looked abandoned, and the other half seemed inhabited by ghosts who could not sweep the dust away, clean the windows, or paint the shutters.

"There it is!" Jim Novy pointed at the house at the end of the lane. "But has no one moved into it? No young couple? I gave it to the community for that use."

Reb Shmuel shook his head. "No one. My dear boy, let us talk over lunch. Your family and friends want to see you."

***

Rosalind stood at the doorway between the small kitchen and the parlor where the dining table had been set up. Even keeping up the pretense of not understanding Yiddish or Polish, she'd made herself helpful to Esther, whose hair, under her kerchief, was the color of the fresh sour cream she plated and whose hands shook from the effort to carry a platter of local fruit into the parlor. The rabbi and his wife were not healthy, nor was anyone else who dropped in to greet the great American visitor.

All of Novy's relatives had come, some with fruit, some with a platter of cheese or hardboiled eggs. One by one they'd embraced him and David, the littlest ones wrapping their arms around Jim's legs, the young girls curtseying and blushing and looking sideways at David. They wore their best *Shabbat* clothes, fresh from the clothesline and ironed to unwrinkled perfection.

One of the girls walked over to Rosalind. She had chestnut brown eyes and hair, and matchsticks for arms and legs. Her cheekbones stood out in her face. She said, in English, "Hello. My name is Clara. What is your name?"

"My name is Rosalind Fisher. Do you study English in school?"

"No. My father has bought the Linguaphone English course. When he plays the records, I am there because I am to learn. I go to see the American films in Bialystok. I want to go to your country to study."

Rosalind took Clara's hand, which had the callouses of an older woman. "You work?"

"I milk the cows, sweep the barn, and carry the pails." Clara stared into Rosalind's eyes as if she knew what secret was there. "Help me go to America."

"How old are you?"

"Thirteen."

All Rosalind wanted to do was grab Clara, put her in her suitcase, and carry her back to Texas. The feeling was so strong that she gripped her hands together until the knuckles were white.

***

When the house emptied of guests, Reb Shmuel ate a last spoonful of cottage cheese from the bowl in front of him and held it up for Esther to take away. "I am afraid they are all living shadows, walking in the valley of death," he said. "I'm not worried for myself. But our community is suffering because of the Polish government. They want to ruin us. Our charitable institutions are almost bankrupt. We're destitute. And yet, we are blamed for the bad economy."

Novy took the rabbi's hand. "I'm giving you the equivalent of $1,500 in US currency in zlotys for the school and the nurse and medicines. And for the free loan society, I'm giving another $2,000."

Rosalind considered the amount—easily a year's salary of a well-paid professional in Austin—but not enough to buttress even this small and deteriorated community against the world's flailing economy, the Polish government's growing hostility towards its Jewish population, and whatever else might come. Why didn't Novy tell his dear uncle, the rabbi of the town, that he had visas for the United States right now?

"I'm truly grateful, dear boy. We can do much with that money. Now though, I must take a little rest. This is a lot of excitement for me." The rabbi stood. "Esther, my love, I am going to lie down. Please escort our family from the United States to see the synagogues. I'm sure they'd love to look around."

"No need to trouble yourself," Novy said. "Rosalind and David and I will be fine on our own. Please, Aunt Esther, rest."

"Let me see to Michal first. I can ask someone else to watch the car so he can rest."

"He can nap in the car. Rosalind will bring in his empty plate of food now."

"Sir?" She tried to react as if she knew her name was being used and that was all.

"My dad said to please help by bringing Michal's plate back in," David said.

Rosalind nodded although she wanted as little unsupervised contact with Michal as possible. Despite his piano skills and smooth ways, he was a beaten man, with a hungry mouth and sharp eyes.

✳✳✳

After she retrieved the plate, the three of them walked slowly down the street. While David looked around with the vague disappointment of a youth promised a horse and given a donkey, Jim Novy kept scanning and occasionally nodding.

"You've decided to act as if you don't have visas and the possibility of escape to America, Mister Novy," Rosalind said quietly as they walked. "Why?"

David shot her a look. "Don't talk like that to my father."

Novy raised his hand. "No, David. She's right. Rosalind is keeping her ability to understand everything that is being said a secret for good reason, and I am keeping the secret of the visas for a similar reason." He rubbed his eyes. It was the only time Rosalind had ever seen him look uncertain.

"If people know you have visas, it'll be a problem for you. I see that. You have fifty-nine relatives just here, from what I counted." She'd scrutinized each family member who'd visited, feeling a lurch in her stomach each time someone looked too old or too frail for such a precious gift.

"There are over two-thousand Jews in this place alone. Some I knew as a child, even if they are not my blood. Who am I to decide who should live…"

Who shall live and who shall die. That was the Yom Kippur refrain.

"My secretarial staff prepared everything that is needed for me to be the sponsor for anyone who receives a visa from me," Jim Novy said a half-block later. "The paperwork is signed and in my briefcase."

Rosalind looked at him. "And I have the visa applications from the embassy, delivered just this morning. Are we sure all that paperwork is safe, sir?"

"It's safe. The money also."

"You're sure?"

"I promised Michal one of the visas." Jim Novy rubbed his eyes again. "I promised him so he would guard us with his life."

Ahead of them, on the other side of a small side street, Rosalind saw a newer brick building with a Star of David on its façade.

"Who is Clara?" Rosalind asked as they headed toward it.

"A Spiwak on her mother's side. Her father is widowed now. He owns a dairy farm, I think, just outside the town limits. Why?"

"She's taught herself English. Is she a relative of yours?"

"All Jews are related, Miss Fisher. All cousins. First, second, third, fourth, fifth, who knows."

She should ask if Clara was a cousin close enough to get a visa. The thought brought her cousin Jakub and his three children to mind, and Rosalind sighed.

Novy stopped in front of the synagogue's door and pulled on the handle, dragging it open. "Let's see this. It was rebuilt just a few years ago when times were better, before the depression, before Hitler. My old *shul* stood here."

In the small lobby, a set of winding stairs led to the women's balcony. Rosalind, who'd reluctantly attended services with Hannah in Austin's Reform synagogue where women and men sat together, walked up the steps.

She peered over the balustrade, with its carved pomegranate ornamentation, onto the *Bima* where the rabbi and cantor would stand. Behind her were benches and a set of armchairs where the women and young children sat for services. She picked up a prayerbook then put it down. Prayer meant nothing to her, just a constant petition to *Save us, save us, save us,* when everyone knew you had to save yourself.

When she rejoined Jim Novy in the lobby of the synagogue, he said, "I'll offer two visas to Reb Shmuel and Rebbetzin Esther. Then…" His voice trailed off.

Even with Novy's financial sponsorship, America wanted only fit, young workers. And *wanted* was an exaggeration. America would tolerate and absorb the Brits, the Swedes, the Belgians and the Dutch, but they didn't even like *them* very much.

"My plan is to bring everyone into Texas and have them work for me," Novy continued. "And for others in the Jewish community."

Rosalind wondered how any of the women she'd seen that day would manage as a clerk in a five-and-dime, but quickly stopped herself, realizing that every immigrant in her parents' generation had done just that—managed to fit themselves, somehow and some way, into a new life.

"So, we start with your uncle and aunt. Then first cousins and their children?" Rosalind asked.

"Yes, a total of forty-three because we must bring in not just the cousins and their husbands and wives, but also their children and *their* husbands and wives, plus their children's children. If we don't, no one will leave."

"Poppa, that's thirty-six just with immediate family," David said. "Three adult children, married, each with three adult children with spouses, and a total of ten children from them. And, of course, the rebbe and rebbetzin." He leaned against the wall as if the very thought was exhausting.

"And Michal," Jim Novy added.

"Thirty-seven then. Is Clara among those?" Rosalind asked, thinking there were only seven precious visas left. Her cousin Jakub had three children.

Jim Novy shook his head.

"May I ask, sir, that she be included?"

"If I consider her, this is the calculation. She has a father and a younger brother who is about ten, I believe. If I take the three—father, daughter, son—who would I not take? Now I have forty visas left and thirty-six close relatives just here. I have first and second cousins in other towns, ones I still must visit on this trip. Those cousins are not as close to me as these people who I grew up with, but still…" Jim Novy sighed and stared through the open door into the empty synagogue. "I'll ask Reb Shmuel's guidance in this matter. He knows my whole family."

"Sir, if her father would just let Clara go, I'll guarantee her a place to live until she is eighteen," Rosalind said. A teacher's salary would be enough for the two of them in a quiet section of Austin, Rosalind thought, although she'd never wanted to have a child who might lose her as a parent.

"I will talk to Reb Schmuel."

"So, we have a plan," David said, his tone lighter.

"My dear son, remember what we say: *Mann tracht und Gott lacht.*"

Man plans and God laughs. Rosalind nodded. She did not need to believe in any God to know that was true.

***

When they entered the house again, Reb Shmuel was sitting in his armchair and Esther had put out a pot of tea and small cookies, as if they hadn't recently enjoyed a huge meal. She hovered in the kitchen door until she was satisfied there was enough for everyone and then took a seat next to her husband.

"Well, Rachele, how well do you understand Yiddish? I could see you listening intently when you thought no one was looking," she said in Yiddish. Her voice was warm and she smiled.

"A *bissle.*" Rosalind felt a slight blush on her cheeks as if her mother had caught her fibbing.

Esther nodded. "An important young woman like you would not be sent into Poland without skills. Yiddish, and perhaps Polish, as well? Don't worry. We'll keep your secret, but in the future you must work on looking less…curious and alert. Now, Shimy," she said in a louder voice, using Jim Novy's old name, Shimeon, "what are you doing here besides visiting and bringing us funds?"

"My dear aunt, you always were the brains in the family. I have forty-three visas for the United States to give out. Rosalind's job is to get the visas authorized by the embassy staff. Without the authorization, the applications and all the supporting documents are just paper to burn in the stove."

"Then those people must get to the United States, to Ellis Island, on their own with Mister Novy's funding," Rosalind said.

Esther leaned over towards her and patted her hands. "Relax, dear girl. I see I upset you before. But I thought it better for me to tell you than to allow you to continue as you were. Remember, as an American woman with a job for an important man, you are a bit of a curiosity.

People will watch you with interest, no matter if you are known to be Jewish or not," she said.

Rosalind nodded.

Novy cleared his throat. "Once we have selected the people, Miss Fisher and I will take care of the rest. I have sponsorship papers all prepared. It will happen."

Novy sounded like the confident Texas businessman he was—a man who wouldn't let a stampede stop him.

Esther pulled a white, ironed handkerchief out of her pocket and wiped her brow and Rosalind caught a whiff of rosemary.

"Your dear brothers who are here still, Shimy. What about them?" she asked. "We try to visit them when we can. A short trip, as distances go, but a long one for the heart."

"Are they well, dear aunt? I should have asked before."

"As well as they can be. Their health declines. Some wounds can never be healed."

"I'll visit them after we leave here."

"And what's next for them?" Reb Shmuel leaned forward in his chair and put a hand on Novy's thigh.

"They'll stay where they are. Where they are treated well, as you have assured me, dear uncle, and I will continue to pay for their care. They have no chance of being admitted to America. None. They will die where they were born."

Reb Shmuel sat back. He said nothing, his eyes downcast in silent acceptance. As he picked up his cup, his hand trembled and the tea sloshed out. "Let's begin now to discuss who leaves. Who is best able to gather the necessary documents, who is best to travel so far…so far… and build a life away from this *Gehenna*."

"You and my beloved aunt are first on—"

"No. We won't go. I can't leave anyone behind. Many will remain and I will also."

Esther nodded in agreement. "We are needed here. If we leave, those who cannot go will feel a rising dread, then a panic. They will be like horses who smell smoke and find the barn door shut."

"What if others won't go just because you're staying?" Rosalind asked in Yiddish.

"The younger people will go. Since when do children not climb trees just because their parents wail in alarm? We'll convince the others if we have to." Reb Shmuel smiled. "I'm sure there is a blessing for this occasion. Esther, dear, bring me my books."

***

Almost two hours later, Rosalind left Jim Novy and Reb Shmuel huddled at the table with a list of names, some with a line through them, some circled. The total was forty-nine and included young Clara Spiwak, but not her father or brother.

"We will ask until we have forty-four, then stop. The only thing worse than preparing this list would be to not prepare it," Reb Shmuel said, but the words comforted no one.

The rabbi and Novy had already debated which port to use—Antwerp, Rotterdam or Le Havre. All of these had service to the United States, but they all required travel through Germany and so there was a huge risk—not of papers being pulled, since the Germans did not want Jews in their land, but of brutality. The port of Gdynia remained in Polish hands, but vessels with direct passenger routes to the United States were few and booked full. Rumor was that passengers slept on the open deck or, if lucky, on the floor of the dining room. Novy said he'd take care of all that with "connections." To what or whom, Rosalind didn't ask.

Now the rabbi, his wife, and Novy would meet with the adults, one by one, and inform them of the visas. Esther left the house and began to walk down the street to summon the first family member.

Rosalind also stepped outside. Michal was leaning back against the car, cigarette in hand. He tipped his cap to her.

"No need for that," she said in English.

"I know you are quite fluent in Polish and Yiddish, Miss Fisher," he replied in Polish. "Your job here is not to be a pretty thing I drive about. Not that I mind."

Rosalind considered how she could be better at hiding her language fluency, how to look stupid or bored while conversation flowed around her. She'd failed to trick the rabbi's wife and, apparently also Michal. She'd botched her primary task in Poland—being nondescript.

She walked up to him. He watched her approach, pushing a lock of black hair off his forehead, blinking once with his dark brown eyes.

In a low voice she said, in Polish, "My job requires that I not reveal all I know, Mister Maltin. Tell me more about you and we'll see where this goes."

He remained a few steps away from her, and replied, "There's not much work now for a classically trained Jewish pianist. I played in Germany, Russia, here, of course, and Belgium. Small, but very decent, concert halls. I have three albums with—and here's the irony—Deutsche Grammophon. As you may be aware, Miss Fisher, they have let all their Jewish musicians and composers fall away. I am fluent in Flemish—don't ask me why—it was a whim. There are no notable classical composers from Belgium, despite what they say."

Rosalind laughed. He smiled, revealing a straight, white set of teeth.

"What will you do in America?" she asked. A conversation with a man close to her age, educated, who made her laugh felt like just the antidote for what she'd left in the rabbi's parlor.

He held out his hands and waggled his fingers as if over a keyboard. "I will play in small, but..."

"Very decent concert halls," she said.

"Exactly. And if not that, the parents of Austin most certainly wish their children to learn to play piano. I also am good with cattle. An asset for Texas, I believe."

He looked perfectly serious when he said it, so much so that Rosalind did not know whether to laugh or ask another question. She opted to nod and tilt her head.

"My father, who was a bit older, and Mister Novy were friends, as you know. After Mister Novy departed from this town, my father continued to work with cattle. I worked with him, which is how I became strong. Not by playing piano, I assure you. Then it was clear, Miss Fisher, that hauling hay, driving a tractor, and shoving cattle onto a train car to be carried away to the butcher was not consistent with my ambitions or talents."

"Yes, I see that. How did your father feel about it?"

"He sold his interest in the cattle business and used it to move us to Warsaw so I could study. Now, I will ask you questions, Miss Fisher."

She nodded.

"How many visas has Mister Novy agreed to give out of the forty-four I have counted in his briefcase?"

"I don't know." Rosalind took a small and silent sip of breath and stayed in her same posture, feigning disinterest in Michal having gone through Novy's things.

"You don't wish to tell me the exact number. Fine. I want one more for my brother, who is nineteen."

"I have no say in who Mister Novy and Rabbi Shmuel select. As you can see, I am outside, here, and they are inside."

"Maybe you have no say. But you're the one to bring the people and the applications and the visas together. You'll guide them through. So you have control of the process and therefore the ultimate outcome. Not Mister Novy. And I'll be there as well. As your trusted driver."

Rosalind remained silent. He had not raised his voice or changed its tone, but his grasp of the situation and his threat lay in each word.

"We'll talk more about this, Miss Fisher. I promise. Don't think you can rat me out—the term is correct, yes, from gangster movies? I'll just tell Mister Novy you are a young woman, prone to drama when all I asked was if there was room for my brother. To which you said, you didn't know. For now, I want a bit more to eat. Please watch the car." With that, Michal walked towards the house.

Rosalind took a deep breath and tried not to feel panicky. Had Novy been too trusting with his old friend's son with piano fingers and a gangster's heart or was this the logical reaction of Michal who had a younger brother to protect?

Her job remained to get forty-four people the stamped visas to get to America, and to get that cylinder to Sidney. She reached into her purse and tapped the lining to reassure herself that the cylinder was still there.

CHAPTER 11

About fifteen minutes after Michal had returned with another plate of food, Rosalind saw David leave the house in the company of three fellows, each with a yarmulke on his head, sleeves rolled up to show tanned forearms. One had a rifle over his shoulder. Rosalind decided to trail behind them, hoping to distract herself from the unsolvable problems Novy and the rabbi faced with the list of people.

The boys took the northwest street through the heart of the Jewish district where *mezuzahs* were posted on every doorpost, past a medical clinic, and then they cut towards the north, into a semi-industrial zone. Rosalind saw the boys dart behind a deserted warehouse.

She stopped, reluctant to follow them farther. A few minutes later, she heard the bang of the rifle firing. Heart pounding, she started to run in the direction of the sound.

"Missed that one, my friend. Let's try again," said a voice in Yiddish.

"Here you go. Another beer bottle." That was David, speaking English.

Rosalind stopped running, overcome with relief that David was okay. She turned and began walking back, wandering up and down the lanes. Soon, she was at the tip of Knishin where the main street slid into a farm lane, giving up its urban cobblestones for trampled dirt and golden fields of hay. The sun was low in the cloudless sky, seeming to hover on top of a distant grove of trees, illuminating them. Turning back to look at the street, she saw windows gleaming with red and green hues from the sun's rays. A woman opened the door of her house and began sweeping the step with a broom. The scene was peaceful in a way she'd never known in Texas.

It was close to dinner time, and she headed towards the rabbi's house. Before she could even knock at the front door, Esther opened it and waved her in.

"This selection is almost more than the mind can bear, my dear. How will you manage it all at the embassy?" Esther asked.

"It's not going well?"

"How could it? And yet, it moves along. One-by-one my beloved husband and Jim Novy have considered the families. In the last four hours they have spoken to six of the men, three of whom are our sons, three of whom are cousins to Jim through his mother. Altogether they represent forty-three of the people."

"Clara's father?"

"She would travel alone as there is no room for her father and brother. But he will not let her go." Esther held up a hand as if to stop Rosalind from crying out. "He understands on the one hand. On the other hand, it is unbearable, and he cannot agree. It isn't as if she were seventeen or eighteen…a young woman…and even then, how hard it would be."

"Maybe if he met me and I could tell him I will be a schoolteacher and can take good care of Clara until he comes to the United States himself?" Rosalind said, struggling not to cry.

"You'll never be a schoolteacher in America while this infection from Germany oozes across borders. Never. Give up that foolish thought, my dear. I see that, even if you don't. You must dry your eyes. It's possible that tomorrow will bring him a change of heart, and there is still time to bring clever Clara to America. Every day is a blessing of new possibilities."

Until it isn't, Rosalind thought.

"I will think more positively," she told Esther.

***

After a light dinner, Rosalind took Jim Novy aside on the porch. "Who's helping these people get all their documents together, sir?" Rosalind asked.

"These are educated people, my dear. Pay their taxes, read the newspapers, listen to the radio, drive cars. Not country…" He paused, a slight flush on his cheeks.

"Bumpkins?"

"Yes, that's the word. They'll have what they need by the end of the week, one way or the other. I will contact the ticket agent for the ship. Now I have time to see my brothers and wish them a last goodbye." He paused. "You will return tomorrow to Warsaw to begin your real task. Michal will drive you."

"Sir, why are you so certain this will go well?"

"How will it help me to have doubts at this moment, Rosalind? What wheel does not sometimes require a little grease? I have that. And I will apply it with the ticket agent, the ship line, wherever it is needed. You have a lesser amount but feel free to let me know if you need more. I would love to think the staff at the embassy will do the right thing because it is right, but I'm not a fool." He went back into the house, closing the door with care.

Rosalind considered the ways of money, how it flowed with forceful certitude towards where it wanted to be, pushing whatever was in its way along if it could, drowning what it could not.

***

Mister Novy and David bunked in the unoccupied house he'd left the community, on clean sheets provided by the rebbetzin. Rosalind slept fitfully on the small couch in the rabbi's front room.

Well into the night, Rosalind decided to keep Michal convinced she would help with his brother's visa. Otherwise, who could say what he'd do? He could take all the visas and sell them, steal whatever Novy had in zlotys, kidnap David—anything a person desperate to save someone he loved might consider.

Rosalind rose at dawn, splashed cool water on her face, ate two hard boiled eggs, and got into the car. Michal delivered her to the hotel in the mid-afternoon after a short stop he declined to explain at a large house in a village. He'd emerged from the house with a small, wrapped package.

"You'll think of a reason to get another blank application for a visa at the embassy. Make up a story about something. Then give it to me so I can fill it out," he said as he opened the car door for her, the perfect picture of a chauffeur.

"Ink spilled on one of them?" Rosalind offered in the most helpful tone she could muster.

"Whatever you decide."

"Of course." She slid out of the car.

***

"Miss Fisher, welcome back. You've had a call." The desk clerk reached into the key cubby and handed Rosalind the key and a slip of paper.

In Warsaw for 3 days. Will be at the Mala Ziemianska 15:00-16:00 each day for you. S.

"When did this come in?"

"Yesterday, ma'am."

The clock above the desk read 14:45.

"What is this?" She pointed to the name on the paper.

"Our most famous café. Wonderful pastries."

"Have the doorman call me a taxi, please." Rosalind turned to leave.

"Wait, ma'am. I have another packet for you." The desk clerk held out a small, sealed manila envelope with a visible bank address. Rosalind thanked him and put it deep inside her purse. More grease for the embassy. Novy hadn't even waited to see if she needed it.

***

In the back of the taxi, she undid the envelope clasp and looked inside. High value zlotys, each worth about a day's wages for a secretary, if her calculations were right. She pushed the clasp down and buried the envelope as deep as she could. Then she tapped the cylinder, still tucked inside the purse's lining.

The short taxi ride brought her to the middle of Wierzbowa Street, where well-dressed women and men strolled in front of retail stores with mannequins displaying the height of fashion—cloche hats and little furs for the coming autumn—and two nightclubs bracketed the cafe.

Rosalind paid the driver. Pushing open the door to the café, she found herself in a hum of conversation from people at small wooden tables densely packed on the floor. A sugar and coffee aroma made her mouth water. She felt normal, that was the only word she could come up with. Normal and hungry.

"Miss, the gentleman over there is waiting for you." A waitress tapped Rosalind's shoulder and pointed to Sidney. He rose from his chair and smiled.

"Hungry?" he asked as Rosalind sat down.

"Very."

"Here's the menu. I'd suggest a few items unless you're not the sort of woman who likes that."

"Go ahead." Whatever Sidney had been doing, he seemed to have slept well and was in fresh clothes, which she had not and was not. Rosalind was content to let him take the lead.

He waved the waitress back and ordered two plates of small sandwiches, two plates of pastries, and two coffees, all in fluent Polish. "I've eaten, so it's all for you except one of the coffees. Glad you got the message."

"Sidney, I…"

"If it's business, let's wait and handle it later. This is a very public space." He spoke so softly she almost didn't hear him.

She smiled and looked into his eyes. "I'm so glad we made our little rendezvous," she said in English as the waitress put down the sandwiches, pastries, and coffee.

It was all she could do not to shove the sandwiches in her mouth. They were delicious, the breads warm from the oven, and the fillings of cheese for one and a fish spread for the other tasted as if the dairy cow and the river were just outside the door. The first pastry, with vanilla cream filling and raspberries, made her moan. Then she took a sip of the strong coffee and sighed. She felt better than normal, a sliver of happiness in her stomach.

"Thank you."

Sidney put down his coffee cup. "Relaxing interlude over," he said in English. "Shall we go?" He waited for her to rise, put a stack of zlotys on the table without waiting for the check, and waved her towards the door.

***

In Rosalind's hotel room, Sidney sat in the desk chair and Rosalind perched on the bed. They'd been silent in the taxi, silent in the elevator, and Rosalind had no idea who should speak first, although that seemed important somehow.

"I have something for you. It's in my purse." She waited for Sidney to say something but he just nodded. She picked at the stitches in the lining of her purse until they loosened. Plucking the cylinder out, she handed it over.

He looked at it, then turned it over and over.

"I got it open."

Sidney stared at her wordlessly. Rosalind wondered if this was something he'd learned in spy school, if there was such a thing.

"If you care, I'll tell you what I found inside."

He rolled the cylinder between his palms. "You ought to have given this to me on the Queen," he said, his voice an angry whisper. "Now I'm in Warsaw with no backup unless we go to the British Embassy. Which would be a very bad idea. The bloke in charge there is… Never mind."

"I was planning to give it to you when you gave me the new gun. That didn't happen when we got off the ship, though. Care to tell me why?" she asked, hoping aggression would loosen his lips.

He shook his head. "Lord, you're an amateur. It's what I get for thinking you needed help—or that I should provide it. I went to some effort to get you exactly what you wanted, which was not in port. You should have…" He stopped and sighed. "What was in it? And where was it?"

"A very long strip of paper with code on it. It was in Heinrich and Hedda's luggage. She thinks I have it and she was here to get it."

"Obviously she didn't." He put the cylinder down next to the chair leg.

"She might be back."

"In that case, I'll give this to you now. Wouldn't want her busting through the door, what with you defenseless."

He reached into the inside pocket of his jacket. Rosalind knew enough about tailoring to see that the pocket was much deeper than ordinary. He pulled out a derringer, as small as the one she'd had, and handed it over along with a jingly packet of bullets.

"Could you make anything of the code, Rosalind?"

She shook her head.

"Of course not." He picked the cylinder up again, tossed it up and caught it like a boy with a ball. "Here's my dilemma, which you have caused. Is this coded message so important that my boss needs to know right now? After all, it would have been in the hands of the Reich three days ago if you hadn't snatched it. And Hedda wanted it back badly enough to follow you here and try to intimidate you."

Was that a note in her favor? She'd prevented the Reich from getting something and withstood Hedda. Rosalind waited, her neck knotting up with distress.

"If you'd given it to me like the good little amateur agent you're supposed to be, we would already know what's on this. We'd be a few days ahead of where we are now." He continued to toss the cylinder up and catch it in a rhythmic, monotonous way.

Not forgiven. She tried a smile which he ignored, so she nodded, all business. "I have a question. How dense is this thicket of spies on both sides?"

"Well, Miss Fisher, I don't know. If I did know, why on earth would I tell you? It's the game of foxes and you are decidedly not a fox."

"When did it start, at least?"

"There are references to spies in the Book of Numbers in the Bible."

"I meant start between Hitler's Germany and Britain."

"Countries always have spies in other countries. The more worrisome the relationship, the more the spies. When Hitler broke the Treaty of Versailles in 1935 and started the *Luftwaffe*, which was strictly forbidden, those in Britain who could see the darkness ahead put in more spies," Sidney said. He rolled the cylinder across his palm. "America has just a few, thanks to your Secretary of State, Cordell Hull, who, in my opinion, wants just enough information to keep America disengaged. We assume the Nazis have done the same as we Brits. They surely have lots of spies in Britain, our territories, and in America."

"Where do you get all your information?" she asked.

"I matriculated from Oxford. But not all from there." A thin wisp of a smile slid over his mouth and evaporated.

"Well…" she paused then plunged on, "certainly, Sidney, despite my error of judgement, you can take this to the British Embassy and find someone who can assist with that cylinder and its mysteries."

"Certainly, Miss Fisher, I can and I will. It's best to get this away from you before Hedda tries to get it again. You succeeded once but that may have exhausted your luck." He paused. "So, let's away. Unless you'd rather remain in your room and sleep? First though, make sure you have your passport. You'll need that official identification. And do change your clothes. You look like you've been in them for three days at least."

"Fine." Rosalind wondered if all British agents were arrogant or if it was reserved to Oxford graduates. She wouldn't be surprised to learn that under his steward uniform, Sidney was a Lord or a Duke.

Her door rattled. Sidney put a finger to his mouth and placed himself flat against the wall, gun out.

"Who is it?" Rosalind asked. Her voice sounded firm to her, despite having leapt out of a trembling body.

"Michal."

"Please go away. I'm trying to rest and then I need to bathe."

"You will remember, Rosalind, that I do not have to be a nice guy. I'm asking for just that one thing, but I can take everything if I want."

"Yes."

"Fine."

She and Sidney waited. Then she walked to the door and looked through the peephole. No one was there.

"You'll tell me about this new Michal problem. After you bathe," Sidney said, shaking his head.

***

Rosalind, dressed in cleaner clothes, her hair in tightened, damp curls, sat next to Sidney in the taxi.

"We'll walk now," he said to the driver, who then pulled over to let them out on a boulevard with huge, well-kept buildings in soft colors.

"The British Embassy is in the former Branicki Palace. Three-stories, rococo style, as befits our great country. Just a few blocks from here is the Vistula River." He took her hand and tucked it through his folded arm.

They were, Rosalind thought, a perfect imitation of a young couple on a tourist stroll. A three-piece suited man in a bowler hat passed them. Sidney nodded and continued in a loud voice, "You may not know this, my dear, but Warsaw is the up-and-coming city of eastern Europe, aspiring to be at the same level as Paris and Berlin."

A small path between the walls of the buildings opened on the right and Sidney steered Rosalind onto it. "The Michal problem, Rosalind?"

"It's not related to this. Really."

Sidney shook his head. "Fine. Have it your way. Now, when we get to where we are going, offer as little as possible. Follow my lead. Brits and Americans are the first cousins at the family dinner who bicker all the time. We should have the same interests, especially at times like these, but…" He shrugged.

The path dead ended in an alley and Sidney turned to the right, continuing between tall walls topped with barbed wire. He stopped in front of a steel door and rang a doorbell, two shorts and a long. Rosalind almost laughed.

"Rings in a special office," Sidney said, noting her amusement. "By the way, we all wear civilian clothes here but don't let that fool you. If I say 'general,' you say 'general.' The fellow we're meeting is a Brigadier General. Second highest rank there is, not that he deserves it. Be aware."

"Got it."

***

"And who is she?" A balding man with a sheen of perspiration on his brow sat behind a desk strewn with papers. He was wearing a gray wool three-piece suit that was much too warm for the room and a green Windsor-knotted tie. Behind him a bookcase held a two-faced clock with both English and mid-continent time represented, a heavy, black telephone, and a ticker-tape feed.

Sidney waved Rosalind into a chair. "Rosalind Fisher, sir. From the States."

The man nodded. "And why is she here?" His gaze flickered over to Rosalind and back to Sidney.

"She's an asset for our limited American partners, new to espionage. So, naïve and makes mistakes." Sidney paused.

Rosalind shifted in her seat, bracing for a recital of her failures, and began to formulate her defense, thin as it was. The Brits would hand her over to the Americans and off she'd go, back to America, without being able to get anyone—much less forty-four Jews—out of Poland.

Sidney gave her a sideways look and the barest shake of his head.

"So? That's the States' problem, not ours."

"Yes. However, she has potential and can be trained. Also, she did make an excellent recovery with our charming duo, Hedda and Heinrich, when I couldn't—that list of names I've given you—and she managed to grab another prize for us. She even got this open without damage to the contents. It's a code, she thinks. Handed it over to me the first opportunity she had." Sidney reached into his capacious suit pocket and handed over the cylinder.

The general picked up the phone's handpiece and dialed a two-digit number. "Come. We have a present for you," he said, then hung up.

In less than a minute, the office door behind Rosalind opened. A middle-aged woman with streaks of gray in her hair and clothing that could only be described as "sensible" entered.

"Yes, what is it?" Her voice was low, each word clipped to its essentials. She didn't look at Sidney or Rosalind and barely glanced at the brigadier general before staring at the blank wall behind him.

"Lieutenant Collins," the general said to Sidney, "you've met our ace decoder before."

"Of course. Miss Lonsdale, an honor to see you again," Sidney said.

"What am I decoding?" Miss Lonsdale asked, holding out her left hand. The general dropped the cylinder in it. "Back in thirty minutes with a report," she said, and turned and walked out the door, leaving it ajar.

Rosalind stood up. It was past seven in the evening, and she had a lot to do before Novy returned with Michal and the names and information of the immigrants to the United States. She had to find staff at the United States Embassy to stamp the visas, and she needed to seek out her cousins and let them know there was nothing she could do for them.

"Do sit down, Miss Fisher. You are not going anywhere just yet. Would you like some tea? Perhaps a cold sandwich?" the general asked.

"I was hoping to return to my hotel. I have people to visit in Warsaw and just a short time to do it."

"Lieutenant Collins will make sure you can do what you need. Just not yet. Where are they, these people?"

Rosalind considered her answer. The general was digging for information, obviously, and she needed to offer something in response, but not much.

"Here." She reached into her purse and found the slip of paper with the address to hand him.

"A good section of Warsaw. Mostly professionals. Mostly Jewish."

"Mmm."

"You wish to visit because?"

"This person is close to someone I know in Texas, and I promised I would see how he and his family were doing if I could."

"I see. And you are traveling in Poland on behalf of an American congressman and with a well-known industrialist also of the Hebrew persuasion."

"Yes."

To her left, Sidney shifted in his chair. The clock ticked. The general nodded and said nothing.

The door opened and Miss Lonsdale stuck her head in. "Norfolk Navy Yard. Heard of it?"

"State of Virginia. Major shipbuilding yard, Miss Lonsdale," the general said.

Miss Lonsdale shut the door. Neither the general nor Sidney seemed surprised or bothered.

After another five minutes, Rosalind said, "Is there a restroom nearby?"

"W.C. out the door and to your right. Sidney will show you."

Sidney was out of his chair and holding the door open. "After you, Miss Fisher."

***

"Will we ever get out of here, Sidney?" Rosalind whispered as they walked down a hall lit by flickering florescent bulbs.

"Most assuredly."

"Why is your commander keeping me here?"

"First, a small correction. He is not my commander although he does outrank me. Second, let's assume that Miss Lonsdale decodes this message. She has an excellent reputation for doing just that. Let's assume it has something to say about your Norfolk Navy Yard of interest to our Nazi neighbors. That cannot be good, right?"

She nodded.

"Because you found this message and because you are here primarily at the direction of Representative Johnson, I believe the good general feels you get some credit, as does Johnson. He wants to know what is on the message and how to get that information to the United States Embassy in the best way. I'm sure he'd like to present it as a sterling example of a joint venture in espionage. A positive gesture of cooperation."

"Fine. Now I really will use the W.C." Rosalind stepped around Sidney and opened the W.C. door.

She considered what Sidney told her as she washed her hands. If Nazis spying on a US naval yard stirred up the US Secretary of War, great. So far, Woodring had remained in lockstep with Hull, advocating for non-intervention. He'd made that clear in interviews that Charles Marsh duly reported in his newspapers.

***

"I must see my cousin tonight or early tomorrow morning at the latest," Rosalind whispered to Sidney as they walked back towards the general's office. "He doesn't even know I'm here so I'd like to call first but I don't have his telephone number and I've had absolutely no time to try to find it."

"I'll handle that. Just give me the name and address."

She'd memorized both and told Sidney. He opened the door to the office, waved her in, said, "Have other matters here. I'll be brief," then shut the door before the general had the chance to object.

Rosalind sat silently across from the general, marking the time on his ticking clock. After twelve minutes, Sidney opened the door, said, "Done," and sat down.

Three minutes later, Miss Lonsdale opened the door. "It's a list of the ships in drydock to be repaired and the ships to be built in the next two years. Their armament capacities, storage, interesting new equipment."

"All of that on that one piece of paper?" Rosalind blurted out.

"It is code, not word after word. If that's all, sir, I'll have one of the other girls type it up." Miss Lonsdale closed the door without any reply from the general.

"There's a spy at that naval yard?" Rosalind asked. The general looked at her with the slightest pursing of his lips and wrinkling of his nose and she bit the inside of her cheek.

"Probably more than one," Sidney said. "Folks of German background are the largest population in the United States and there is that American Bund crowd eager to help Hitler along. In addition to the spies Hitler has already sent over, of course."

"This may be more than Miss Fisher wants to handle at her embassy. We'll send it over to them. All credit to you, of course, Lieutenant, for bringing this to us as you should," the general said.

Rosalind registered the left-handed insult and took a breath to steady her voice. "I'll turn this information over to my embassy. Lieutenant Collins is welcome to come along. All credit and thanks to you and your staff here, of course, for decoding it first."

The general gave the briefest of nods. "Escort Miss Fisher over to our counterparts and be certain they understand we are helping them," he said to Sidney. "Then you are free to go back to whatever it is you do."

Sidney stood up.

"And make sure they understand this was our operation. Thank them for Miss Fisher's assistance, however. Goodbye, Miss Fisher."

***

The sky had settled into dark with no hint of sunset left. Streetlamps lit up small puddles of sidewalk. Sidney again tucked her arm into his. As another couple approached them, Sidney said, "If we're going to make our dinner engagement, we have to hurry."

At the next boulevard, where restaurants and clubs clustered, Sidney stepped to the curb and raised his hand. Within seconds a taxi pulled over.

Handing the driver a small piece of paper, Sidney said in English, "We're going to this number."

In the cab, Rosalind turned to ask him where they were going. He put his finger to his lips. They drove in silence through what Rosalind assumed was Warsaw's downtown area, with department stores, restaurants, a massive library building, and well-tended apartment buildings. The taxi pulled over.

"There it is," the driver said in Polish.

"Sorry, don't speak Polish and neither does my wife."

"There, there." The driver jabbed his finger in the direction of a uniformed doorman. "Jews live there." Sidney handed the driver a wad of zlotys and they got out. He slipped another bill into the hand of the doorman, smiled at him, and said, this time in perfect Polish, "We need to step into the building to find someone. Government business. There's a good man."

Once inside, Sidney waved her towards the stairs rather than the elevator. "Up we go to floor five. Your cousin awaits."

Rosalind's mind wandered as she climbed the stairs behind Sidney. She remembered a photo of her father at his bar mitzvah, remembered the color of her mother's hair and the sound of her voice, the snip of her father's scissors, Hannah washing her hair and letting her read for hours on end when another income, even from a fourteen-year-old, would have helped the family's finances so much. Rosalind had benefitted all her life from the care of her family and now she had the opportunity to pay that kindness forward, if she could only pull it off.

***

"There you are. You go on in. Best if I stay out here." Sidney pointed to a varnished oak door with the number 51 on a brass plate and a small *mezuzah*, enameled in bright blue and green, attached to the doorpost.

Rosalind knocked on the door. A boy opened it and peered out through a small crack. "Rosalind Fisher?"

"Yes."

The door opened enough for her to slide in. She was in a small entry way, decorated with a table, mirror, and umbrella stand.

"Hello," the boy said. "Do you understand Polish, Cousin Rosalind?" She nodded.

"I am Tomasz. I am pleased to meet you." He held out his hand and Rosalind shook it. "My father and my sister and brother are in the parlor."

"Tomasz, bring our cousin in already," a man's voice called.

Rosalind followed Tomasz into the sitting room, where Jakub, her cousin, was sitting. He stood up and opened his arms. "Dear cousin, let me hug you. How good of you to come."

Jakub was taller than she'd expected. She let him wrap his arms around her and then kiss her on both cheeks.

"And this is Zofia and Andrej." At their father's introduction, another boy and a girl stood up. The girl, in a simple blue dress, curtsied and the boy, in his school uniform, bowed.

Jakub said, "Please, Rosalind, sit down."

She took a seat in a blue brocade wing chair opposite the floral-covered sofa where the children and their father sat.

Zofia stared at her with eyes so dark they seemed black in the sitting room's light. Her curly hair sat at shoulder length, dark brown with not a hint of red. "Do you speak Polish, esteemed cousin?" she asked in English.

"Yes. I speak, write and read it. Please call me Rosalind."

Zofia nodded. "I would prefer to speak in Polish, please. I have only English for year five, six and seven."

In Polish, Rosalind said, "And you are now entering grade eight?"

Zofia shook her head. "Father, please explain."

"Last year," Jakub said, "the universities imposed bench ghettos, so all Jewish students must sit apart from others. This will, we fear, infect our secondary schools, even our primary schools." He lifted his palms in the air. "And after the boycott two years ago of our Jewish businesses and professional people, I have almost nothing left to send my children to the Jewish schools which remain safe for now. No one has."

"My father wants me to study at home with his help and work in his office," Zofia said.

"I do not want this. I do not. But I see no other choice." Jakub's voice broke.

"My brothers will continue to go to school." Zofia offered this to Rosalind as if she were explaining a simple fact.

"Your brothers are younger than you are." Jakub reached for a piece of paper on the table to his left. "This is your letter, which arrived three days ago. I have all the documents needed. I went that day to your embassy because our dear cousin, Hannah, agreed to sponsor us. I told them she is putting together what she needs in Texas. Austin, yes? Will she send those soon?"

Rosalind nodded. Hannah and her husband, both working, could barely keep food on the table, the rent paid, and some money in the bank. There was no way she could sponsor a family of four. No need to mention that. Maybe Hannah had a trick up her sleeve, a co-sponsor.

"I was told to return to the embassy only when Hannah had sent all the information. Did she give it to you, perhaps?"

Rosalind shook her head.

"I have gone to the British Embassy, the French, the Spanish, the Portuguese, even China. The ones who hold out any hope at all. Sometimes they smile, sometimes they sigh, and they put me on the list. The endless list with the endless seven-year wait."

"I'll work on getting visas approved for you and the children. I will let you know as soon as I can because if I am successful, the exit date will be in less than a week."

"We no longer hope. If it happens, it happens."

"You'll need cash." She reached into her purse and pulled out the bank envelope. "Here's some," she said, handing it over without counting it. "Do I have your office contacts, an address, a telephone?"

"Since the troubles began, all my money is hidden here," Jakub said, holding up the zlotys. "Thank you for this." He sighed. "I work from home now, too. Zofia's former bedroom—that's why the children share. So just call our home."

***

"How'd it go with the family?" Sidney asked when they were safely back in a cab.

"They want out."

"Don't they all."

The rest of the ride back to the hotel was silent.

CHAPTER 12

The next morning in the backseat of the taxi, Rosalind scanned the list of names she'd been given as contacts in the embassy and memorized them.

Jim Novy and David were due back in tomorrow, chauffeured by Michal. She might need Michal's help, Rosalind knew, because she had an idea she felt Sidney would not approve of. Not that she trusted Michal, or that it was any of Sidney's business, but he was the only spy she knew, and she might need an ally.

The driver pulled up in front of a four-story building sitting on two streets that met at a forty-five-degree angle. A single United States flag hung outside a double door half-way up one of the streets. At eight-thirty in the morning, a line of people already stretched up the road and into the next block.

Rosalind paid the driver and walked up to the front door with her papers identifying her as Representative Lyndon Baines Johnson's staff.

"Clerks and secretaries enter down the street," said the Marine guarding the entrance.

"I'm neither. Staff to Congressman Lyndon Baines Johnson and here on official House of Representative business."

"Regarding?"

"I'll explain to the person I need to see. May I enter?"

The Marine stepped aside and pushed open the door. "See the receptionist first."

"United States identification and documentation that you are here on official government business, please," a man behind a half-circle desk said, holding out his hand.

Rosalind pulled her passport and the document on LBJ's letterhead, signed by him, identifying Rosalind Fisher as a member of his staff on special assignment to assess conditions in Poland and requiring all appropriate cooperation from the United States Embassy. It closed with a warm personal message to Ambassador Biddle on behalf of Charles Marsh, inviting the ambassador to visit Longlea again whenever he was back in the Washington DC area because Marsh had a polo pony he was certain Biddle would love to try out.

"Fine. Do you know where you are headed, Miss Fisher?" The man returned her documents to her.

"I'm to provide Representative Johnson with an assessment of the efficiency of the visa process."

"Because?"

"Because that's my assignment. I'm sure you understand assignments."

"Ours is not to question why." The man smiled.

"Ours is but to do or die," Rosalind said, completing the line from the "The Charge of the Light Brigade" and returning his smile.

"See George Fried. He's the Vice-Consul foreign service officer over-seeing the staff. Third floor. He can also pass Representative Johnson's greetings on to Ambassador Biddle."

"Is the ambassador in today? Maybe I can do that myself."

"You need to ask Mister Fried that." He turned and pointed up the stairs.

***

"I must say, Miss Fisher, I don't understand your assignment. Representative Johnson has no perch in any committee working with foreign affairs or immigration." The balding, stiff-backed Fried stared at her from his seat behind the desk.

"Vice-Consul Fried, sir, Representative Johnson, who is a good friend to Charles Marsh, has required my services for this small assignment. Mister Marsh is a friend of Ambassador Biddle. You see his invitation to the ambassador there, in the papers I just gave you. Mister Marsh is also interested in the current state of visa processing in Poland."

"The current state is we are swamped. Sit down." Fried glanced down at the documents she'd handed him.

"Yes, of course. Mister Marsh wants a newspaper story on how hard our Americans here are working on the problem."

"We are understaffed. And people come without the right documents, without a sponsor in America. You have no idea the headaches we have."

"Absolutely. We don't fully appreciate all you do. That is one reason the good representative sent me here, so we might help the public understand." Rosalind waited for a reaction, but none came. "Also, a British officer, Lieutenant Collins, will be coming here sometime today with very important information for the ambassador. Very important and highly confidential. Lieutenant Collins will be asking for me at that time."

The tips of Fried's ears got a bit pink and his lips tightened.

Rosalind wondered if she'd pushed too far. "When Ambassador Biddle hears what Lieutenant Collins has to say and views the documents, he'll be quite thankful to you for facilitating the quick meeting. I'll be certain to mention how helpful you are, not only to him but also to the good congressman from Texas."

"And who shall I say you are when Ambassador Biddle asks, Miss Rosalind Fisher?"

"Me? I'm the person Representative Johnson sent here. I'm just doing my job, like you are."

He looked at her before lowering his gaze to the papers on his desk.

"I'll just begin, then," Rosalind said. "A few questions about the process by which visas to the United States are issued and how well that process is working now. And who on your staff you'd hold up as excellent employees in these tough times."

"Will you be taking notes?"

"I have an excellent memory, Mister Fried. Better than writing anything down, wouldn't you agree?"

He nodded, face blank, then said, "The line of people outside our embassy want visas. They bring the paperwork in to us, to our front-line consular officers."

"How many officers?"

"Two. Each has a secretary and an office, for privacy. The applicant is interviewed, and the paperwork is checked carefully."

"If the applicant has children?"

"They are interviewed, as well, or, in the case of the very young, observed."

"And then?"

"They wait." Fried sat up, an almost imperceptible movement.

Rosalind shifted the cross of her ankles, tilted her head, and sighed.

"Do you require more information, Miss Fisher? I do have other matters to attend to."

"Who is in charge of approving the final documents? What does that entail?"

"As the senior vice-consul for this embassy, I have the final approval. I review the documents."

"And then…" Rosalind tilted forward a bit in her seat as if the last words of the last act were coming.

"The visa, properly filled out, is stamped with the seal and handed to the immigrant."

"By whom?"

"By whom?" Fried raised his voice.

"I'm asking, sir, because Representative Johnson wants a full report on how the process works. He is…he *was* in charge of the Works Project Administration for all of Texas. So, he understands this type of situation. Administration, I mean, and how complicated it is," Rosalind said, her stomach lurching. If Fried didn't tell her, she'd have to ask around and risk him discovering she'd pursued the information he didn't seem to care to give her.

"Complicated." Fried repeated the uninflected word which now sat like a mountain between them. "Once I've approved the documents and consulted again with the counselor clerk about the potential emigrant, I have the responsibility of placing the seal on the visa. It's a real seal of melted red wax. Then I give the documents and the visa back to the counselor clerk. He arranges for the person to return to the embassy and receive them. Then, of course, it is up to the new emigrant to manage a way to the United States."

"So the final step happens here?" Rosalind looked around the office which was fairly bare. A large oak desk, one matching file cabinet, and a picture of President Franklin Delano Roosevelt on the wall.

Fried's phone rang once. "Yes? Fine. I will tell her." He looked at Rosalind. "Lieutenant Collins is here."

"You will want to meet him, sir, hear what he has to say and consider how it will be useful for you, and for our great country, once the ambassador is given the information."

"Send him in." Fried put down the receiver.

Sidney entered the office in service dress uniform, a sextet of medals hanging from his jacket, hat tucked under his left arm, small briefcase manacled to his right wrist. "I've come at the request of the British Embassy, Mister Fried."

"As I've been told. Please sit."

Sidney perched at the end of the chair, placed the briefcase on his lap and dangled the hat, like an afterthought, from his left forefinger. "Miss Fisher inadvertently came into possession of top-secret information of great importance to the United States."

At the word *inadvertently* Rosalind raised her eyebrows.

"Go on."

"It's best if you review the documents. You are in the best position to decide how to bring them to Ambassador Biddle's attention."

"You Brits saw this before us?" Fried's voice rose and he glared, first at Sidney and then at Rosalind, lips pursed.

"I'm happy to explain, Mister Fried. Do you want the explanation now or after you read what I've brought?" Sidney said.

Fried held out his hand. Sidney opened the briefcase and handed over three typed pages.

After a few minutes, he looked up from the papers. "This is quite concerning. American spies—traitors—sympathetic to the Third Reich. Details on our ship production and repairs. And how did Miss Fisher come into possession of this?"

"Let's just say Miss Fisher located an odd small metal container in her handbag which had been placed there by a party we prefer not to name. The plan had been to extricate the container and hand it over to our person, but the plan went awry. Miss Fisher had the foresight to open the container, realize the importance of the coded message, and hand it over to our embassy at her first opportunity."

"Why not our embassy?"

Sidney sat up even straighter. "The Queen Mary is a British vessel. Our territory, as it were. What is found on our territory belongs to us. And she had no way to know that a coded message pertained to American concerns."

"She seemed quite certain I would want to see this and forward it to the ambassador."

"Of course. We contacted her and wanted her to know her efforts were valued. She was inadvertently involved and yet acted with great foresight and care."

Both men looked at Rosalind. She smiled, blushed, lowered her eyes, and thought poisonous thoughts about both of them.

***

From what Rosalind had been able to discover, Ambassador Biddle had come to his post in the way of most men of wealth and connection. No college degree, no working his way up the ranks, not even a single successful business to his name, just inherited money and money he'd married into that he then handed over to politicians who subsequently won elections. He had a reputation for good manners and superb taste in clothes. He'd first gone to Norway. When it was clear that he might have found his true calling, he was promoted to ambassador to Poland, landing in Warsaw just fourteen months before Rosalind's appearance at the embassy.

He rose from behind an eight-foot-long mahogany desk when Rosalind entered his office, followed by Sidney, briefcase still locked to his wrist, and Fried, holding the papers.

"Miss Fisher, a pleasure. I'll be sure to tell Charles Marsh that you were diligent in delivering his invitation as well as Lydon Johnson's introduction. Please make yourself comfortable. Lieutenant Collins, welcome. And, Mister Fried, I understand we have a gift from our British cousins. What is it?"

Rosalind sank into a deep leather-clad chair, one of three that faced the desk, and looked at Biddle, a handsome man with dark brown hair just graying above the temples, brown eyes, and a suit that was obviously tailored to his athletic build.

Fried handed the papers to Biddle and waited as Biddle sat back, then took a chair himself.

"You'll get our radio dispatcher on this as soon as we are done here. Our great thanks to your embassy, Lieutenant, for moving so quickly to decode the message and to bring it here," Biddle said finally, putting the papers on his desk.

"Of course."

"Eton?" Biddle asked.

"Yes, Ambassador," Sidney said. "Then Oxford. And now, as you see, service."

"Would you explain the role Miss Fisher had in all this?" Biddle asked.

Rosalind tensed up. Men would once again be explaining her to each other.

Sidney turned towards her, the side of his mouth tweaking up, and shook his head. "Ambassador," he said, "I've found Miss Fisher perfectly capable of explaining herself and, indeed, handling herself admirably in a difficult situation. I believe that is why she was hand-picked by your Representative Johnson for a job much different than the one she found herself dealing with."

"Please, Miss Fisher."

"As Lieutenant Collins explained to Vice-Consul Fried, I found myself in possession of a mysterious metal canister of obvious importance."

"How did you know that?"

"First, sir, it was sealed. Second, I was followed here to Warsaw and an attempt was made to find it among my possessions."

Sidney looked at her, a slight frown on his face, then returned his attention to the ambassador.

"I see. And then?" Biddle asked.

"I managed to pry the thing open."

"With?"

"A pair of scissors—embroidery scissors—sharp, narrow blades. I found a coded message, and—"

"If I may, Sir, I had told Miss Fisher, whom I'd met on the ship, that I would be on assignment to our embassy in Warsaw and that I would be pleased to escort her to dinner one night if she was free from her other responsibilities," Sidney interjected. "It was under those circumstances that she told me what she had found. Because the whole matter involved our sovereign territory on the Queen Mary, I took her to my embassy. I gave her no choice."

"All's well that ends well," Biddle said. "Excellent work, Miss Fisher." He nodded to Sidney. "Our thanks again to your embassy's decoding personnel. We'll see that this gets on its way to where it should be. And, Vice-Consul, you can see that Miss Fisher gets the assistance she needs to do whatever it is that Representative Johnson wants."

"Yes." Fried started to rise. "I'll be with her every step of the way, or one of my staff will be."

"Of course. And, Miss Fisher, perhaps you and the lieutenant would like to join me and my wife this evening for a small cocktail party? If Mister Novy is back, we would love to have him as well, and anyone else in his immediate group."

"Thank you, Ambassador." Rosalind tried to sort through the competing messages as she walked out of the office. Fried's 'every-step-of-the-way' statement had been said with an undertone of intention and suspicion, she was sure of it.

"Give me a moment, Miss Fisher, Lieutenant." Fried stepped back into Ambassador Biddle's office and shut the door.

"What are you not telling me, Rosalind? Why are you really here?" Sidney's whisper was hot and fierce in her ear.

She shook her head.

Sidney shrugged. "I'll see you tonight at the ambassador's, Miss Fisher. I'll leave you with your tasks to complete, whatever they might be." He walked down the stairs.

***

Fried introduced Rosalind to a clerk, Hank Martin, then Fried, Martin, and Rosalind retreated to Hank Martin's office so Martin could explain the interview process, review of documents, requests for more documents, and final processing. While they spoke, twelve people holding paperwork sat on benches in the hall flanked on each end by an armed US Marine.

"I'm able to process three an hour, four if everything is in order, which it is mostly not," Martin said, shaking his head. "Then it's all sent up to the Vice-Consul. I answer any additional questions he has. If he approves, the visa is stamped, and I arrange to have the person return for it."

"So, a bit more than twenty a day?" Rosalind asked.

He shook his head. "You have to consider the people, the crying, the pleading. It just sucks up so much time."

"The line this morning looked like it was more than a hundred."

"Closer to two hundred."

"A little more than ten thousand a year," Rosalind said. "Less than half what you're allotted."

"Miss Fisher, are you planning to file a critical report with Representative Johnson of the House of Representatives?" Fried asked.

"Critical? Absolutely not, Vice-Consul. These are difficult times for all of us who work for the government. Too few of us, too much to do." She saw the senior clerk nod his head. "In the meantime, I am taking up far too much of Mister Martin's valuable time."

"Then let's go so he can work."

"My instructions are to observe the process. I am to sit in the office and watch until I think I can write a report on what happens. Did you want to sit with me?" Rosalind asked Fried pleasantly.

"We've told you what happens." Fried flushed.

"Yes, yes. It's just, the…"

"Routine?" Martin offered.

She nodded.

"Fine, then. Just sit here. Don't interfere. I'll see you tonight at the ambassador's. You and Representative Johnson's wealthy friend." With that, Fried turned and walked out of the office.

"Well, have a seat in the corner there, Miss Fisher. The office is small. We'll have to make do."

She sat on the hard chair.

"I'll begin by saying we need a minimum of four times the staff to process legal visa requests. And we need people who speak Polish. Now we need people who speak German because Germans, especially Jews, are fleeing Germany and trying to get visas here. All pretty sad. Everyday we're in mud up to our knees. We shovel it, but the next day it's back."

"Where are you from?"

"Right up against the Mississippi in Hannibal, Missouri."

"Mark Twain's hometown."

He smiled. "Fine writer and observer of the human condition. Now, I must work."

Three hours later, he had ushered nine sets of people—men and women, all dressed in their best day clothes, and six children, four in pinafores, two in sailor suits, two swaddled, crying infants—in and out of the office. Of those, two sets met the exacting standards for paperwork and timely filing.

Rosalind could not tell how Martin felt about what he was doing. Maybe that was his training—a look of complete neutrality, a voice of tempered calm, repeating the instructions in the exact same way, all in fluent Polish. Rosalind could not imagine maintaining that emotional distance from people whose desperation seeped into the slightest shift of their posture on a chair.

"Lunch time, Miss Fisher." Martin stood up and stretched. "There's a café just down the street if you want something light."

"Where do the folks who work here usually eat?"

"Cafeteria in the basement. More the clerks and secretaries, not the…"

"Bosses?"

He nodded.

"I am supposed to give a greeting to Wanda Wieroski from a friend."

"Wanda is no longer at the embassy."

"Oh. Why?" Wanda was one of the four people who might have pushed the forty-four people, paperwork in hand, to the head of the line. That was concerning.

"She emigrated herself, to Australia."

"And Antoni?"

"Good fellow, Antoni. Went over to the Swiss Embassy. Better promotion opportunities there."

"I see. What about Amelia Stuind? Henrich Bukker?"

"Amelia is my clerk. Lovely woman. I didn't know she had friends in the States." He paused. "Anyhow, she's taken her summer holiday. This is August, after all, and some folks get a break. Feel free to leave her a note. I'll be sure she gets it."

"Of course. Henrich Bukker?" She worried about the questioning tone that Martin had taken on, as if he wondered about her and the people she named. She tried a slight laugh, a shake of her head, as if this was an expected outcome.

Martin held the door open for her and motioned her out into the hall. The chairs had refilled with people.

"Bukker might be in the cafeteria. We'll look for him," Martin said.

"Does he still work for the other senior clerk?"

"No. Nice guy, Bukker. He got a temporary promotion of sorts when my counterpart returned to the States. We're waiting for a new guy. In fact, I sort of thought maybe you were him. Or her."

They'd reached a set of stairs and began to head down.

"Promotion to?" Rosalind asked, lips dry around the word.

"Yeah, doing this job. He's the only Polish national, although he's fluent in English, of course. Mostly unsupervised although I wave at him from time to time just to keep the boss happy."

Rosalind could not believe her luck.

***

Henrich Bukker dipped his spoon into the cold beet soup in the bowl in front of him, his napkin tucked into the neck opening on his white shirt, blue tie flipped back over his shoulder, the picture of careful precision. He looked younger than Rosalind had expected, early thirties at most, with sandy blonde hair and blue eyes. When Martin and Rosalind approached him with the clear intent to interrupt his lunch, he rose from his seat.

"George, would you both care to join me?" His English was almost unaccented. Rosalind guessed he'd begun to learn it early and practiced it often.

"Rosalind Fisher, Henrich Bukker."

Rosalind held out her hand. "A pleasure, Mister Bukker."

His grip was firm, no effort to ease off because she was a woman. When he smiled, his eyes did not, as if observing her was more important. It was unnerving.

"Are you new to the staff here, Miss Fisher?" Bukker asked.

"No. I am here on behalf of Representative Lyndon Baines Johnson of Texas to observe the process of handling immigration visas."

"Interesting."

"Miss Fisher is to visit your office next, my friend. I'm off to see what food remains from the hungry horde. Miss Fisher, may I bring you some soup and bread?"

At Rosalind's nod, Martin got up and walked away.

"I was asked to bring you greetings from friends in the United States," she said to Bukker.

"By whom?"

"John Smith."

Bukker nodded.

A pale, black-haired woman about Rosalind's age approached the table. She wore a dark skirt, white blouse, and a black shawl across her shoulders even though the cafeteria combined the warmth of the August day outside with the steamy heat of soups in pots.

She smiled at Rosalind. "Are you a new staff person?" she asked in Polish.

Something in Bukker's face changed, a heightened attentiveness, slight inbreath.

Rosalind smiled back. "I'm sorry, I don't understand Polish."

Bukker, his face again immobile, translated for the woman, who nodded, and said in accented English, "I just wanted to say hello. Have you come from the United States, then?"

"Yes, but only to observe for a day or so and bring a report back."

At that the woman stiffened. "We are hard workers here. Not like the socialists, the unionists. Or—"

"Yes, I see that, even in the little time I have been here." Rosalind wanted to cut her off, stop her from naming the other groups she disliked, since Jews were surely among them.

The woman held out her hand. "Nice to meet you."

"And you."

Bukker leaned in and whispered in English, "Poland is splitting between those who love Hitler and those, well… I can't help Mister Smith and his friends anymore. Too dangerous."

"But…" Rosalind looked at Bukker's rigid mouth and tightened eyes. How much of Novy's money, snug in its envelope in the depths of her purse, would it take to change his mind?

"And here's your soup, Miss Fisher." Martin put a bowl of cabbage borscht down, then sat himself. "Have you been entertaining her with stories about our embassy, my friend?"

"Absolutely," Bukker said.

"I'll be visiting Mister Bukker's office next, Mister Martin." Rosalind ignored the squeak of the chair as Bukker slid backwards and coughed.

***

Rosalind sat in a folding chair with a hard metal back in the narrow space behind Bukker's desk. The hall outside had filled up again with people seeking visas.

"When I gave you Mister Smith's greeting, I was unable at the time to expand. Now that we are in your office alone, I need to tell you more."

"No."

"You are being asked to expedite visas for forty-four people. That is all."

"That is all! Do you understand anything, you people in America? This is a horror movie that will not end. My wife's mother is Jewish. I can't risk anything. My children…" Bukker whispered at Rosalind.

"I have resources," she said. Then she switched to Polish. "Tell me how much it will take for you to do this."

He shook his head, his expression remote, as if her suddenly speaking Polish was expected, part of the plot to undo him.

"I need to see my next set of people, Miss Fisher," he said in English. "If there is any question you have, please ask. I can translate for you if you wish. We will have no further discussion of other matters."

***

The last applicant left at 4:30. He was a young architect, with papers in order and a sponsor waiting in Minneapolis, a distant cousin—not that it mattered, but the architect emphasized the relationship with a solid business running a beer distillery. Bukker told him the visa would be processed and waiting for him in five working days.

"Return that day, keep your papers close, be ready with a ticket to leave."

The architect nodded, stood, and reached over to shake Bukker's hand. "Thank you."

"It is my job. Only that. No 'thank you' needed."

Bukker shut the door behind him and began to tidy the already immaculate desk, moving the blotter to an exact position only he could see. Rosalind reached into her purse, pulled out the envelope stuffed with zlotys, and centered it on the blotter.

"All that is for you for just speeding up the forty-four visas for Mister Novy. The goodwill of Representative Johnson goes with it. He is a powerful man, as is Mister Novy."

"Please tell John Smith that I cannot help for the reasons I gave you earlier. Do not ask me again. When—not if—I am betrayed by someone here for helping Jews skip the line, all those zlotys and all the goodwill of people in America won't protect me or my family."

"Yes, I understand. You could take four of the visas for yourself. And the zlotys."

"I cannot leave Poland. Poland will not fall. We will wait this out." He pushed the envelope back towards her.

She picked it up, feeling its dead weight as she slipped it back into her purse. What was a situation so frightening to people that money could not fix it? She had failed.

CHAPTER 13

At five-thirty, Rosalind returned to her hotel room. She wrote a note to Jim Novy on the hotel's stationery, giving him the essentials of the invitation to the cocktail party that night at Ambassador Biddle's house. At the front desk, she told to the clerk, "Be sure Mister Novy gets this the minute he arrives," and slid the equivalent of half a clerk's day's wages into his open hand. In response, she got a definitive nod.

"A message for you, Miss Fisher. It just came in." He reached back and handed her an envelope with the seal of the British Embassy embossed on it. She turned away, tore it open and read, "*Called away to the west. Will make sure Frau B receives a version of what she lost courtesy of Queen Mary. Should send them on a wild goose chase. S.*"

Rosalind felt a wave of disappointment that Sidney wouldn't be at the party. She nodded at the clerk and walked upstairs.

In her room, she stripped, turned on the water in the bathtub, and watched it fill. When would she get the list of those Novy had selected for visas, a blessing promised but unfillable because there were no willing helpers at the embassy? Was there a word for a blessing that never happened? Ah, yes. *Jewish luck.* That was it.

When the water was warm, she sank into the tub, lathered up, and then ducked under the water to wash her hair and rinse off, grateful to not be troubled by other boarding house women knocking at the door or her landlady's glowering reminder that hot water was a limited commodity.

As she toweled off and began to prepare for the evening, Rosalind wondered if a direct approach to Ambassador Biddle might work. She could just tell him Johnson wanted these visas handled and let Biddle assume that Charles Marsh knew and approved, that the exquisite Alice Glass was all for it, and that the State Department was not a problem. With all of those people in support, how could the State Department object? She could keep Jim Novy and the Jewish angle out of sight and arrange for Johnson to call Biddle. It would be a straightforward request from a politician with wealthy connections.

She slid the chartreuse dress with the plunging neckline over her head and down her body, then she applied a light amount of make-up, using mascara to emphasize her eyes. Looking at herself in the full-length mirror, she was amazed at how completely poverty vanished with a silk dress, a cashmere scarf, and a great pair of shoes. "Ambassador Biddle, just a quiet word, if you please," she rehearsed.

Someone banged at her door. She looked through the peephole and saw Michal. "What do you want?"

"We are back. Mister Novy got your note from the front desk clerk. He told me to wait here until all three of you were ready. Where are you going?"

"Surely Mister Novy would have told you if he wanted you to know beforehand."

"Some areas are dangerous for Jews in Warsaw. Day by day the sewage rises. Don't be a stupid woman."

"To the residence of the United States Ambassador. I assume that is a safe neighborhood."

"Who will be there at this house? Maybe the Nazis with their tricks?"

Rosalind hadn't thought about the other guests, just her plan to speak to Biddle. Now she considered Nazis, their uniforms, their German voices. "It's possible."

"Let me in. I will behave. But we can't continue to talk through the door."

She unlocked the door and stepped back.

"We have the same interests, you and I," Michal said, closing the door behind him. "Keep Novy and the boy safe. Make sure the visas are approved. Get Novy and David out of the country and back to Texas so he can support his forty-four Jews." Michal looked around the room. Seeing nowhere to sit except the bed or sole desk chair, he leaned back against the door.

"Our interests narrowly overlap," Rosalind said. She stood near the desk. Her purse lay reachable on the desk chair, with the little derringer tucked inside.

"I wish to make a deal with you, Miss Rosalind Fisher of the United States." Michal lowered his voice and looked into her eyes. "We will make the paperwork of five of Mister Novy's selected people disappear from the files. Files, I remind you, that are in the car he has entrusted me with. We will substitute the documents for our people—yours and mine. That is four for you—your cousin and his three children—and one for me, for my brother. Good for you and me."

"And how will this be reconciled at the United States Embassy? The names, the necessary paperwork?" She didn't know if her questions were designed to buy time and convince Michal she was considering his proposal or if she was, in fact, serious. She had no one who would review all those documents, health records, and property records, and get Vice-Consul Fried to drop the melting wax and seal the process.

"You will find a way to do what's necessary. You are more like me than you want to believe underneath that dress. In which you look lovely, I must say."

She felt his gaze raking across her face and throat.

He motioned towards her face. "You are unadorned. No necklace or earrings?"

"No."

"I will fix that. I will have baubles for you by the time we are driving to this fancy house for your fancy party." He turned, opened the door, and left.

Rosalind sank onto the bed.

***

An hour later, the four of them stood next to the car, Michal holding the keys. Novy and David were dressed in identical charcoal gray suits, Jim with a white handkerchief and aqua tie, David with a dark gray handkerchief and red tie. Their shoes were polished to a glowing black satin. The housekeeping staff at the hotel must have worked overtime to get every piece steamed, ironed and gleaming.

"Give me just a moment, my dear Mister Novy. I have brought a necklace of my beloved mother for Miss Fisher to wear tonight." Michal reached into the pocket of his light summer jacket and pulled out a gold chain from which an emerald the size of an olive dangled.

"What a beauty," Jim Novy said. "Both the necklace and you, Miss Fisher. And your mother came upon that how exactly? A gift from your father, I assume?" Rosalind heard the knife edge of disbelief. Novy was a businessman with not an ounce of naiveté about the showpieces of wealth and how they were obtained. And Michal's father had been a friend of his.

Michal paused, then laughed. "I thought to say that it was my mother's was a gentler story."

"Still a story."

"I have borrowed this for tonight. From a fellow Jew, an industrialist, in exchange for limited services after you depart, sir. This is just my gesture of thanks to you and Miss Fisher."

Novy nodded. "I shall remind you once more that I did not leave my brains in America."

"Yes, sir. Quite true." Michal shifted from his left to his right foot and held the necklace up. "Miss Fisher, do you wish to wear this?"

Novy stared at her.

"No, I think not. It's far too valuable to risk."

Michal shrugged and dropped the necklace back in his pocket. "Let us leave then."

Other than the soft drumming of Novy's fingers on the back seat, the car ride was silent.

***

Inside the ambassadorial residence, a few dozen people were spread out from the large entry hall into the living room and adjoining rooms. French doors opened onto a patio lit by the sinking sun. The chairs and sofas were in the mid-European Art Nouveau style, all soft palettes and sinuous lines. Rosalind stood near the doors to breath the fresh air because the center of the party was dense with perfume, men's aftershave, cigarettes, and chatter that seemed to silence when she approached.

The Novys, however, had been whisked into the center of the room for introductions by Ambassador Biddle. Novy was smiling, David was sipping a cocktail and snagging appetizers whenever a plate went by.

Novy said something to David, who nodded and looked over at Rosalind before walking over to her. "My father wants you to join us."

"Of course."

Novy put his hand under Rosalind's elbow to pull her into the circle. "Representative Johnson graciously loaned us his staff person, Miss Fisher," he said. "She's observing the European situation and our embassy's work for him."

"Yes, I know. Miss Fisher and I met earlier today. I assume our staff is cooperating, Miss Fisher? That's a substantial task for someone as young as you," Biddle said.

"Your excellent staff is very cooperative, sir."

Biddle turned towards Novy and lowered his voice. "There are three guests from the German Embassy, Jim, that you may wish to steer clear of. Easy to know who they are with the swastika pins on their lapels. Bad fashion choice, but what can I say." He turned to Rosalind. "Miss Fisher, I know Lieutenant Collins is unable to join us. I hope you'll find other people here to your liking."

At the mention of his name, Rosalind longed for Sidney's smile, the feeling of her hand tucked into his arm as they walked through Warsaw. Stupid girl, she chided herself as she smiled back.

"Let me introduce you to my wife, Margaret. She'd love to hear any gossip from DC. Absent that, a friendly chat about anything American would be welcome. If you've gone to the American Museum of Natural History in New York, you might mention her father's collection of rocks, minerals, and gems. The museum got it a few years ago as part of his bequest."

"Thank you, Ambassador."

To her right, Novy stood scanning the room looking for incriminating lapel pins.

"I'd like to meet with you briefly alone tonight or tomorrow at the embassy, sir," Rosalind murmured to the ambassador.

He shook his head. "So sorry, Miss Fisher. Not tonight and I have an all-day meeting tomorrow at the French Embassy here in Warsaw. Vice-Consul Fried can assist in my absence. I doubt I'll be back until after dinner." His face was already turning away from her towards other, far more elevated guests, a smile at the ready.

"Yes, of course," Rosalind said, her throat tightening.

***

The gems on Margaret Biddle's neck and wrists were astonishing and Rosalind tried not to stare as the ambassador introduced Rosalind as "one of the House's up-and-coming young aides, here on government business, my dear."

"Welcome." Margaret introduced Rosalind to the three other women while Rosalind settled into the sofa next to one of them. Two Germans, one Pole—unclear who they were attached to—all speaking passable English, and therefore well-educated. Ilsa, Gerda, Lidia, in order, each smiling, knees tightly together, legs tilted to avoid bumping the coffee table in the middle, all dressed far more conservatively than Margaret. And more conservatively than Rosalind, who, having failed at her one important job, now felt almost naked and a bit tawdry.

Lidia was there because she served as a translator at the embassy whenever Biddle needed her, Margaret told her. According to Margaret, Lidia spoke and wrote in five languages. The two other women were wives of men at the party, men whose roles were vague within the German Embassy. Cultural Attaches or something.

"Do tell us what is going on in Washington on the street. I have only been able to read the *International Herald* and listen to the radio."

Margaret's flat mid-western accent was oddly comforting to Rosalind. If she could join in the discussion, possibly Margaret would have a way to reconnect her with Biddle tonight. Or tomorrow night, if the ambassador returned in time. But Rosalind's experience of Washington had been limited to the few days before she left. What could she say?

"The tourists are out in droves, of course."

"Of course." Margaret nodded.

"Department stores are bustling. You'd hardly know there is still a Depression."

"Indeed."

"As you know, Mister Marsh and Miss Glass have a lovely townhouse. The paintings…" She was draining out her limited experience in short sentences.

At that, Margaret said, "The Ambassador and I brought a few of our art pieces with us to Europe. Would you all like a tour?"

The three other women brightened at the diversion. Rosalind could only imagine how hard small talk in another language could become over the space of an hour.

The group moved from room to room, Margaret Biddle providing commentary on the paintings, which were a staid array of mid-level European and Hudson River Valley artists, all absent nudity, themes of war, or signs of poverty.

One of the women whispered to the other in German, "Just what our dear Führer would like." Now Rosalind could match them to whatever men wore little swastika pins in the main rooms. She noticed that the word *Führer* caused a slight wrinkling of Lidia, the Polish woman's, nose, as if she'd smelled skunk, quickly masked with an astute question in impeccable American English about the New York landscape around the Hudson River.

When they returned to the main room, Lidia said, "Mrs. Biddle, I am going to go onto the lovely patio for a few minutes. The cigar smoke… Rosalind, would you like to join me?"

The three other women looked up with varying levels of quickly masked surprise.

Rosalind said, "Of course."

They walked out without speaking. Lidia took Rosalind's hand and pulled her towards the farthest end of the patio. She leaned close and began speaking Spanish in a whisper, "Do you understand me?"

Rosalind nodded.

"Good. No one else will. Stop what you are doing. You asked about people at the embassy specifically when you were there, people sympathetic to the Jewish situation. Then you tried with someone whose own standing is perilous at best, with his wife's family having a Jewish background. Did you think word wouldn't get around? We know our own and we talk."

"I'm new at this."

"It shows. Naïve. And from a country with no interest, vested or otherwise, in the dangers of middle-Europe. They put a man like Biddle—foppish and weak—in charge of a basket full of vipers and expect him to keep the lid on." Lidia shook her head.

"I need visas stamped."

"Of course." Lidia shook her head and laughed. "We all do. Truly, you'd be better off hiring a burglar. You won't get any cooperation from the Polish staff. Too scared. And none of the Americans want to violate Hull's agenda, which is to avoid filling the Eastern European visa allotment altogether."

"You're scared?"

Lidia leaned towards Rosalind and gave her an air-kiss on the cheek. In Polish she said, "Thank you so much for letting me speak in Spanish with you, Senorita Fisher. Your accent is not Castilian but only a Spaniard would pick that up. Maybe I will see you again."

Rosalind smiled, continuing in her apparently Texas-Mexican Spanish, "I'll be at the embassy tomorrow. Do you have a visa application in?" Maybe she could bribe her.

Lidia switched back to Spanish. "I was born in Spain. I have two passports. That will get me out of here. Lucky me. Others, not so much." Lidia gave her a second air-kiss and walked away.

***

Rosalind stayed on the patio, wondering how on Earth she would get forty-four Jews out of Poland. She hadn't cared which ones before she met Jakub and his children, but now… If no one at the embassy would help, she'd have to find help elsewhere.

She walked out the mansion's front door, past the US Marine standing watch. Michal was leaning against the car, smoking a cigarette like he was in a Bogart movie. With a slight smile forced onto her face in front of clenched teeth, Rosalind approached him.

"Party over?" He threw the cigarette onto the gravel and ground it out with his heel.

"No. I'm considering your offer to help in exchange for another visa."

He tilted his head. "Go on."

"That is, if you can help me solve a problem that will prevent you and anyone else from getting one."

Michal remained silent. Rosalind said nothing. The quiet stretched out to include a few owl hoots and the shush-shushing of tires on the road where all the cars were parked. Guests were leaving.

"What's the problem?"

"It isn't suitable for discussion here. A quiet corner of the hotel lounge around eight-thirty…"

"I will take you to a restaurant."

"No." She wouldn't be on her own with Michal. She didn't trust him and apparently neither did Novy. Better to try her luck again at the embassy despite what Lidia had said.

"I'll go back in and wait for Mister Novy." She turned.

"Fine. The hotel lounge. Eight-thirty."

***

As they prepared to leave, Novy pointed David to the front passenger seat. He took the seat behind David, leaving Rosalind the one behind Michal.

"Put on some music, Michal," Novy said.

The radio had two stations, one of which was playing something classical, with an earthy, rhythmic undertone, that Rosalind didn't recognize.

"Tchaikovsky. Symphony number two," Michal said. "Enjoy." He turned the volume up and waved his right hand as if conducting.

"Pay attention to the road, please."

With that, Michal put his hand back on the steering wheel and turned the music up another notch.

Novy shook his head. Then he leaned in towards Rosalind. "What news from your day at the embassy?"

"I met the ambassador…"

"Yes. Not that news."

"Nothing. I am working on another plan."

"How much will it cost?"

"I don't know, sir."

"Do whatever it takes. Cost is not an object."

"I will."

"We have only two days left. And the ambassador told me something that will drastically change our plans to return home, and possibly yours and Michal's and the others', as well."

"Sir?"

"I will tell you later. After I have taken care of the business I need to." Novy turned to stare out the passenger-side window at the passing scenery, then pressed his forehead into the glass. "You were right, my boy," he said over the music. "We should have brought your camera to take pictures. A once in a lifetime experience that we now have only in our heads."

"Yes, Poppa."

***

She'd had a single glass of champagne and two small cheese appetizers at the party. Now, despite all her worries, Rosalind was hungry. She changed quickly into a simple dress unlikely to draw attention and went to the lounge. There she ordered a dinner plate of fresh trout with potatoes—potatoes being, along with beets and cabbages, constant presences in Poland. As she put the last forkful into her mouth, Michal walked in and came over.

"Do you know anything about Novy's change of plans?" he asked, sliding into the seat opposite her.

"No." She took a sip of water.

Michal picked up the last thumb-sized piece of bread from the basket on the table, swabbed it with butter using her knife, and popped it in his mouth.

"I didn't eat much tonight," he said.

"The lounge has a menu."

He shook his head. "Overpriced food for foreigners."

"Can we talk about the important issue?"

"Sure, Rosalind. You know what it is. I don't."

"I cannot as yet find someone able and willing to help with the visas at the embassy. If I can't by tomorrow, say mid-morning, I will need a plan to find the visa seal, use it on our applications, forge the vice-consul's signature, and move on."

"Interesting. Complicated." Michal held his hand up as the waiter passed. "A scotch on the rocks."

A man who wouldn't eat overpriced food but who would drink overpriced liquor. Life was full of choices, Rosalind thought.

"Of the contacts at the embassy, one is on vacation, one now is at another embassy, and one has immigrated. The other is a Pole who was recently promoted. He was supposed to be our best hope, but he is scared because his wife has a Jewish parent. I tried to talk to him, but he shut me down. He's probably persuadable with money and time. I offered money, but we have no time."

The scotch came and Michal downed half the glass. "Anyone else in the direct visa chain?"

"An American. Very by-the-book. Not on my list."

"But you should try him, my dear Miss Fisher." Michal smiled at the scotch on the table. "Cheers," he said, then drank the rest in one gulp.

"No. Too dangerous if he decides to tell the vice-consul or ambassador. I need your help, Michal. Who do you know who can burglarize Vice-Consul Fried's office, find the seal, and stamp the visas with me? Who can imitate Fried's signature?"

"You've seen too many American gangster movies, read too many spy novels."

"You can comment after I finish."

He raised his hand to bring the waiter over.

"I'd prefer you sober." Rosalind waved the waiter away.

Michal looked angry for a half-second before he shrugged. "Fine."

"At lunch, the Americans leave the embassy, including Fried, so far as I can tell. Hank Martin—the by-the-books guy—didn't leave today because of me, but I'll figure out a way to make him go tomorrow."

"They head for a bar, the Americans and the Brits. Drown their sorrows, moan about the Poles," Michal said.

"I'll take your word for it. They are gone for a good hour-and-a-half. During that time, it seems the Polish employees relax in the cafeteria. The people waiting are ushered back outside to make do as they can without losing their place in line. This leaves time to break into Fried's office, get the seal, use it on our visas, and leave." She sat back to see his response.

"And the signature?"

"We'll need a forger. Fried signs them, so tomorrow, somehow, I will get a sample of his signature. You show up at eleven. I'll tell them you're coming because Jim Novy sent you for some reason. I'll make it up."

"I'll have papers for you. That's the reason. And I have someone who can help with the signature. Another Jew, an artist, well-trained," he said.

"I have lots of zlotys."

He shook his head. "She's not a fool. She'll do this for a visa."

"Sure." Another Jew. What did it matter in the end? The immigrants would come in through New York and the ones Novy didn't know would scatter to the winds. Novy might ask questions, but Rosalind would have a story, or she'd scatter to the winds, too. Blow herself to Chicago or California or Oregon. Start all over.

***

Rosalind laid back on her pillow, wishing she were back in her boarding house room with her no-account job at Woolworth and her few classes left to go until her BA. She rolled back and forth, pounded the pillow, slid under the covers, then tossed and turned until her eyes finally closed.

A knock at the door awakened her. "Yes?"

"Dress and come to my father's suite."

"What time is it?"

"Five-fifteen. The time he's always up to start the day."

"David…"

There was no answer.

***

In the sitting room of his suite, Novy pointed Rosalind to a chair by the table where coffee and a plate of bread and cheese were waiting. Rosalind poured herself a cup of coffee and began to sip.

"Ambassador Biddle received credible warnings that we should not return to port through Germany or Austria. We are effectively limited to the Polish major port of Gdynia, to the north. You will go with us to Gdynia, of course. We will not go on to Palestine, sadly, but will return to America."

Rosalind continued to sip her coffee while she considered the news.

"There's a threat to us even though we're citizens of the United States?" she asked, setting her cup in its saucer.

"There is a threat to me because I am a rich Jew. The Nazi dogs can grab me in Germany on a pretext, hold me in a prison—and David, as well—and demand a king's ransom to release me, which my wife would pay. They'll have no trouble making it seem legal. German judges have become puppets in this Nazi circle of hell."

David walked over to where his father sat to put a hand on his shoulder. To Rosalind, in those few steps, he'd become a younger version of his father, face set, mouth firm.

"And how easy will it be for our forty-four Jewish visa holders to leave Poland, then?" Rosalind asked.

"The Poles will be happy to see them go, especially because they will leave everything behind—houses, gardens, farms, factories, synagogues…" Novy's words caught and he stopped.

"You visited your brothers, sir. How are they?" Rosalind worried that Novy would decide to bring his brothers to America after all, two more to worry about.

"My brothers, oh my brothers. Aged beyond my recognition. Fragile in their bodies and in their minds. We'll rescue those who understand what they are leaving. Those who can live beyond this rising filth. Not my brothers." Novy's voice shook. He took a sip of water from a glass. "No, I have my list of forty-four healthy, capable adults and children. I'll give it to you today."

The acrid taste of the coffee made Rosalind's stomach queasy. She felt Novy had aged years in the time they'd been traveling, lines of worry etched into his brow, eyes squinting as if some event in the distance had to be brought into focus. The affection she felt for him and David surprised her. But she had four people of her own to get into America and Michal had his brother and the forger. Six people from Novy's list had to stay.

"I'll need the list as soon as possible, sir."

"Yes. When the visas are ready, you'll tell me. I'll have them notified. It'll take a day for them to get to Gdynia. They have their bags packed and know who they are handing the keys to the homes and businesses over to."

"They'll also leave through that port?"

"Yes. I thought at first Germany and on to the Atlantic seaboard, but if it is known that they are my people, there is the worry that they, too, might be held for ransom. And I would pay. The French ports are far away and perilous to get to. So, it must be this Baltic port. They'll go through and out. Tickets are being held at the manifest office for them there. With a bonus, of course, to the ship's agents for that."

"You have thought this through very clearly, sir."

"I didn't make my millions being stupid, Rosalind. My folks better all show up in Texas or I will find out why."

David nodded behind his father, a slight flush on his cheeks, then put his hand on his father's shoulder again.

"I need to return to my room and get ready to go to the embassy this morning. If at all possible, I'd like to have the list now, sir."

"Of course." Novy walked over to the small desk, picked up two sheets of paper with handwriting on them, and gave them to her. Rosalind took them, surprised that the weight of forty-four lives was so light.

***

She returned to her room, sank to the bed, and wrapped her arms around her body.

The phone on her nightstand rang. "This is your six-thirty wake-up call. And we received an envelope for you last night." The front desk staff person's voice was female, familiar, cool. The *Heil Hitler* woman from the first day.

"I'll be down to get it." Rosalind kept her voice cold, dismissive, the way she imagined a woman of higher rank would treat a mere hotel employee. She put down the receiver, checked her face in the bathroom mirror, and left the room. The walk to the lobby was short and cleared her head.

When Rosalind reached the desk and saw the package Matilde handed to her, she knew immediately it had been tampered with.

"Did you try to open this? I am a citizen of the United States. How dare you!" Rosalind pointed at the slight tear on the seal flap and a rumple where the gum hit the paper.

Matilde tried glaring back but quickly dropped her eyes.

"You've made a terrible mistake messing with my mail. Where is the manager?"

"Madam, please wait."

"What, then. Who did this?"

"Do you understand any Polish? I could explain better if you did."

Rosalind shook her head 'no.' She wasn't going to give up her advantage just to hear a weak excuse.

"*Glupia krowa*," Matilde whispered, a slight smile creeping onto her lips.

She'd been called worse than a stupid cow in her life. And Matilde had just lost any credibility. Rosalind imitated Matilde's smile and deepened her Texas accent so Matilde had to lean over the counter to make sense of her words. "I don't know what you said and I'm still waiting for you to explain the tear in my envelope."

"It was like that."

"Unlikely. Who brought it in? Someone from the embassy, perhaps?" Rosalind sighed, shook her head, a picture of incredulity by a connected American. She was rewarded by Matilde's sidewise glance towards the door to the back office.

"I think not the embassy. Too early," Matilde said quietly. "Around five-thirty this morning. A man. A Polish man—well-dressed, spoke like an educated person from Warsaw. He was maybe mid-forties. He only asked for you and gave us the envelope when we told him you were asleep."

"Did he tip you?"

"In zlotys. Only enough for a coffee." Matilde shook her head.

Rosalind didn't need to press for more details. She'd gotten enough from Matilde's glance to the back office to think that the hotel was crawling with staff sympathetic to Germany. Staff well-placed enough to keep underlings in line. Staff who had access to all the rooms.

She'd need to alert Novy that any paperwork he had that he did not want in the hands of the wrong people had better go into the car guarded by Michal. And she'd try to alert the right people at the US Embassy today that anyone should be cautious if they stayed here—if, that is, she could figure out who the right people at the embassy were.

Rosalind walked back up the stairs with the envelope. Once she rounded the steps and Matilde couldn't see her, she studied the flap again. She knew nothing about steaming envelopes open, next to nothing about how it would look to reseal one. But in her boarding house, some women would swear they'd taken an envelope out of the wrong cubby by accident, opened it, and resealed it once they knew it wasn't theirs. And if a distant aunt had sent a few dollars to help tide someone over and one of those dollars had been miscounted, wasn't that just like an old person to not count well?

Once in her room, door locked, she opened the letter. In an elegant European script, the letter read: *Dear Cousin Rosalind, We are increasingly confined to our apartment and at risk. In two days, if we do not hear from you, I will take the children to Gdynia and use all my resources to flee to Sweden by ship. I have sold my apartment and whatever is in it. I have cash and will find someone who will help us. We will start anew. I am, after all, a physician.*

Rosalind felt a mixture of relief and worry. Jakub saw the situation for what it was. Flee through any door, break it open if he had to. But how sure was it that he could bring himself and the children into Sweden? She'd ask at the embassy.

***

Michal opened the door for her and then got into the driver's seat. "I'll drop you at the embassy. I will return at eleven and we will do what we need to."

"Yes. I think I will not need four visas. You can do what you want about your brother. I won't say anything to Mister Novy."

"Your cousin has changed his mind? Foolish man."

"He has money and will go to Sweden with the children in two days."

Michal brought the car to a stop at a light and shifted into neutral. He tapped his long fingers on the steering wheel and Rosalind remembered, with a start, that he had been a concert pianist.

"Rosalind."

"What?"

"I know you do not trust me. But your cousin is taking a blind alley. Sweden will send him back."

"He's a doctor!"

The light changed. A car honked behind them. Michal shifted gears and their car moved on.

"The students at the Uppsala University in Sweden have gone on strike against Sweden admitting more Jewish doctors. The Swedish government has tightened its refugee policy yet again. Your cousin will not get into Sweden. And he will have no money."

"He might get in." Rosalind gripped her thighs through her skirt.

"He might get in." Michal's voice was high, whiny. "Just like our great professors, artists, and musicians might get in the United States, too?" He scoffed. "How rare is it to be an Einstein? Even a Doctor Loewi?"

"Loewi?" Rosalind asked, remembering the story of the Viennese conductor Eric Leinsdorf Lady Bird Johnson had told her, rescued by Representative Johnson only because of Charles Marsh's intervention.

"Loewi is a German Jew who won the Nobel Prize in physiology in 1936. In March of this year—this year, Rosalind! —he was arrested by the Nazis in Germany. June, he is freed and off he goes to France to teach, minus his prize money, his house, his possessions, even his research. All signed over to the thugs. Voluntarily, say the thugs. Do you think in Warsaw we don't read the papers, listen to the news? I repeat, your cousin is a fool if he tries to go to Sweden."

Her cousin was a fool and so was she, Rosalind thought. There was no chance she would be able to pull this off.

"Let's go through the names and the papers Novy gave us, Michal. Maybe there are five who somehow can't go or have change their minds."

"Six. We need a forger and the forger will demand a visa."

Rosalind nodded. The burden was on her to find the visas and the seal, to get Michal into the embassy, and then to disappear so Novy and Lyndon Baines Johnson could never find her.

"Please get word to my cousin not to leave or to give his money to anyone." She wrote out his name and address on a sheet of paper. "He has a telephone."

"I'll go in person, I promise. I am not a bad person, Rosalind, just a desperate one."

Rosalind could see Michal's smile. She tried to smile back.

CHAPTER 14

"Representative Johnson, acting for the House of Representatives of the United States, demands that I have a step-by-step understanding of the visa application process," Rosalind told Hank Martin. "This means knowing where the visas are stored in the embassy, who does the interviewing, what the common errors are, how those are fixed in a timely fashion, and finally, how the visas receive the seal and are returned to the applicants." Rosalind kept her voice flat and tried to act like a long-suffering employee of a demanding boss. "Unfortunately, I did not obtain all of that information yesterday."

Hank Martin clamped his lips together, his retort flushing his cheeks but not making it out of his mouth. Instead, he nodded.

"Because I have to type up my notes, I will not join you and the other Americans for lunch. It's the only time I will have. You'll provide me with a desk and a typewriter in a quiet space. That should not be a problem since I have clearance to be here."

"Miss Fisher, the only desks are in our offices. There aren't any typewriters in them. Those are in the secretarial pool."

"Well, then, I'll have to be in one of your offices and you will need to find a typewriter for me to use. And because the report I'm working on is confidential to the representative, I need to be able to lock the office if I have to exit. Otherwise, I'll be carrying my notes and everything all over the embassy. Unacceptable. Finally, Mister Novy's chauffeur, who has provided safe transportation all over Poland, will be coming to deliver papers. Michal Maltin."

"Michal Maltin, the pianist? I heard him play Beethoven's Concerto Number Five."

"Yes."

"I suppose it's a tough life for classical musicians now."

"Indeed. We're clear about what I need?"

"Crystal."

***

One after another, seven family groups entered Martin's office, where he interviewed them, inspected the paperwork they'd brought, and sent them away for another bank statement, a different certificate from the doctor, a new date on the military clearance form. One couple had to start over because their baby had been born in the eight months since they began the process and now required papers of his own.

Rosalind expected more drama, crying and threats, but it seemed to be buried under the weight of resignation, the expectation of delay, and the thick gray cloud of bureaucracy.

One couple had everything in order. They were young, maybe in their thirties, dressed in clothes so new Rosalind wondered if the store tags were still on them. The man gripped the woman's hand with a fierceness that turned it white. A Polish last name, which meant nothing about whether they were Jewish or not so far as Rosalind knew—with an aunt and uncle in Maryland who owned a set of drug stores. Rosalind acted as if she didn't understand Polish and the wife, who'd majored in English literature at the university, translated for her. Then she added, in English, "We are so relieved."

"I'll need to watch every aspect of the provision of the visa," Rosalind said. The couple acted as if they'd be thrilled to have an onlooker, as if she were witnessing their wedding.

The couple, the unsealed visa, all their forms, and Rosalind walked upstairs to Ambassador Biddle's floor accompanied by an embassy guard. They stopped at Biddle's secretary's desk, always staffed whether Biddle was in the embassy or not.

"Take these over to Mister Fried," she said. "He'll do the final check, sign, and put the official seal on. Hurry before he leaves for lunch."

***

"Congratulations," Fried said as he took the paperwork, glancing at Rosalind. "We need to be careful because there are some forged visas out there."

She clasped her hands to keep them from shaking. Fried knew nothing of her intentions, she reminded herself. He was only saying that for the benefit of her report to Representative Johnson, to let him know the embassy was diligent.

Fried took a pen and signed the visa. Then he unlocked the drawer on the top right of his desk and pulled out a seal and a red wax stick with a wick. Lighting the wick, he watched as wax dripped onto the lower left corner of the visa.

"Amazing how hard it is to get just the right amount for the seal," he said. He blew out the wick, stamped the visa, and left a perfect impression. He handed the sealed documents to the wife. "Wait a minute for it to harden. You don't want to ruin it."

"Will I see you at lunch, Miss Fisher?" he asked when the Polish couple turned to leave.

"No, Vice-Consul Fried. I have a report to write while the information is fresh in my mind."

"Indeed." He put the seal back in the drawer, locked it, and put the key in his jacket pocket.

***

A guard had told Rosalind that Mister Novy's chauffeur was waiting for her at eleven. By noon, Martin had interviewed a total of twelve sets of applicants, of which only the young couple had made it through. Martin pushed his chair back from his desk.

"Is that typical of your day?"

"Some days no one has it right all morning and it creeps into the afternoon. Then it's like a streak of bad luck hits them all and it can go on for a few days. It's too bad, really. Miss Fisher, I don't care who goes to America and who doesn't," he said, shrugging. "I care about doing my job right. If the rules change every hour, I change."

Martin got up, went to his office door, and said, "Miss Kaminski, please bring your typewriter in here and put it on my desk."

A sturdy, dark haired woman picked up her typewriter, walked in, and put it down. As she did, Rosalind saw Michal sitting on the bench farther down the hall.

"Michal, Mister Martin is a fan of yours," she said in English. Martin repeated the sentiment in Polish, adding his own compliments to the pianist. Michal rose with a smile and took a slight bow. As Martin walked towards the exit, Michal accompanied him, heads tipped slightly together. Rosalind heard Michal laugh. Then he returned to Rosalind, the office, the typewriter, and the problem of the visas.

"We need the forger," Rosalind whispered. "And something with Fried's signature. Also the visa seal. How good are you at breaking in without leaving a trace?"

"Passable. My brother is better."

"Your brother is not here. How did the talk with Jakub go?"

"He will postpone his effort to flee to Sweden for a day and wait in Gdynia for you starting tomorrow. He has contacts who are in Stockholm but if he is delayed too long—a day, I don't know—that opportunity disappears in the mist. Since I believe it was a phantasmagoria, nothing will be lost, especially not his money."

"And his papers?"

"Here." He pointed to a weathered, tan briefcase. "I told him I would return them to his apartment this afternoon if we did not have the visas and call him—three rings, hang up, two rings—if we did."

Rosalind shut Martin's office door and she and Michal walked up the stairway towards Fried's office. The front office staff had left; only the building's entry doors were guarded by security.

***

As Michal studied the lock on the door, Rosalind grabbed a letter from the Outgoing Mail box on Fried's secretary's desk and opened it. She smiled. Fried's signature, or at least his secretary's facsimile, was on it. "Look," she said, showing it to Michal.

Michal nodded and returned his attention to the lock, working it with a small pick. Rosalind felt she was in another world. "Quickly," she whispered, and Michal shook his head as if the word would bounce off it.

"Now." He opened the door. They slid inside and closed it behind them.

He opened the briefcase. "You find four people who will not go, and I will find two. I've thought about this, and I don't think it matters. Except that families should be together."

"Agreed." Rosalind felt nothing about his idea except relief as if a path in a thorn hedge had been hacked out for her.

In five minutes, Rosalind had a set of four unaccompanied men set aside. Not only couldn't she split up a family, but someone in the family would certainly know a member was missing and complain to Novy or worse. She put back three others, including two women, who stated on their applications that Jim Novy was a cousin who was hiring them into one of his businesses.

Rosalind had refused to read the applications closely, to avoid any detail that might impact her decisions. She firmly believed what you did in life defined you and then you died. This act of dividing the saved and the doomed would be her definition. It wasn't a role she would have chosen for herself, but now that she was in it, there were no options but to forge ahead.

"Where's the seal, Rosalind?"

"Top side drawer of the desk. You have to pick that one, too."

Michal snorted, hunched down, and wiggled his pick. She heard it clicking, then heard him tug on the drawer, which came out partly then stuck.

He pulled again. Still stuck.

"Wait, wait. Let me see if something's jamming the drawer." She slipped four fingers in and swept them around as best she could.

"Hang on. There's something in there. I'll try to tip it over. Oww!" She pulled her hand out and inspected her finger, which was nicked and pearled with a drop of blood.

"A boobytrap or a letter opener gone rogue? Let's see." Michal pushed the pick inside and moved it around. "There." A kitchen knife stood on end. "Not a well thought out snare. You Americans have much to learn." He pulled out the drawer and plucked out the seal and wax and the knife. "All will go back in order."

"Let me see who you pulled out for your brother and the forger, Michal. I will need to know the names in case Novy asks me where they are." Rosalind sucked the blood off the tiny cut, wrapped a small portion of her black skirt's hem around her finger, and looked around for blood spots on the floor. There weren't any she could see.

Michal began to heat the wax and drip it onto a visa form. "I've thought about it. If he asks you about anyone, you say there was a paperwork problem at the very end. There's always a paperwork problem."

"What if they go to Gdynia ready to leave?" Rosalind handed him another visa.

"I will try to call the unfortunates to tell them we have no visas for them because of the paperwork, and we ran out of time. Maybe they've not yet abandoned their homes and livelihoods. If I fail, they will be in Gdynia and…"

Michal let his thought go unfinished and concentrated on applying the wax seal to the visas. It seemed the time it took to finalize saving a life was amazingly short—thirty seconds at most for each visa. When all the visas had seals, they replaced the seal, wax, and the knife, then shut the drawer and Michal relocked it.

Standing outside Fried's office, Rosalind hid Michal as best she could as he tried to get the lock to the outer door to catch. After four tries, he gave up.

"You must go now, Michal," she whispered. "Get the forger to work. I will stay and finish out the day as if nothing has happened. Maybe Fried will think he forgot to lock up."

"Be safe." Michal turned and walked down the stairs with the forty-four visas in his bag.

Rosalind peered over the balustrade. She watched him stride toward the door. As she began to turn away, she saw Michal come back inside. He was walking backwards, and a US Marine was pointing a gun at his chest.

"What are you doing?" Rosalind yelled as she ran down the stairs. "You there, with the gun!"

The Marine shook his head and pointed Michal towards a bench. Michal settled onto it and crossed his legs, the handle of the bag still in his left hand.

"Foreign nationals leaving our embassy with bags is my business," the Marine said. "Now how is this any of your business, ma'am?" The guard—young, sandy blonde hair and blue eyes, a Norman Rockwell kind of kid—spoke in a flat mid-western accent.

Rosalind weighed her options. If she told this guard she worked for Representative Johnson and Michal was her driver and then he found the visas with the stamps, it would be a disaster for everyone, including Johnson, probably. But the longer she took to explain, the more likely Fried would return to his unlocked office and put out a cry of alarm. That would also be a disaster for everyone.

"I'm…an aide in the House of Representatives. I had the pleasure of going to Ambassador Biddle's reception last night. Were you there?"

She got a head shake.

"This man is my driver. In his bag he has documents related to the dire situations of just forty-four of the applicants for visas to the United States. These are accurate *copies*—I emphasize they are copies—of what the people have submitted here. We may release them to the newspapers and radio stations in the United States to…"

"Won't help, lady. This here is a slow-moving operation, staffed by folks who care about their paychecks. Problems get worse, we'll all go home to the States and Poland can figure it out on its own. It's a little country in a big continent."

Michal shifted forward on the bench.

"Good thing my driver doesn't understand a word of English."

"Yeah? So how do you give him directions?"

"Polish. Listen." She turned her back to the guard and said, in Polish, "Reach slowly into the bag and pull out just two visa applications. No stamped visas. Act dumb."

She turned back to the guard. "I've just told him to show you the copies of the visa applications we have," Rosalind said in English.

Michal handed two sheets of paper over. He'd managed to pluck a father and ten-year-old boy out.

"See here, lieutenant… It is lieutenant, right?"

"Corporal, ma'am."

She smiled. "Corporal, you see, this is a family. That's all. Just papers."

"I have to look through the bag."

"Those papers are my property, not the embassy's. So, I think not. I've shown you everything I'm going to. Now let my driver go. We are on a deadline, and I have more work to do and a report to draft. If you don't let us go immediately, I'll make sure the ambassador knows about this." She drew herself up to her full height and stared at the corporal.

"Well, ma'am, if what you say is true, and I have no way to judge that, then this fellow can wait for Vice-Consul Fried to return from lunch and you can both explain. Meantime, I won't look in the bag."

"*Co zrobisz?*" Michal asked her.

She didn't know what to do.

"You will excuse me so I can return to the office I am using," she said. "I need to lock the door."

"No, ma'am. You're part of this. In fact, I'd like to see you on the bench next to your driver where I can keep an eye on you both."

"Corporal, you are making this much harder than it needs to be."

"Just sit down." He waved his gun towards her.

"*Zastrzel go.*" Michal's tone of voice was surprisingly normal as he told Rosalind to kill the Marine.

Rosalind considered this. All she had to do was reach into her purse for the derringer tucked in its lining. Michal would escape. But a young man, just doing his duty, would be dead. And she would have to explain.

"Colonel, let me have him show you a few more papers. Michal, *kiedy się do mnie zwróci, znokautuj go i uciekaj. Możesz to zrobić?"*

Michal sighed. "Jeśli to nie zadziała, wiesz, co robić."

She nodded. If her plan to have Michal knock the guy out didn't work, she'd have to kill him.

"Showing me more paperwork won't change a thing, lady," the corporal said. "I'm not in charge."

Michal slammed his right fist into the man's blonde head. As the corporal tilted away, Michal finished with an uppercut to the stomach. The man's gun fell to the floor.

"For God's sake, hurry!" she hissed at Michal, who turned and ran.

Rosalind knelt, shoved the gun far under the bench away from the downed soldier, and then checked to see if he was breathing. He was. She sat on the floor next to him, cradling his head in her lap. She was close enough to read his nametag. "Poor Jerry," she said and patted his cheek. Then she began to think about how to explain herself, the lack of a report she was supposed to be working on over lunch, and why she'd chosen a driver like Michal—or why Novy had.

CHAPTER 15

"I cooperated completely with the corporal when he stopped us. Corporal Jerry Hank, right? I explained that this man, Michal Limowitz—I think that's his last name—was a driver for Mister Novy and for me, if Mister Novy didn't require him."

She watched Fried write Michal Limowitz on a notepad and prayed that Martin, who knew Michal's real last name, wouldn't be asked about this incident.

"Go on," he said.

"The driver had a satchel with copies of visa applications. Examples of families who'd applied and were still waiting final approval. You know, Mister Fried, that is what Representative Johnson and his good friend, Mister Marsh, are interested in—among other issues impacting America, of course."

"How were you involved, Miss Fisher?"

"Just like Corporal Hank asked me to, I was giving instructions in Polish to Mister Limowitz. I don't know why he knocked the poor corporal out."

"And I don't suppose you know why he ran or why my office door was mysteriously unlocked?" Fried's words were icy.

"No."

"You were the only non-official personnel left in the building, Miss Fisher. He was your driver. So, logically, my suspicions rest on you."

"I can understand that. But really, the cafeteria was full of Polish employees, plus there was Corporal Hank and another guard at the front door, if I'm not mistaken."

"Let me correct myself. You are the only one who's not been carefully investigated. The only one who doesn't have others vouching for her whereabouts."

"Ah." Rosalind crossed her left leg over her right and pulled down her skirt, grateful again that the black hid the blood from her finger. "Since you have those thoughts about me, I'd prefer to continue this discussion with Ambassador Biddle present. Really, this whole situation is dreadfully stressful." She felt her stomach turn in confirmation, bile moving to her throat. Forcing a swallow, she said, "I need to go to the lady's room."

"No."

"A…" She was going to ask for his wastepaper basket, but her stomach protested again. She turned away from Fried and vomited onto the rug.

"My God." Fried pushed himself back from the desk and stood up. "Have you no self-control, woman?"

She pulled her handkerchief out of her purse and wiped her mouth and nose, blew, and wiped again.

Fried stepped around the other side of the desk. "Miss Jankowski, in here now."

His secretary looked up from her typewriter. "Sir?" Unaccented American English, so probably a US citizen from birth, Rosalind guessed. Polish ancestry, though, from her last name. Impossible to know where her sympathies lay.

"And the janitors, immediately. All of them. There's been an unfortunate event in my office caused by Miss Fisher here."

"Miss, are you alright?" Miss Jankowski stood next to her, the smell of vomit apparently not a deterrent to carrying out her duties.

Rosalind shook her head and looked pathetic, which was how she felt.

"I'll take her to the ladies' restroom, sir. Clean her up best we can. Is that good for you, Miss Fisher?"

"Please." Rosalind stood up.

"Leave your purse and any identification here, Miss Fisher." Fried pointed to the chair.

Rosalind hesitated.

Miss Jankowski said, "Sir, possibly Miss Fisher will need something in her purse." She offered it in a quiet, hesitant way—the mouse speaking to the lion.

"Fine. Take it."

"Not coming down with something, are you Miss Fisher?" Miss Jankowski whispered as they turned right in the hall.

"No. I think everything got to me. All the people trying to leave—hundreds of them with so little hope. There's the whole problem with Hitler, and then that poor young man beaten up by my very own driver."

Miss Jankowski nodded and put her arm around Rosalind's waist. "Not to mention the Depression, the Dust Bowl… This world is not for the faint of heart."

Rosalind sighed. "We women—single and fending for ourselves—we have to stick together. Did Mister Limowitz take anything from anywhere? Anything important? How much trouble do you think he's in?"

"Nothing's missing that I know of. Vice-Consul Fried's door was unlocked but everything was there, he said. And I looked around my desk—all in order."

"How odd." Rosalind's relief eased the stomach cramp.

"Isn't it? Maybe your driver's got other problems he doesn't want to be found out for. Like in the movies, ya' know. Gangster connections, the black market. Here's the restroom. Let's get you as cleaned up as we can. And can I say something just between us?"

Rosalind nodded.

"Fried—he's a dyed in the wool bureaucrat. Anything out of place, out of the ordinary, and he's like a wet cat. So good luck," Miss Jankowski whispered.

"Hmm… Gangsters, black market. I wouldn't be surprised. After all, these are hard times. Crime is up everywhere. Thank you for your help," Rosalind said, then stepped into the bathroom.

***

An hour-and-a-half later Rosalind, Vice-Consul Fried and the only attorney the State Department had assigned to the US Embassy in Poland sat in a conference room. Rosalind had stacked a thin sheaf of typed papers from her desperate key-slapping in Martin's office on the table and laid her passport on top. Her purse was on the table, too, emptied of everything except the derringer, still tucked under the bottom lining, light enough to be mistaken for part of the purse's weight.

"Who are you supposed to be helping here?" She turned to the attorney, whose name tag read Herbert Small.

"My job is making sure everyone is protected and the laws are followed. An attack on a US Marine has taken place on United States property. You're a witness."

"I've told you what I saw."

"You saw nothing suspicious in the building beforehand?"

"I was just coming out of the woman's restroom when I heard the ruckus. I'd been trying to type a report in Martin's office just before." She waved at the papers.

Small tapped his forefinger on the table. "What committee of the House authorized you to come and do a report, Miss Fisher?"

"Committee?" Damn Eleanor for not preparing her for this question. "I'm sorry, sir. Did I ever say I was making a report for a committee?" She didn't think she had but the blood pounding in her ears made it hard to hear the sound of her own voice.

She was rewarded by a slight clenching of the lips and no reply.

"The Honorable Representative Lyndon Baines Johnson of Texas hired me because of my linguistic skills. I was to come to Poland with Mister James Novy and his son, accompany them through their travels, and make a report on what the situation was in the smaller towns of Poland, especially impacting those of the Jewish faith."

"So why are you in the embassy?"

"I was also asked to report to Representative Johnson on how the visa process was going. Both he and his friend, Charles Marsh, the owner of several newspapers, are concerned…" She let her voice trail off.

"Why did Representative Johnson take this on himself, rather than just ask the people who are in charge to tell him?"

"Mister Small, I…" Anything she said would bring another question. She saw that now. "I can't tell you why, sir. I was asked to do this, and I agreed. It seemed interesting and a way to better myself. I just want to be a high school teacher when I get back to Texas." No need to suggest she understood anything except American English.

Small nodded. "All right. I won't pursue that more right now. If we need to, Ambassador Biddle can make a few discreet inquiries."

Rosalind kept still.

"I want to ask you about a shooting incident on the Queen Mary now, an incident that resulted in a death."

She sat back as if a gaping, black hole in the floor had opened in front of her and put her hands up to her face.

"This has nothing to do with that." She shook her head, feeling her curls bounce back and forth, then she dropped her hands to her lap.

"Still, Miss Fisher, I want an explanation. You have been nose-to-nose with two, let's say *dramatic*, events in less than three weeks. Possibly it's just bad luck."

"Fine. A man on the Queen Mary with a gun followed me to my small cabin and pushed his way in. He wanted…he wanted…" She stopped, watching Small's cheeks pink up, his gaze now on the wall in back of her.

"Continue, Miss Fisher," he said, then he cleared his throat.

"I fought him off. As I did so, I gripped at his hand which held the gun. We were, Mister Small, struggling on the small bed. He was on top of me, pulling at my panties. In that terrible moment, the gun went off."

"How did that happen?"

"How do I know? I was underneath a man who outweighed me by fifty pounds at least, fighting not to be…violated." Rosalind felt her own cheeks flaming, her heart beating. She glared at Small, invested in her story.

"The ship's captain exonerated you of all wrongdoing. Still, it's odd, isn't it, to have two men harmed—one fatally—within three weeks of each other? Both US citizens, both with you around."

"I'm used to not being lucky," Rosalind said, shrugging. "My parents died before I was thirteen. I lived with an overwhelmed cousin, graduated from high school at sixteen, and moved out when I was eighteen. I support myself with low-wage jobs when I can find them, and I am trying to finish college so I can teach."

"Do you know how to shoot a gun?"

"Doesn't everyone? Just pull the trigger."

"Don't be smart with me, Miss Fisher." He looked at his pocket watch. "The ambassador will be back by four, I hope, and I need to report to him. Answer my question."

"I'm a Texas girl. I know how to shoot a gun," Rosalind said, doing quick calculations in her head. If she was detained until Ambassador Biddle returned, there was no way she would have enough time to do everything that needed to be done.

"Ever own a derringer yourself?"

The question floated in the air. Rosalind tried to recall how many people knew and, of those, how many would reveal it if asked in the right way under pressure. Only Sidney knew she had a derringer in Europe. He wouldn't tell.

"I own a gun. I don't have my gun here in Europe. If I'd had a gun on the Queen Mary that scum wouldn't have pushed his way into my cabin, would he?" She gave Small a tight-lipped smile.

There was a discreet knock at the door. "Yes?" Small asked.

"The ambassador is coming."

***

Ambassador Biddle put a well-manicured hand, ring finger sporting a large gold and ruby ring, on Small's shoulder. Rosalind took the briefest note of his tailored blue linen jacket, blue-striped cotton shirt, and red tie.

"I understand someone's punched Corporal Hank's lights out. Why aren't our guards here tougher? Recovering though, I'm told. Why are we interrogating Miss Fisher?"

"It was Mister Novy's driver who did it. She's an eyewitness."

"And?"

"She says she instructed the driver, a Michal Limowitz, to hand over documents as Corporal Hank demanded. Then this Limowitz slugged him twice and bolted. Says she doesn't know why because all he had were copies of visa applications."

"And?"

"She had a serious incident on the Queen Mary, as well, so I'm suspicious. I also want to interview a janitor who was down the hall and might have heard something."

Rosalind cursed inwardly. If the janitor was Polish, he might have understood every word.

Biddle sighed. "Mister Small, Miss Fisher did our country a great service on the Queen Mary. I even sent a letter to Representative Johnson applauding her work—although I didn't say what it was or how she did it, as its nature is top secret. She's here to help one of the representative's good friends, a man I just had to my home, along with Miss Fisher. A fine, philanthropic gentleman whose given thousands of dollars to benighted Polish communities and brought a lot of positive press our way. I say all this to suggest that Miss Fisher is not the person you should focus on."

"If that's your wish. Although I will say that a woman capable of doing secret work is…"

"That's my considered opinion and my order, Mister Small, based on a great deal of information."

"In that case, Miss Fisher, you're free to go. Take your papers, your purse, whatever you brought with you." Small pushed himself back from the table and stood up.

"Miss Fisher, a word in private." The ambassador waited until the door closed. "My apologies. As you see, I'm out of the meeting at the French Embassy much earlier than I thought, thank goodness. You and I could have met, but now it seems it is too late."

She nodded.

"I've warned Mister Novy not to go back through Germany. Find a ship—any ship—out of here."

"He's told me, sir. We are planning to leave."

"Excellent."

"Will Germany invade?" Rosalind asked.

"There are enough Nazi sympathizers here already, infesting the government and all the social institutions. Invasion may not be needed, although I'm sure it will come. In the meantime, there are many ways to hold a man like Jim Novy and accuse him of anything. He's made too much of a name for himself."

"They'd take his money."

"Of course. Arrest him on a pretext, make me beg for his release. I don't want to do that, Miss Fisher. Neither does our Ambassador Wilson in Germany. Like myself, he's just stepped into the position."

"I understand, sir."

"Meantime, tell Mister Novy that our corporal has given us a description of the chauffeur. In turn, my people have handed it over to the Warsaw police, who will issue their equivalent of an all-points bulletin. Terrible stuff, a Marine doing his duty attacked in our very own embassy. Need to keep that story out of the newspapers. Why'd he hire a thug?"

"Good help is hard to find, sir."

"Indeed."

She'd just have to pray no one asked any of the American staff if they'd seen Michal there. If Martin knew he was Michal Maltin, the pianist, perhaps others had seen and recognized him, as well.

"Will you be asking Mister Small or anyone else to ask the Americans here about this driver?"

Biddle looked at her. "Our American staff were at lunch when this unfortunate event occurred. What would be the point?"

"Yes, sir." That's what Ambassador Biddle was doing. But Fried? She could only hope she and Michal were on the ship and gone before the false last name rotted and stank.

CHAPTER 16

All the car windows were down in the heat of the late afternoon and the air smelled of city—exhaust fumes, dust, and garbage out for pick-up. Still, it was cooler than Austin. She wore a short-sleeved blouse and light linen skirt that she'd changed into at the hotel, but her legs still stuck to the seat whenever she moved around.

In Novy's hotel room, Rosalind had told him the bare bones—security wanted to search the briefcase, she'd told them it wasn't necessary, and then Michal grabbed it and fled. Novy's private property, what Michal had been hired to guard. The less Novy knew about the details, the less he'd have to explain or cover-up if he was ever questioned. It could just all fall back on her.

Michal's back was under her feet, his rear end and legs under David's. Grzegorz "just call me Greg," his brother—a Michal with shorter fingers, dark curly hair, and barely accented English—drove the car. Its gears groaned and hesitated in novice hands. Six hours of this to the port.

"You're sure he knows how to get us to there?" Jim Novy asked.

"Yes. And as soon as we're clear of Warsaw I'll drive," Michal replied.

"Too dangerous," Greg shouted.

"Well, I knew it wouldn't be easy to get those visas stamped and signed," Novy said. "My thanks to you both for whatever measures you took. How happy I'd be to embrace these people at the port. But David and I have to get out of here. Our ship leaves tomorrow morning." Novy held up the manila folder with the visas inside.

Rosalind had tried, and failed, the night before to keep the stamped visas out of Novy's reach. But he viewed them as the treasure he'd traveled to Poland for, risking his life and David's. She'd only just persuaded him to take out the top twenty, stare at them with the tenderness of a father for a newborn baby, and then return them.

In the twenty-one hours that Michal had the visas to himself, he'd kept his word. He'd seen her cousin, Jakub, and brought her a signed note from him. He'd found a forger, who'd made an immaculate copy of Fried's signature on each one, loops and swirls in carefully blotted black ink. But now Michal would have to leave with Novy and David, and Rosalind would have to stay and hand out the visas—and watch the six people who would not go collapse while her cousins and Greg and the unknown forger boarded a ship and floated away.

"I want to stay and help Rosalind, Dad," David announced suddenly.

Rosalind and Novy turned to look at David. "No," they said in a chorus.

"I'm not a child. I'm almost the same age as Greg and look what he's doing—driving us out of Warsaw while cops look for his brother."

Rosalind understood David's thirst for adventure. Espionage on the Queen Mary, trouble on the train, interviewing family and friends for visas that had to be snuck out of the embassy, and now a fugitive hidden in the car—what sixteen-year-old boy wouldn't want to be part of it?

"It would kill your mother and then she would kill me," Novy said.

In response, David turned to stare out the window. After a few miles of intermittent factories and fields, he said, "I want to help more in the business."

"Yes. College first. Then work."

***

"What ship are we on?" David stood next to Rosalind on the dock, watching his father and Greg walk towards a large ticketing building.

Novy had his passport and David's, as well as Michal's visa. Michal was still lying down in the car, now on the backseat with a blanket over him. He was to join Novy only when Greg told him to. Meantime he had his gun to keep him company and the briefcase with the visas to guard.

"Back in the town, what were you and the other guys talking about, if I can ask?" Rosalind said.

"Yeah. I can understand enough Yiddish to know the guys were talking about taking out Nazis if they ever tried anything around them." He turned, held up his right arm as if sighting down the barrel, and said, "Bang."

"I'm sure there are young Jewish men all over who feel the same way. But Nazis have guns, too."

"You can die trying or just die."

"You're right." That is why the young men fight wars and the old men sit behind desks and plan them, she thought.

She turned to see Novy and Greg heading back towards them.

"Let's get our baggage, David," Novy said. "We have three tickets. Not luxurious but leaving tomorrow morning directly for New York. Otherwise, it's a ferry to Stockholm and find a vessel there."

"What kind of ship, sir?" Rosalind asked.

"The steamer Polonia. Completely sold out. I pushed myself into the office through a thicket of desperation. Found the person who took my zlotys and got three tickets. What a person may do in times like these…" Novy pursed his lips, and Rosalind could see the bull of a young man he'd been.

"Poppa?"

"Rabbi Meier Berlin, of the Mizrachi organization—the president—was in there, with a ticket for a tourist cabin. Was that not the hand of the Almighty reaching out? He has agreed to share it with us. A blessing for which I will repay him thousandfold. Michal will sleep on the deck with others. Money smooths our path."

"Swell," David said.

Rosalind smiled, surprised at the level of relief she felt that David would be safe.

"What's the Mizrachi organization, sir?" she asked. For a world with not a lot of Jews, they always seemed to have some group to belong to.

"Supporters of Zionism, the return of Jews to Palestine for a country of their own. Very religious people, not like me, not Reform or modern. *Tzitzit.* The whole works. Nevertheless, we are still all one people."

"So, I guess he'll be eating hard-boiled eggs and apples the whole way over?" David laughed. "No kosher kitchen on a steamer."

"You will not make fun of this man, David." Novy's voice was stern. Then he motioned to Greg. "You have the tickets for everyone else."

Greg held up a manila envelope emblazoned with *Baltic America Line The Direct Line.*

"They are for tomorrow, the ones I put on hold before I knew David and I would have to abandon our trip to Palestine. Everyone knows to be here no later than nine a.m. Michal still guards the visas in the car. You, Greg, and Rosalind will now have the responsibility for giving out the tickets and the visas."

All the responsibility for telling six people expecting to leave that they would not, plus the getting Greg and her cousins and the unknown forger onto the ship without causing mayhem, was now hers.

"Will you return directly to Texas, sir, or wait for your relatives in New York?" Rosalind held her breath for the answer. If he stayed in New York, she'd have to flee the moment she stepped off the ship.

"Return to Austin. Make sure the preparations are finished. I left it to others but now that I will be back sooner than I thought, I prefer to do it myself. I also want to write to the Jewish Joint Distribution Committee about the dire conditions here, especially in the small towns. We have to do more." He sighed. "And you, Miss Fisher?"

"I'll go to DC and report to Representative Johnson's staff. Then I'll see."

"You have your last semester of college."

She shrugged. "There may be other work for me to do for Representative Johnson. Sir, did anyone try again with Clara's father?"

He shook his head sadly. "No, Clara's father decided for her." He leaned in close to her and waved David further away towards the dock. "This has been a greater burden to my soul and to the blessed Reb Shmuel's than anyone could have imagined. I truly believe those who remain are condemned. Those who believe this will turn around are deluded." He exhaled audibly. "I will need two lifetimes of good works to begin to cleanse myself of the stain of choosing who will live and who will die, a job that even the Almighty can only bear to do one day of the year."

***

None of the four hotels catering to steamship passengers had any rooms available. Michal and Greg slept in the car, with a gun, guarding the visas and the luggage. Jim Novy paid what would have been the price of four rooms so that David, Rosalind and he could take three armchairs in the lobby of the best of the hotels to sleep in overnight. Rosalind also saw him hand over a stack of zlotys to guarantee her a room for the next night. Greg would guard the car.

In the morning, red-eyed from lack of sleep, she watched Novy, David and Michal join an ordered and quiet line of passengers, all holding visas or passports for inspection. She waited for five hours on the dock for all two-thousand passengers to board, afraid that if she moved David would vanish with all his sixteen-year-old promise.

At last, the *Polonia* steamed away on its five-day voyage.

Greg tapped her on the shoulder. "Tomorrow by six a.m., we will go to the plaza by the ticket office. That's where everyone will come. We'll wait."

Rosalind turned to look across the promenade where hundreds of people once again stood in line at the office. She had only a vague recollection of what Novy's people looked like, but she knew they would look like everyone else in that line: desperate for the gangplank to freedom.

"How will we know who they are?"

"They will know you, Miss Fisher. We've told them what to look for. Curly red hair, blue eyes, American clothes. Just sing *The Star-Spangled Banner* and Novy's people will find you."

"Many others will notice me too," she said in Yiddish. Did she have to make a spectacle of herself at this late juncture?

Greg laughed, then stopped abruptly. "Police are heading this way. Also a man in a suit," he said.

"Go to the car. Lock the doors and don't open them unless I say so."

He nodded and, gripping the folder with the tickets so tight that she could see his knuckles whitening, walked towards where the car was parked.

Rosalind continued to watch him, back to the police, until someone tapped her on the shoulder and said, in American English, "Miss Fisher, we need to talk."

She turned. "Vice-Consul Fried. Are you traveling back to the States?"

"No. And until I have the answers to my questions, neither are you." The two uniformed men with him were not Polish police but US Marines, young, like the unfortunately punched corporal.

"Well, my ticket isn't until tomorrow and Mister Novy and his son are safely away, just like the good ambassador warned them to be." She hoped Biddle's concern for Novy would throw enough water on Fried's fire to finally drown it.

"The ambassador has a lot to do. I understand phone service from here to Warsaw is pretty intermittent so I wouldn't count on reaching him, or really anyone, at the embassy today. So let's hope we resolve this before your ship leaves."

A line from Dickinson sprang into her head. *Hope is the thing with feathers.* Did that mean hope fled, frightened away like a small bird at the feeder? Rosalind had a bad feeling she would soon find out.

***

"We interviewed the janitor, the one cleaning the floors when your driver punched out Corporal Hank." Fried sat back in the chair across the table from Rosalind in the corner of the hotel's dining room that he'd commandeered. The two sergeants stood behind him.

Rosalind said nothing. She'd learned now that the more she said, the more rope she gave Fried, and people like him, to hang her.

"Says he heard you say something like 'punch him hard and run.'"

She shook her head.

"You're denying that?"

"Yes."

"Our lawyer wants to talk to you again."

She considered that. The lawyer wasn't there. How badly could he want to talk to her if he didn't speed up to Gdynia with Fried to catch her before she left? A long bleat coming off the water rattled the window and made her jump.

"I'm on edge, Vice-Consul Fried. This trip to Poland has been much more than I thought it would be."

"I'm sure." He tapped his fingers on the table.

How long could Greg hide in the car without being seen and without food or water? Novy's forty-four would start to arrive—some tonight, she was sure, anxious not to miss the *Estonia*'s departure. She was supposed to tell six unlucky men that their paperwork was incomplete and better luck next time. She was supposed to find her cousins. She was supposed to watch over every soul as the steamer headed for the Statue of Liberty.

"*Give me your poor, your huddled masses yearning to be free.*" She sighed the words.

"What did you say, Miss Fisher?"

"Just quoting Emma Lazarus, Mister Fried."

"So you're sympathetic to unfettered immigration to the United States during a time of great financial despair? I'll be sure to make a note of that."

Rosalind decided to say nothing else. For the next twenty minutes, she sat in the chair watching Fried fold and unfold his hands on the table opposite her as if he could not find a comfortable resting spot for his fingers. She could see people coming into the lobby of the hotel with suitcases, toddlers gripped firm by the hand, babies swaddled in arms, the men in suits, the women in fur coats despite the heat. People who still had money—the last of it on their backs and in their bags. Passengers for the *Estonia* to America or the ferry to Sweden.

"This is your last chance, Miss Fisher. Where is Mister Novy's chauffeur?"

"I have no idea where in Poland the man might be, sir." She shook her head. "That is the truth and you asking me another six times or six hundred won't change the answer."

"We know you gave us the wrong last name. As soon as Mister Martin heard about the situation he came to us and told us that the man was a Michal Maltin, concert pianist."

Rosalind bit the inside of her lip. What could she say that wouldn't get her in more trouble? Nothing came to mind.

"Miss Fisher, I don't care why Ambassador Biddle thinks well of you or even that he does. He'll go away at some point and I'll still be here in Poland. I care that one of my men was attacked and that my office was broken into." Fried stood up and addressed the Marines. "Keep an eye on her. I'll be back."

The two young men slumped into chairs but continued to watch her.

The air was damp with the stink of fuel, seaweed, and smoke. Even with the windows open in the dining room, Rosalind sweated. How in the world was Greg coping?

Fried returned. "If you have a weapon now, Miss Fisher, best to let me know. I will search you if I need to."

"In my purse. Tucked in the lining at the bottom."

Fried picked up the purse from next to Rosalind's right foot, stuck his hand in, and thrust around.

"It's loaded. Be careful when you take it out," Rosalind said.

Fried put the gun on the table in front of Rosalind. "A derringer. Interesting."

"For defense, sir. After the episode on the Queen Mary, I was frightened."

"Now, I'd like to see your hands, Miss Fisher."

"They're right in front of you." She plopped her hands down on the table, right hand folded over left. "What are you looking for, Mister Fried? Next thing you'll be asking me to strip."

"I'm looking for whoever broke into my office."

Rosalind had no idea if Fried could arrest her or otherwise detain her, but she knew she wouldn't find out if she kept sitting there answering the same questions over and over. She'd have to try something else. So far in this exchange, she'd invented nothing, said nothing that wasn't true, but it was wearing on her—even remembering the truth and a few lies with the stakes so high was exhausting.

"I really have nothing else to say to you and I have a ticket to leave tomorrow. I'll be going to my room now."

She pushed her chair out from the table and stood. One of the Marines took a step towards her.

Fried shook his head. "I'll get our attorney on the line, Miss Fisher."

"Fine, sir. When you do, let me know and I will speak to him. As long as I'm not already on the ship. Not that I'll say anything I didn't already say. Meantime, I'll take my purse and my gun and my passport. If you need to know more about Mister Novy's chauffeur, please ask him."

"Mister Novy is on the *Polonia* heading back to New York, Miss Fisher. As we both know."

"True. At the insistence of Ambassador Biddle. You're aware that Mister Novy received a threatening note on the Queen Mary? We were harassed on the train coming into Poland, then told to cut the trip to Poland short and return directly to the United States. The United States can't protect our Jewish citizens in Europe, it appears." Rosalind took a step away from the table and past Fried, who looked up at her.

"That hotel where we stayed—the one your office recommended—is staffed with Nazi sympathizers," Rosalind continued. "Those sympathizers spy on our citizens when they're out, go through their briefcases, ransack their suitcases and whatever they've put in the hotel safe." She watched Fried's face for a reaction. "They tried to steam open a note to me. The good representative and his friend, the newspaper publisher, will be interested in that. Maybe they will start thinking about long-time embassy staff. How capable they are, how efficient, how sensitive to the Nazi threat. Something to take up in Congress, or with the President, or in the papers."

Rosalind picked her gun up off the table. "Goodbye, Mister Fried," she said, and walked towards the door. Fried's chair scraped as he stood up. Maybe she shouldn't have added that last threat, but it was too late to take it back. She pushed the door open, walked into the lobby, and got the key for her room at the desk.

"My men will keep an eye on you until you leave, Miss Fisher. To be sure you're safe and all," Fried called out to her as she walked up the stairs.

Rosalind cursed under her breath. How would she give out the visas?

***

Rosalind found her suitcase, delivered by a bellman, seemingly unmolested in her room. She used the bathroom, and then hurried out to the car, managing to avoid Fried's young Marines. She knocked on the passenger side window, alarmed at Greg's slumped body.

"I fell asleep." Greg opened the door and took a deep breath. "I'm hungry and I really need to use the W.C." He reached in his pocket and handed her the car keys. "You guard for a while."

"Get something to drink. Not alcohol!"

He walked off in the direction of the hotel. As Rosalind rolled down the window to get a breeze off the water, Fried's men strolled towards her.

"Greg, come back." She leaned out the window and called to him.

Once he was back at the car, she said in Yiddish, "See those two fellows? They're supposed to guard me. See how distracted you can make them, please."

"Let me practice my English with them after I return from the W.C. Maybe they're thirsty."

She watched Greg as he passed the Marines, nodding to them, and saying something she could not hear. They laughed, shook their heads, and stood, staring at her in the car. Greg walked on. They continued to stare at her.

"Fine," she muttered and looked away. She leaned her head back against the seat. Eleanor had been right when she recommended coloring and straightening Rosalind's hair. She would never be inconspicuous.

After a few minutes, she heard Greg's voice. "Hello, guys." Greg had returned with three bottles of soda and three Snickers bars, which were now—along with American jazz—all the rage in Europe. She saw that he'd positioned himself so the two Marines were turned away from the car. They were tipping the soda bottles together like lifelong pals.

She took her purse and the folder that held the visas and the applications and slid out the passenger door, which she closed with as little bang as possible, and locked it. Walking at the same pace as the few other people in the square, she made it to a store with several mannequins dressed in high fashion in the window.

Not more than fifteen minutes later, she reemerged in trousers held tight onto her waist with a belt into which a new notch had been whittled, a white linen shirt, a gray-and-white striped blazer, boat shoes, and a fedora with a deep brim on her head. Underneath, her curls were wrapped in a black scarf. The shopgirl had laughed and said in Polish, "You look like Greta Garbo now—pants on a woman!" as she handed her a bag with her other clothes.

Rosalind walked within a few yards of the car. The Marines had realized she'd left apparently, since they'd also vacated the square. She hoped that her disguise worked well enough to keep her invisible in the growing throng.

Greg was nowhere to be seen. The line at the ticket office had grown by at least several hundred and once again Rosalind wondered how she was ever going to find Novy's people.

"That's an interesting look on you, Miss Fisher." Fried had come up on her left while she was looking around the square. "My men, they're not trained for this sort of thing. I, however, spent time during the Great War looking around, honing my observational talents."

Rosalind turned to stare at him. She felt empty. Out of ideas.

"Your young driver is with my fellows. He says he's got a ticket and a visa for the States leaving on the next ship. Part of that folder you've got a grip on?"

She said nothing.

"This will not end well for you, Miss Fisher. I believe you have fraudulently obtained visas for the United States and that an employee of yours assaulted a member of the United States Embassy staff. You'll go to prison. And that congressman you work for will pay a price, as well."

Rosalind thought about the people lined up outside the embassy, paperwork in hand, waiting for a visa that would never exist. Johnson had only wanted her to find a sympathetic employee who'd accelerate the process for just forty-four people, nothing illegal—just a push to the front of the line, a power play, a slight bending of the rules. The practical politics of the powerful. She'd decided on her own to break the law when she couldn't find anyone to help, and now she'd have to face the consequences. But not before the forty-four people she could help got their visas.

"Thanks for noticing the new clothes," she said. "I needed them because of the abrupt end to our trip to Poland and such different accommodations returning to New York. Pants are better for some things, as I learned on the Queen Mary." She was trying so hard not to sound threatened and to keep her voice low that she could barely hear herself through the pounding of blood in her ears.

"Stop playing games and hand that file over to me, Miss Fisher."

The two Marines turned and walked over to stand behind Fried as if summoned by an invisible hand. Behind Friend's shoulder, Greg shrugged and walked towards the car. Rosalind gripped the file and shook her head.

"I don't know exactly what the rules are, Mister Fried. Maybe you can help me. If I work for a member of the House of Representatives and I have papers that belong to him and you are a member of the State Department and you ask for them, do I have to hand them over? I was told I reported only to Representative Johnson."

"This is a criminal investigation, Miss Fisher."

"Yes, of course. I've told you what I know. The driver punched the soldier and ran. I'm not the criminal."

A half-dozen assorted people, three holding large suitcases, had gathered. One man took out a small Brownie camera and started snapping pictures.

"Move the crowd away," Fried said to his men.

They began to shoo people away, but this only drew more people's attention. Within half-a-minute there were a dozen more, drawn by the boredom of a long wait in a quiet square. Two more started taking pictures.

"*Co tu się dzieje?*" a woman called out in a clear voice.

"What did she say?" Fried asked.

Despite the warmth, his face had paled a shade, Rosalind thought. A disadvantage to not speak Polish. A double disadvantage to have to rely on Rosalind to translate. "She's upset by the military uniforms and wants to know what is going on."

"Tell her not to worry."

"I don't think that will work, Mister Fried. From what I can see, more people are coming over."

The center where Rosalind and Fried stood staring at each other was a magnet drawing in loose shavings of people. Why they were not concerned about their place in line wasn't Rosalind's business—maybe a child or a spouse was standing there, waiting for a report back on the lady in the trousers and the American Marines.

"*Co oni mówią?*" This was from a man standing in back of the taller, blonder soldier.

"Miss Fisher?"

"He wants to know what nationality we are." Rosalind felt that if Fried didn't know a simple question like "What are they doing?" then he deserved to have a translation that better fit her purpose, which was making Fried more uncomfortable.

Fried pursed his lips. "I don't want to have an international incident here. Come back to the hotel, Miss Fisher. We can talk privately."

"I've talked privately with you. I explained my situation to Ambassador Biddle. The ambassador believed me. What would be different in another conversation?" Rosalind looked around. More people had gathered.

A man, wearing a long-sleeved white shirt tucked into dark black pants, and holding a stenographer's notebook, strode over and stood next to Rosalind. "*Jestem z Gazety Polska,*" he said.

"This fellow, Mister Fried, is a newspaper reporter with the Gazeta Polska."

"Does he speak English?"

The reporter understood enough to shake his head "no" in response. He continued to watch Rosalind and Fried, his pen poised over paper.

The newspaper was a right-wing supporter of fascism, good only for taking out the garbage and deciding who to avoid in a café if they were reading it. It had only taken her the few days she'd been in Poland to figure that out. Fried must have known that as well because his lip curled with distaste.

Fried looked around at the crowd, which had now grown to over fifty people. He stared for a second at his two young fellows—the ones so easily distracted with Snickers bars.

Then he leaned over and spoke to Rosalind in a harsh whisper, close enough to blow spittle onto her cheek. "It appears, Miss Fisher, that you need the ongoing protection of the United States Embassy. Regardless of whether you were somehow involved with the incident of your driver, one thing is clear: neither you nor I want an incident involving the press—especially not this one. You'll return to the hotel, to your room, and my men will be instructed to keep an eye on you. You will stay there until your ship is boarding tomorrow. They will continue to guard you until you are on board. This is an order from your government. Is that clear?"

"I don't want to be guarded."

"My job, Miss Fisher, is to protect the citizens of the United States in Poland. You're free to believe that or not. It's your right. But I will protect you until you leave on that ship tomorrow."

A tugboat blew its horn loud enough to be heard over the murmuring of the crowd. To her right, the reporter was conferring with an onlooker and to her left, the two young Marines, grim-faced from their dressing down, stared at her.

Rosalind nodded. As she began to walk away, the crowd dispersed, most turning in the direction of the ticket office.

She took a deep breath of salted air and began to look for Greg. Behind her, Fried called out, "We're not done. I'm arranging for you to be among the first on the ship tomorrow and my men will stand guard until the bloody thing sails off. I'll see you in Washington. We'll finish our discussion there."

CHAPTER 16

Greg had vanished for the night, but he would have to return. Rosalind had his visa and ticket in the folder with everyone else's. It was five-thirty a.m. She hadn't slept at all, tossing the blankets off and turning over and over.

She patted the manila folder under the pillow to assure herself it was still in her possession. If she couldn't give out the visas, Greg would have to. She'd have to tell him to be discreet, and how to handle the six people who'd been removed from the list to make room for her cousins, the forger, and him. What would they do when they were told the visas hadn't come through? She imagined Greg on the ground, bleeding from his nose, clothes torn, while faceless men ran up the gang plank.

She sighed. Greg couldn't give out the visas. It was a stupid idea to transfer the responsibility to him. She'd have to do it before she boarded. Surely the first-class passengers would get on before her, and even if Fried watched her standing in line, there was no bucking first class privilege in life. She'd have time. But what if people were late? What if the Marines marched her onto the ship? What if they realized what she was doing and yanked the visas out of her hand? She groaned.

✳✳✳

She sat on the bed staring at the clock, that measure of time with its soft, steady, fatal click. Five forty-five in the morning. She could hear Fried's two fellows through the door. One of them was speaking to someone in the hall.

Rosalind heard a woman's soft, apologetic reply.

"Hey, I need new towels," Rosalind called through the door. "And it's real stuffy in here. Maybe she can open a window for me."

"I said she can't come in."

"Sergeant, do you know who I am?"

"No, ma'am, I do not. And I don't care."

"I am on the staff of the House of Representatives. I'm someone Ambassador Biddle invited to his elegant home. I have…" What did she have, really? A short-term job she'd bungled terribly.

"Ambassadors come and go. Embassy staff live forever."

Rosalind heard the door next to hers open and close and then the muffled snorting of the vacuum cleaner. She pushed the window open, letting in a salted breeze, and looked down. She was just on the third floor, with a fire escape ladder to her left, but it would be a long drop if she mis-stepped.

The ticket office was only half a block away, and already the line was snaking around the square.

"OK, fellows," she called. "I give up. If I need a bath, I guess I'll use these towels, wet as they are."

"Wait up." The door rattled. "Fried said to take care of you proper."

The door opened and one of her guards stood there, towel in hand.

"So, here is how it will go, Miss Fisher. You'll go into the bathroom and bathe, door shut, of course. I will stand here to make sure you don't try to get out an open window or some nonsense like that. Then you will sit back down on that bed and not get up again unless you have a good reason."

"What is your name?"

"Baker."

"Corporal Baker, let me see what you mean by a good reason. I need to be in line with all my belongings for that ship. The one out there, blowing its whistle, with all the people lined up. That one."

"Exactly, ma'am. You'll let me know when we need to leave, but not a moment before that. Me, not White, there. He's an alright fellow but this is as far up the ladder as he'll go. Bottom rung. He's a KP-duty kind of guy."

"So you're the brains of this operation?" Rosalind smiled.

"Miss Fisher, I'm accustomed to being underestimated due to my youth. When the judge said choose between enrollment and juvie, it was no decision. My career is this here Marine Corp. My goal is to be a lieutenant or even higher."

"An ambitious man."

"I've already lost points with my superiors because I let myself be distracted by soda and candy. Like a child. That's made me angry, if I can be honest with you."

She nodded noting that his voice had gotten even lower and his grip had tightened around the towel. A fuse lit up, he'd blow. When he took a step towards her, she stepped back, banging the back of her calf against the bed frame.

"We only meant that as a good-will gesture."

"Don't play me, Miss Fisher. I grew up on the hard side of St. Paul. No work for my dad, so I dropped out at thirteen and began lugging pails of nails for money you wouldn't think about if you dropped it on the street. I know the score."

"O.K." She forced herself to look at his face. She knew young men with backgrounds like this, lurking, angry, bust-your-jaw guys. Who knew what they could have been without the Great Depression, the Dust Bowl?

"Take your bath," Baker said and took a step back. "Then put on your clothes and come back out. I'll be right here, waiting."

***

Rosalind used the four minutes soaking in lukewarm water to consider and discard her options. Fleeing the room using the fire escape would be impossible—the drop was too far, and Baker was too close at hand. Even if she managed the drop, she'd have to get to the square, distribute the visas, and return to the room as if nothing had happened, which meant getting back up the fire escape which was at least six feet off the ground.

Greg had vanished. If he returned to talk to her, he'd be detained by the soldiers. Another disaster. What would Michal do to her if Greg didn't make it out of Poland?

And what if Fried insisted on getting the folder? He'd backed off once, but she couldn't count on crowds and fascist newspaper reporters the next time. She'd been running on luck and felt certain she'd used it all up.

Rosalind slapped the water and stood up, furious that neither Eleanor nor John Smith had prepared her better. They'd assumed that the people she was supposed to contact would be there, that Sidney would be a simple one-time connection who'd just hear what she had to say about conversations in first class and be done with her, that Jim and David Novy could finish their grand tour of Europe and sail off to Palestine so she'd have the time to get these forty-four people out. And, worse, they'd assumed that the American staff at the embassy would see more clearly the danger Hitler posed, would want to help, and would be more aware of the dark leanings of some of the Polish staff they'd hired and the staff of the hotels they used.

Drying herself off, she began to consider the Marines outside her door, turning the little she'd picked up about them over in her mind. She'd need to figure out what motivated them, and from there, how to get what she wanted.

***

"Corporal Baker, what time do you think the passengers begin boarding for the departure?" Rosalind called through the door. She was gripping the folder with the visas, and tapping her finger on her derringer, which was again loaded and in its purse nest behind the lining. It had been thirty minutes since she'd bathed and dressed. The clock read six-ten a.m.

"I don't know."

"Would one of you please check? I can see the line growing outside and I'm concerned."

"We're to escort you onto the ship. You won't miss it."

"Please ask your colleague to find out. I'd be grateful."

She heard muttering outside the door and then one set of footsteps walking away.

Five minutes later, just as she'd hoped, the other soldier hadn't returned.

"Can you come in, Corporal Baker? I want to talk to you but I can't shout through the door. What I have to say is too confidential."

"Fine." The door opened and he stood in front of her. "What is it?"

"Please take me down to the dock now. You can guard me all you want, and I promise I'll stay right by you. But I don't want to be rushed up the gangplank with two Marines. There's a newspaper man there and people with cameras. It won't look good for Representative Johnson and he'll be furious. He'll…" She paused.

"What?"

"He'll want me to report back on everything that happened. Everyone who was involved in treating me like a criminal."

"Including us?"

Rosalind paused as if considering this for the first time. "Yes, including the two of you. He's very important and influential, knows powerful people. Real kingmakers. And he'll be one, too." Damn. She should have said "is one."

"I could highlight you as a real positive in this mess," she continued. "You seem like just the kind of young man Representative Johnson has tried to help. Or I could tell him I explained my situation to you, and you still treated me like a criminal."

"I can do what you want. Up to a point." The lad was tempted. She could tell by the way he'd slowed his speech, seemed to pick his words. "But nothing that'll get me in hot water with my lieutenant or Fried."

"Well, seems like you've got a choice. In trouble with a powerful man who can protect you from men like Fried or…" She let her words trail off, then said, "Look, I'm just a cog in the wheel, like you. Trying to keep my job, move up the ladder."

"So, if we go outside right now—you, me, your stuff—what then?"

"You let me talk to some of the people Mister Jim Novy, Representative Johnson's good friend, came here to see. They have tickets for this ship, too."

He nodded. "And you have…?"

"Paperwork for them, courtesy of Mister Novy, that guarantees he'll cover expenses for them if they get to the United States. I have to give that to them."

"You just want to talk to these folks and give them papers, right? Then you'll get on the ship without a hassle?"

"There's nothing I'd like better. I'll be good, promise."

"And for me helping out…"

"I'll put in a very good word on your behalf with Representative Johnson and ask him to let the right people know how helpful you were."

"We have a deal."

CHAPTER 17

On the square, Rosalind surrendered her suitcase to a porter wheeling a large cart stuffed with other passengers' luggage, some saggy and weary with ropes around them, others so pristine she wanted to wipe away the scuff marks they'd just been subjected to.

"Second class and here's my cabin number," she said in Polish and then immediately translated to English for Baker. The porter nodded and she tipped him in zlotys.

"How much did you give him?" Baker asked.

"About a dollar."

"Big tipper."

"No one's got anything these days. And, anyhow, it's not my money."

"Government's?"

"No. It's Mister Novy's. He just wants me back safely. So it's grease, you know."

"More where that came from, then?"

"Not for me. I work for the United States government, like I said."

Three people, two men and a woman, began to walk towards her from where they'd been standing in line, leaving another woman to stay in their spot. The taller man called out, "Miss Fisher?" in accented but clear English.

"Yes."

At his question and her reply, six other people, two of them girls who reached just to their mother's chin, also began to walk over. The same woman now guarded nine spots in line.

The handoff of the visas went fine. Less than three minutes to verify names, flip through the papers she had in the file, hand them over. Ten of the forty-three were done, thirty-three to go.

Baker stared off across the square as Rosalind dealt with the visas.

At the far edge of the square, she thought she saw her cousin and his three children but couldn't be sure. The light off the Baltic Sea was startlingly bright under the cloudless sky. She made a visor with her hand and squinted to get a better look at the man, who raised a hand to wave at her.

As he did, a Polish *Policja*, uniformed and armed, walked towards Jakub with his baton swinging. Jakub grabbed the hand of his younger son and lowered the suitcase he was carrying to the ground.

It was like watching a horror show in pantomime. The policeman opened the suitcase, tossed the clothes onto the cobblestones, tore out the lining, and took out a pair of shoes. He dug his hand into the toes, wiggled the heels, and dropped the shoes on top of the shirts. Then he walked over to the girl, grabbed her face, turned her head back and forth as if she was a mannequin, and spat on the ground in front of her. Having accomplished this, he strolled towards the café whose umbrellaed tables sat in the square's corner.

Jakub directed the children to pick up, shake out, and replace the clothing in the suitcase. He took a handkerchief out of his pocket and handed it to the smallest child, who must have been crying, although Rosalind couldn't hear him. The boy wiped his cheeks and handed the handkerchief back. Then Jakub picked up the repacked suitcase and the family continued towards Rosalind.

***

Jakub nodded at Rosalind and said in Polish, "We are here. The Poles are happy to see us leave. That policeman was just making certain we knew not to return. It just alarmed the children, is all."

"Not me, Poppa," Zofia said. She still had red marks on her cheek from the officer's fingers.

"Here are the visas. And the declarations that you need of sponsorship."

Jakub took them, his expression somber. "And what did you have to do, Cousin Rosalind, to provide these to me?"

Rosalind remained silent.

"It isn't for me to judge or even to ask what the price is for my benefit and my children's," Jakub said. "We are obligated to ransom the captive. What do the sages say if we haven't enough money to ransom them all? They say do not encourage the taking of more captives by paying more than any captive is worth. But they also say you may pay more for a captive if that captive is your relative. And what do the sages say if millions are held ransom? They say nothing and we are left to figure this out on our own."

"Yes, well, there's no time for religious debate," Rosalind answered in English, then turned to the soldier. "Baker, this gentleman is a physician who is immigrating to the United States with his children. He will receive the sponsorship of Mister Novy and I have to provide him with those sponsorship papers as I did the previous folks. Please give me a moment to speak to him in Polish and then I will translate for you."

Baker grunted. "That was a lot of Polish just to ask you if you had his papers. And somehow religion got into it, you said. I'd like the translation."

Dealing with Baker was like negotiating wet rocks across a raging stream. "He said it was of course very expensive to sponsor refugees, and he thanked God for the chance to leave."

"Whose God?"

"I believe there is only one."

"Nah. There's the Catholic one, the Lutheran one, the one those Mohammadians have…lots of gods. So which one is his and those kids? What god are we letting into our country, Miss Fisher?"

What was Baker? He was white—a white guy with a white religion. Saw his God as white. A God who spoke American. A God he probably seldom visited or even thought about until foreigners were about to come in.

"This man is a physician who treats sick children, Corporal."

Baker shook his head.

"I haven't asked him his religion."

Jakub was staring at her. Better than staring at Baker for certain. Then he dropped to one knee and gathered the children closer to him.

In Polish he said to them, "*Złóż ręce i udawaj, że modlisz się tak, jak robią to twoi przyjaciele.*"

The children knelt and put their hands together in prayer, imitating their former non-Jewish friends.

"Is that some Catholic gibberish he just told them?"

"Not at all. He asked them to pray in Polish."

"And…"

Zofia began in Polish, "*Chleba naszego powszedniego daj nam dzisiaj.*"

Baker shook his head. "Can she say it in English?"

Could she?

Knowing she was being singled out to perform, Zofia nodded. "Please give us bread today and forgive our sins." The English was halting and the translation lacked poetry, but apparently it was good enough for Baker, whose life undoubtedly lacked poetry but who knew what it was to want bread and forgiveness.

"Fine. Somethin' I recognize from when I was young. Carry on." He nodded and smiled at the children.

Rosalind handed Jakub the four visas and the other papers and explained what they contained. When she was done, he walked as fast as the children could keep up with towards the line for the ship.

Striding in the opposite direction came Greg, with Corporal White pointing a rifle at his back.

"I didn't know where the hell you went to," White shouted at Baker as he drew closer. He jabbed the rifle into Greg's back and Greg took a short stagger forward. "Don't you move, Polish guy. Tell him, lady. He don't move, I point my rifle elsewhere. He moves, I shoot."

Greg nodded his head, but Rosalind translated into Polish to be sure and added, "Don't let him know how really good you are in English."

Greg nodded again.

"He's just my driver," Rosalind began to explain, but White turned in her direction. "You don't talk, lady. You get on your boat back to the blessed United States of America and tell whatever bigshot you work for that it's all fine here. You did your work. You file your report and then you're done. Got it?"

"The guy only gave us soda and Snickers. What's your problem, White?" Baker asked.

"I think he's got somethin' to do with Corporal Hank getting beat up back at the embassy. Once he confesses, I'll be in for a commendation. Maybe even a promotion."

"'Geez, buddy," Baker said, shaking his head. "And if he doesn't, we've arrested a Polish citizen."

"Yeah, well, I'm willing to risk it."

Rosalind sighed. Greg's chance to go to America was being blocked by the barrel of an overeager Marine's rifle. And there were still nearly thirty visas to give out.

There was no time to waste, Rosalind decided. She grabbed Greg's visa out of the folder, shoved it at him, and said in Polish, "Here's your visa. Go! He won't shoot in this crowded place."

Greg started off at a fast trot. White raised his rifle.

Baker pushed the muzzle down towards the ground. "Don't be a fuckin' idiot," he said.

Immediately, Rosalind created a distraction by taking off at a fast pace towards a group of people she recognized from the rabbi's house. She didn't turn to look at Greg, hoping he'd take advantage of the small window of opportunity to join the line for the ship. As soon as she started walking away, White and Baker followed her.

She got the families their visas and the papers guaranteeing Novy's support as quickly as possible. Two mothers told three children to thank Miss Fisher and then God, which they did in unison, then the fathers grabbed the luggage, the mothers took the hands of the children, and the group hurried to join the line of passengers.

A young man came up to her next. When he said his name, Rosalind knew he was one of the six who had been replaced.

Rosalind thumbed through the visas in her hand, shook her head, thumbed again. Her fingers felt like ice.

"It's not here," she said in Yiddish.

"Nisht dart? Vi ken dos zeyn?" Not there? How could that be?

"Ich veis nisht. Ich hab nor die." I don't know. I have only those.

He asked again. She repeated in Yiddish and English that she didn't know where his papers were. Eventually the young man dragged his suitcase back to the bench and sat, watching her give out five more visas.

Rosalind numbed her feelings for the people getting the visas, ignoring their thanks, kisses and hugs as best she could. If she let any emotion in, she would crack and the whole operation would fall apart.

After forty minutes, the six men without visas stood in place. They stared at each other and at her. One finally said, "But we sold everything we had and left our jobs."

"I will give you money," she said, pulling the envelope stuffed with zlotys out of her purse. "Here. Why not go to Warsaw? There are jobs there."

The tallest man spit on the ground in front of her. "There are no jobs there, you stupid woman. We will have to return to Knishin and ask the rabbi for guidance. He will surely contact the blessed Mister Novy and have some answer for us."

Rosalind shivered. Of course, Novy would find out. She would go to prison for what she had done.

"Let me see what I can do at the embassy. I'll change my ticket for a later sailing and join you here," Rosalind said although she had no intention of doing anything other than charging up the gangplank and boarding the ship as soon as possible. In New York, she would have to disappear and hope no one cared enough to find her.

The young men looked at each other. The tall one who'd spit at her said, "I'll come with you. A woman alone is at risk."

Rosalind shrugged. "Fine. Remind me of your name, please." She continued speaking in Yiddish so all the men would understand.

"Joe. My American name will be Joe."

"Great. Do you speak much English, Joe?"

"I practice. Not much yet."

"I'll need to speak English when we go to the ticket office."

"We are in Poland. You will trick me with your English." Joe's cheeks flushed with anger.

"I'm a citizen of the United States. They'll expect me to speak English. If I speak Polish too well, they will ask me a lot of questions."

He sighed and turned to the other men. "I'll walk with her over to the office."

One of them, Rosalind thought, had been with the fellows shooting at cans with David in Knishin. He shook his head and looked down. "A fool's errand, Yosef. You shouldn't bother with her. What does she know except she doesn't have our visas? Why should she even return to the embassy? They won't have the visas either. No matter what, we need to go back and start all over. Novy, may he be blessed for eternity, tried to help us skip the line, but we can't."

Two of the other men nodded in agreement.

"Ahron is right, Yosef," one said. "It's not righteous behavior for us to take another's place or threaten this woman who is doing her job. Let her just get on the ship. She'll be more help to us in America than here. What do we have now? Our rifles are back in Knishin along with our hammers, paint brushes, Grischa's violin. Do you have your diploma with you?"

Yosef nodded. "I do, Issur."

"Then, let's return. Another chance will come."

"Yids! Break it up." A Polish policeman walked towards the group from the hotel's patio, baton in hand.

"They were just helping me find my way to this place," Rosalind called out in Polish. "I need to tip them and then they are leaving. I'm a citizen of the United States."

At that, he stopped his advance and lowered his baton. "You need to find better help, Madam. These are Jews, and country Jews at that. How is it you know that language of theirs? Are you one of those American Jews come to make trouble? Giving out money, making us look bad to the world. I read in the paper about that Novy—all over the countryside, with his bags of gold just for the Jews. Like always."

"I'm with the United States government as a translator of many languages. And I was just at our embassy in Warsaw and now I'm returning to New York." Rosalind reached into her purse, pulled out her passport, and held it up as the police officer walked a few steps closer.

"You'll come with me. I'll take you to the office and you can board the ship."

"I promised a tip."

"I'll take the tip and make sure these Yids get their fair share."

"You'll stand there, away from me, while I finish my business and watch these men leave the square safe and sound. If you don't, I'll report you and make trouble for you."

The officer snickered. "Quite a mouth on you."

"I have enough for a generous tip for you as well for your trouble in getting me safely across this square and to the ship."

Rosalind motioned to Yosef. Without a glance at the officer, he stepped towards her. She grabbed zlotys out of the envelope and then handed the envelope, still bulging, to Yosef. "Go now. Quickly. We will try again to help."

Yosef and the five others grabbed their suitcases and walked fast out of the square towards the train station. "L'hitraot," she called to them, and one lifted his hand in acknowledgment of her goodbye.

Rosalind reached into her purse, took hold of the derringer's handle, tugged it out of the lining and put it in the body of the purse, next to her passport and ticket. She kept the purse in front of her, hands clasped around it, as she let the police officer guide her to the ticket office. There she handed him the equivalent of two days' pay in zlotys, twelve U.S. dollars. Turning towards the boarding officer, she said, "Here is my ticket and my passport. My luggage is already onboard."

He looked at the documents and at her, nodded, and waved her up the gangplank.

CHAPTER 18

My dear Hannah,
   I hope our cousins from the east have found you in Austin. I…

Rosalind put her pencil down and stared out the dirty window at the building opposite. She'd been in New York for five days, avoiding the reach of Jim Novy and Lyndon Baines Johnson. Who could find her in the almost solid grey-brown masses of people flowing back and forth and up and down and in and out? Putting her forehead on the glass, she sighed and let a wave of dizziness pass.

The second day in the city, at the New York Public Library, she'd found a copy of the Austin Daily Texan just four days old. No story about Jim Novy, or about the thousands of dollars he'd given to Jewish causes in Poland, or cutting his trip to Palestine short. No obituary either. She'd assume he and David were safely home.

I am not returning to Austin. She paused, erased *Austin* and wrote *Texas*.

   Please go to my boarding house and take my small trunk back to your house for safekeeping. Show Mrs. Agostini this letter. She'll give it to you. I'll be in touch.
   With love, Rosalind.

She folded the paper, stuck it in an envelope and wrote her cousin's address and left the return address blank. All anyone would learn from inspecting that little envelope was that it was postmarked in New York, where the ship had docked and where she had watched her cousins, Greg, and the other immigrants board the ferry to Ellis Island for further review. No one would know whether she was still there or had left.

On her way to the neighborhood delicatessen where she'd gotten a behind-the-counter job—sheer luck seeing the *Help Wanted* sign just as

Mrs. Levy put it in the window—she dropped the envelope in the mailbox. She'd fallen right into the rhythm of underpaid work, irregular hours, and the desperate camaraderie between employer and employees trying to keep their leaky boat afloat.

When she arrived at the deli, she stepped behind the counter, draped a long apron over her clothes, and wrapped the ties twice around her waist before securing them. Her wardrobe was too elegant for the deli, having been chosen for the Queen Mary and the embassy. Even the outfit she'd worn to Knishin was too new. In a day or two, once she'd caught her breath, she'd take them all over to the local second-hand shop and trade them for more dreary, worn, and suitable attire. She'd be sad to see them go, especially the trousers. She was sure Eleanor would figure out how to make her friend whole for the evening gowns. Then she'd deal with her hair.

At the end of her day, she walked over to the little library that the city had begrudgingly stuck in a former empty store and filled with books that looked as if they'd been remaindered from at least two libraries before landing in the tenements. She dropped her Austin Public Library copy of *Rebecca* in the Return slot. Let the librarian figure out how it mysteriously got there.

This library had nothing new—no *Brave New World* or *The Great Gatsby*, like she'd seen in the bookshop window. Although she had forty-three dollars of Novy's money left, it wasn't to be wasted on such indulgences. She sat at a small desk and read until the librarian shooed her out. No library card, no permanent address to offer, just a little piece of flotsam on the Hudson.

Returning to her boarding house, she passed by the landlady's open drawing room door.

"Miss Fisher, come in." The words were warm, thickly Yiddish-inflected. Mrs. Stein was maternal and prone to making hot, thick bean and barley soups even now at the end of August.

Rosalind walked in. John Smith sat in a chair, sipping from a china cup as if he'd known Mrs. Stein forever, a small plate of homemade rugelach on the coffee table in front of him.

"Hi, cousin. Thanks for letting us know you were coming to New York. Mom and Dad will be so happy to see you." Smith rose and smiled.

"I'll leave you two to your family reunion. So good when we find each other after a long absence." Mrs. Stein stood up from her chair, walked out, and shut the drawing room door behind her.

"True, Rosalind, don't you think?" Smith's voice was calm.

"How did you find me?" She sat down in Mrs. Stein's vacated chair, feeling nauseous and sticky in the heat.

"Where would a nice Jewish girl try to hide after she got off a ship in New York? Let me think… Tall, red curly hair. You really need to change that color, you know. Oh, and we have a copy of the picture of you from your passport to show around."

"Let me explain what happened—" she began.

Smith put a finger up to his lips. "Not here." He got up and grabbed her elbow. "You shout up to Mrs. Stein that I'm taking you to your aunt and uncle's."

She did.

***

"Welcome to your aunt's." Smith pointed to an office door where *JOLLY IMPORTS* was painted in fading white letters. He knocked twice, waited, and knocked three times and once more. Then he unlocked the door.

The door's opening was noiseless. Smith put his hand on her back and propelled her inside. The room had two large windows, venetian blinds tilted up against the sun, mismatched kitchen chairs, a desk, and on it, a telephone.

"We also lease the office to one side and the office above and below, so I'm pretty sure no listening devices," he said in an almost normal tone. "Sorry about the cloak-and-dagger routine. We just want to get your complete story."

"Am I under arrest?"

"Jesus, no. What makes you think that?" Smith sat down with a thump on a kitchen chair and waved her into another one.

"We should have told you to come back to DC."

She nodded.

"We assume that without those instructions you thought your job was done and you were on your own. And that you decided to stay in New York because…well…why not?"

She nodded.

Smith stared at her for half-a-second. "Fine. That's what I'll tell them. The less said, the better. Now, for what happened in Poland, Rosalind."

She rubbed her hands together in her lap. She was hungry and her back hurt from being on her feet all day.

"This is what Michal has told us. Are you ready to confirm or deny?"

"Michal?"

"He was the only one close enough to…well, let's call it Operation Texas…to give us a report until we found you. He was on the ship that sailed before yours with Mister Novy."

"Look, Mister Smith, who are you representing here?"

"Representative Johnson, in part. But he has nothing at all to do with…" He paused. "Our affiliations with Sidney and like-minded folk in the US and England. Oh, I forgot to add, Sidney says hello."

"Not a government group?" Rosalind said, feeling her mood lift at Sidney's hello.

He shook his head. "Some of us work for the government. But this is our calling, if you will. This is what we have to do. Hitler will end the world."

"Yes," she said. "Yes, he will. So it's you and Eleanor and…"

"Others. Rollins is one. He's a great amateur spy for creeps internal to the US. Anyhow, doesn't matter."

She sat back, relieved that Smith didn't appear to be there to arrest her.

"Michal told us that no one on Johnson's list at the embassy was available to help with those visas. He said you found a way to get the seal and put yourself at great risk to get as many visas completed as you could."

No number forty-four, Rosalind noted.

"And? What happened next?" she asked.

"It's yours to tell."

"No, no. I want to hear this from Michal's point of view."

Smith nodded.

"Employees started returning from lunch. You were both concerned about being discovered so you had to stop well short of forty-four visas."

"We got thirty-eight done."

"Yes. Not what Novy had hoped for. But then when the corporal tried to stop Michal, you told Michal to slug him and run, and you went over and blocked him from shooting Michal."

That was embellishment, Rosalind thought.

"And then Mister Novy and David had to leave urgently. Ambassador Biddle had some intel—I'll get back to the Ambassador in a minute—so, Michal, who was supposed to do the visa distribution, left it all to you. He told us about Fried coming from the embassy, about the Marines and the police. And yet somehow you managed to give out all thirty-eight visas, Rosalind. You had to choose who to leave in Poland. According to Mister Novy, those left behind were six healthy, single young men. Men with the best chance to survive. Then you got yourself and thirty-eight people safely to the United States."

He smiled at her. Rosalind felt as if she'd just been told a great adventure story about someone else. A heroine, not someone who'd traded six innocent lives for six innocent lives.

"And here, Rosalind, is maybe the most interesting part of the tale for you. About Ambassador Biddle. Apparently, you obtained stolen information about our Navy and got it to Ambassador Biddle. I'm guessing Sidney helped."

She nodded.

He went on, "Biddle then praised the good Representative Johnson to FDR, who then passed it on to Johnson."

Smith sat back. Rosalind dropped her gaze to her hands, folded in her lap. She was listening, but her mind was stuck on the fact that Michal had altered the story so they only had thirty-eight visas. Novy would not be angry with her. Only the Almighty would weigh what she'd done.

"So, we'd like you to continue to work with us. In LBJ's office. Maybe other places." Smith was staring at her, obviously waiting for a reply.

"In Austin?"

"We'd prefer DC. If we have to send someone back over whose got good translation skills and other abilities, DC's the place. Or if there's something going on in our nation's capital we need that package for. You need more training, of course. How to be invisible in a city, for one example. I'd suggest, again, a different hair color." Smith shot her the briefest of smiles.

"But I only have a semester left for my teaching credential." Her left hand drifted up to her hair in farewell.

"How does American University sound? I'll get Eleanor on it when we get back."

"Will she put me up for a while, too?"

"I'm sure she's good for it. But, really, Rosalind…"

"What?"

"That semester's going to get interrupted again." He paused. "I do have to remind you that you owe Charles Marsh a long, dramatic eye-witness report, which we will edit with care before handing over. So, are you up for this new job?"

Rosalind thought about the life she was giving up, a boarding house room and her only relatives in the world. Then she thought of the possibilities in front of her. Adventure. The possibility of seeing Sidney again. And, most importantly, the chance to do some good in the world.

She glanced at Smith, who was looking at her expectantly. "So the red hair has to go, huh?"

Smith nodded. "I'd say so, yes."

"And you'll make sure I can finish my degree?"

Smith smiled. "Absolutely."

Rosalind was quiet for another minute. Then she looked up. "Well, Mister Smith. I'd say it's time we go to Washington."

ACKNOWLEDGMENTS

I want to thank my husband, Dan Metlay, for his ongoing support. My writing group has been with this novel from the start and offered invaluable critiques. And my editor, Corey Stewart, helped to clean, polish, and eliminate redundancy, all while keeping the novel's intent in mind.

This is historical fiction. I relied on the following resources to shape the story; if the list is incomplete or I failed to accurately represent facts in the service of drama, the fault is mine:

Bernstein, Arnie. *Swastika Nation: Fritz Kuhn and the Rise and Fall of the German American Bund.* St. Martin's Press, New York. 2013

Caro, Robert A. *The Years of Lyndon Johnson: The Path to Power.* Random House. 1983

Chapin, David, Editor. *The First Jew of Texas: The Life of Jim Novy.* Virtual Bookworm.com Publishing, College Station, Texas. 2012

Dallek, Robert. *Lone Star Rising: Lyndon Johnson and His Times, 1980-1960.* Oxford University Press, New York. 1991

Farago, Ladislas. *The Game of Foxes,* David McKay Company Inc., New York. 1971

Jeffreys-Jones, Rhodri. *The Nazi Spy Ring in America.* Georgetown University Press, Washington, DC. 2020

Johnson, Lady Bird. *A White House Diary.* Holt, Rinehart and Winston, New York. 1970

Smallwood, James. *Operation Texas: Lyndon B. Johnson, The Jewish Question and the Nazi Holocaust.* East Texas Historical Journal, Vol. 47, Issue 1. 2009.

I also used Google to research everything from the stateroom décor on the Queen Mary to weather in Warsaw in August 1938. Thank you to Wikipedia for photographs and a description of pre-World War II Knishin and for more information on Charles Marsh and Alice Glass. Thank you to the archives of the Holocaust Museum of Washington DC for providing access to original Ph.D. dissertations, more information on Knishin and on LBJ's concern for Jews in Europe and the US, and for just being there.

ABOUT THE AUTHOR

Anita Lampel is the author of *Helen*, published under the name Anita Mishook in 2016, called "a fascinating and most intriguing must read" and given a five-star review by *Foreword Magazine*. *Operation Texas* is her second work of historical fiction. Lampel has a Ph.D. in psychology, which she finds a most helpful tool for both research and writing. She lives in the Washington DC area and can be contacted through her website.